"Wha[...]n love, not[...]

How do I explain this to a ten-year-old? Marian wondered. I can't very well tell her that you want him to kiss you and never stop, that you want to be alone with him in a room and stay for at least a week.

She chewed on her lower lip. "You have to remember that I'm new at this, Rebecca. I've never loved anyone before I loved your brother."

"Did it just happen? I mean, did you just see him and you fell in love?"

Marian thought of that first moment, when she'd opened the door and seen the tall, handsome stranger smiling at her. She had tilted her head back to look at him and then his smile had disappeared. Something had come into his eyes, something that touched her all the way down to her toes.

"I did, Rebecca. I didn't know it was love right then, but after a while I knew I couldn't live without your brother in my life."

Dear Reader,

Families have always intrigued me. I collect family stories the way other people collect dolls. We moved a lot when I was growing up and we saw our relatives only on special occasions. I had to gather in as many stories as I could during our visits and the habit grew, so that I now collect stories wherever I go.

I would sit in a kitchen corner, listening to the women. They would talk as they fixed meals, bringing up relationships, children, jobs...all the ingredients of life. I'm not sure if the stories I believe about my family are real, based on those kitchen conversations, or ones I embellished after I was discovered and sent from the room.

Love and marriage were always vital elements of those stories and it was natural for me to write about relationships. I enjoyed creating the story of Frank and Marian and hope you enjoy meeting them in the pages ahead. Their love is an example for the generations that follow and Hannah, their great-granddaughter, is determined to celebrate their lives.

I would love to hear your thoughts about family and love. You can contact me at tessa@tessamcdermid.com.

Happy reading!

Tessa McDermid

Family Stories

Tessa McDermid

*May your
life be filled
with dreams that
come true

Tessa McDermid*

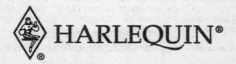

HARLEQUIN®

TORONTO • NEW YORK • LONDON
AMSTERDAM • PARIS • SYDNEY • HAMBURG
STOCKHOLM • ATHENS • TOKYO • MILAN • MADRID
PRAGUE • WARSAW • BUDAPEST • AUCKLAND

ISBN-13: 978-0-373-65410-9
ISBN-10: 0-373-65410-3

FAMILY STORIES

ABOUT THE AUTHOR

Tessa McDermid has been listening to stories and telling them since she was a child in Des Moines, Iowa. As an adult, she's written children's books, educational materials and romance novels and has won various awards for her work. She's particularly pleased to be writing for Harlequin Everlasting Love; she likes the possibilities of exploring long-term relationships, having witnessed so many in her own life. Tessa, who also has a career in teaching, lives in the U.S. Midwest with her husband and two sons.

To my family, through birth and marriage

ACKNOWLEDGMENTS

My thanks to the Joplin Writers Guild for their support and encouragement; the Joplin Public Library for resources and answers to questions; Gloria Harchar for critique and computer help; my editor, Paula Eykelhof, for direction and wonderful editing; my sons, David and John, for giving me a reason to keep telling my stories. And to Bob, my husband, who always believes and provides love and support throughout the writing process.

Prologue

Summer 2004

Hannah scrambled up the last few rungs of the rickety ladder and then tugged her brother into the attic. "You've got to be quiet, Preston," she whispered. "We don't want Grandma to find out we're up here."

"Wow!" He straightened, his head bumping the single light-bulb. Shadows danced around the walls, creating silhouettes of a forgotten Christmas tree, complete with decorations, a dress-maker's dummy, a rocking horse and other remnants of the owners' lifetime in this house.

"Didn't anybody ever throw stuff away?" He stepped over a broken chair, the arms crooked, and bent to examine an old chest, its lid askew and clothes spilling out.

"I don't know. But we're not here to look at the junk." She

headed for a waist-high pile of boxes stacked neatly against the far wall. "We need pictures. Lots and lots of pictures."

She sat cross-legged on the floor in front of the boxes. Preston plopped down next to her. Dust flew into the air and he sneezed.

"Be quiet!" She held her hand under his nose. "We're almost directly over the kitchen. If Grandma hears us…"

She opened the top carton. Inside were stacks of folders, each labeled with a date from decades past and kept together with colorful rubber bands.

"Here, you look at these." She handed him a stack, then pulled out another one for herself. She slid off the rubber band, and photographs spilled into her lap.

Several minutes passed quietly, the only sound the soft rustle of paper. "Okay, these might work." She flipped over a photo of a man standing stiffly behind a young woman seated in a stuffed chair. "G.G. labeled all of them on the back, with the date and the names of the people in the picture. I think these are G. G.'s mom and dad. Our great-great-grandparents."

She held the photograph by one corner, peering at her ancestors' faded expressions. G.G., her great-grandmother, was 93. That meant the picture was more than a hundred years old.

"How do you know who any of these people are?" Preston shuffled through his photographs, barely pausing at any of them.

"Because I listen to stories. Stop it, you're gonna rip them." She scooped the pictures out of his lap and carefully placed them back in their folders.

"I don't want to look at old pictures. Hey—some of this stuff is probably worth a fortune now." He crawled over the floor to a wooden trunk perched under the window.

"Fine. I don't need your help, anyway." She'd actually invited him because the attic made her nervous. The few times she'd managed to slip up unnoticed by her grandmother had been at night, with only the single lightbulb for illumination. With the afternoon sun shining through the small oval window, the room seemed less eerie. She could have left Preston downstairs.

Except that he might've gone looking for her, which would have alerted their grandmother to her absence. She sighed and opened another box.

Her great-grandmother hadn't filled this one with neatly cataloged folders. Instead, Hannah stared at old albums stuffed with envelopes of pictures and loose bundles of photographs all tumbled together.

"Well, crap."

"Umm." Preston scooted back to her side. "Mom doesn't like you to use that word."

"Oh, shut up, Preston." She squinted at the top picture. Not even a date from the developing. "Okay, this seems more recent than the others but who are these people?"

Preston peered over her shoulder. "Maybe Grandma and her sisters?"

Hannah glanced at him in surprise, then studied the black-and-white picture again. "I think you're right." Three girls, wearing frilly dresses, stood hand in hand. Behind them was the fuzzy outline of a house and a tall tree with a few leaves on it. "Easter," she said out loud. "The trees are budding."

"Or maybe autumn, with the leaves falling off."

She'd give him credit for guessing the identity of the three girls, but these leaves weren't the dry leaves of fall. "We'll go ask Grandma if she remembers this picture."

Preston jumped to his feet. "But if you show her the pictures, she'll know we were in the attic."

Hannah shrugged and stood up. She thrust two boxes of pictures into his arms and gathered two for herself.

"You don't care that she'll know we were up here?" he continued. "Then what was that big deal about being quiet and everything?" His steps left footprints on the dusty floor.

Hannah carefully deposited her boxes near the attic entrance.

"I wanted pictures. Now that I have them, I don't need to worry about being caught."

"You're crazy." He grabbed the sides of the ladder and made his way down the steps.

Hannah leaned over the edge and passed him a box of photos. When all the boxes were stacked in the hallway, she followed him down. She pushed the ladder back up.

"Come on, let's show Grandma." She didn't wait to see if he was behind her, knowing he'd be curious to find out whether she got into trouble.

Their grandmother sat at the kitchen table, her two younger sisters on either side. She stopped talking when Hannah and Preston entered the kitchen. "You've been in the attic. Hannah, you're not supposed to go up there without telling me."

"And then you say it's too dangerous and I shouldn't go up at all." She placed the boxes on the table. "Grandma, I'm sixteen. I know how to be careful. I'm not going to fall through the ceiling."

"Your father did and he was a grown man."

Preston giggled. "Dad fell through the ceiling?"

His grandmother nodded. "It wasn't funny. He could've been hurt." But a corner of her mouth lifted in a lopsided grin. "He was here for Christmas and said he'd get the tree out of the attic for us. We were sitting in the living room and suddenly, a leg came right through the ceiling. Your great-grandparents still lived here. G.G. screamed and Grandpa Frank couldn't finish his TV show. He had to help your dad."

She tapped the box in front of her. "So, tell me what you found."

Hannah settled on the chair between her grandmother and great-aunt Alice. This was the part of the visit she always enjoyed most. Hearing the stories. "Pictures. Lots and lots of pictures. We can use some for the party."

"Mom and Dad don't want a party," Aunt Alice said.

"It doesn't have to be a *big* party." Hannah wrapped her own hands around her grandmother's worn ones. "Grandpa Frank and

G.G. have been married for almost seventy-five years! Doesn't that deserve a celebration? I mean, people hardly stay married for a decade anymore, let alone seven of them!"

Aunt Margaret chuckled. "You can be pretty persuasive, Miss Hannah. But I don't think even you can convince Mom and Dad." Her expression sobered. "Mom got very upset when we mentioned a family dinner at the retirement home for their anniversary."

"The party for their sixtieth anniversary was the last time we had any kind of celebration for either of them." Aunt Alice picked up the photograph Hannah and Preston had been studying earlier. "Oh, look! The dresses we wore for the wedding of some cousin. Mom spent all week sewing them."

They lowered their heads over the picture. All three were mostly gray now, but strands of their natural hair colors still peeked through. A blonde, a brunette and a redhead, their appearances just as different as they were inside.

Another picture caught Hannah's eye. A tall, dark-haired man stood at attention in his navy uniform, his eyes bright and his bearing rigid. One corner of his mouth curved up as if he were having a hard time staying serious for the photographer.

Grandpa Frank. Her great-grandfather. The father of the three women sitting at the table. The love of G.G.'s life.

She reverently touched a finger to the picture, her mind racing across the years and past the generations as she recalled the family stories she'd heard.

FRANK'S STORY

Chapter 1

Winston, Missouri
July 1929

Frank Robertson leaned against the railing of the neat frame house and studied the door. The setting sun slanted across it, reminding him that he hadn't eaten yet and that he still had to find a place to sleep that night.

"Just one more," he promised himself. He was going to prove himself to the merchant whose wares he carried. When Frank had proposed going from town to town with a selection of items the man displayed in his general store, Mr. Samson had expressed nothing but skepticism. He'd finally agreed but only after requiring Frank to leave a security deposit, in addition to paying for each item he carried away from the dingy building.

Frank jingled the loose coins in his pocket and used his foot to shove the worn suitcase away from the doorway, scowling at the memory. His first reaction had been to deliver a pithy discourse on the man's antecedents and then slam out of the store. But he had hesitated. He was hungry, he was miles away from the next town and none of the other shopkeepers had listened to even the beginning of Frank's practiced spiel.

Taking a deep breath, he'd acquiesced to the old man's terms. Now he stood in front of the last house in the small village he'd trudged through during the long day. His sales had been successful, even better than he'd anticipated, but he was tired and ready for his dinner. The women he met were eager to invite him into their houses and browse through the things he pulled out of his case but they weren't prone to buying on impulse.

Of course, maybe they just wanted to visit with a handsome young man, he thought with a grin and a jaunty toss of his head.

While he knew that his technique was good, he wasn't foolish enough to think he'd sell a thing if he didn't present a polished appearance that appealed to the women who answered the door. After years on the road, he'd learned to cultivate his dashing good looks. The other salesmen he met teased him about the amount of time his grooming took but he didn't care. His sales record spoke for itself.

He smoothed down the gray suit that comprised his wardrobe and brushed his hands over his dark hair. Satisfied, he rapped on the door with his knuckles and let his lips curl upward in a slight smile as he waited.

When the door opened, his prepared greeting spilled out of his mind and landed in a heap at the feet of the young woman standing there. The late-afternoon sun glinted on hair as shiny as the sun itself. He stared at the sparkling curls escaping from the loose bun and dancing across her soft cheeks.

She tilted her head to one side and watched him, drying her hands on the apron tied around her narrow waist. Her arms were tanned and a dimple showed in each elbow. "May I help you?"

Frank cleared his throat. "I—I—I…"

A dimple appeared in the smooth skin of one cheek, matching those on her rounded arms. "If you're here to see the reverend, he isn't in right now."

Frank swallowed and forced himself to glance away from the bright sheen of her blue eyes. He lowered his gaze to her soft red lips, then wrenched it back to the relative safety of her eyes. "I'm looking for the lady of the house," he managed in a more normal voice. "Is she in?"

The lovely creature in front of him held the door open and took a step backward, her actions inviting him into the dark hallway beyond. "I'll see. You can wait in here."

She ushered him into a dimly lit room. Some sort of workroom, he guessed from the sparse furniture. He wasn't offended. Salesmen weren't high on the social scale and while he knew that his scruples were as high or higher than any of the store owners he met, he accepted society's judgment for now. He wouldn't be a salesman forever.

As he waited for the lady of the house to join him, he wondered if he should start thinking about more serious work now, maybe a job that didn't require so much traveling. For the past five years, he'd lived on the road, leaving home when he was sixteen. Twice a year, he wired his mother and gave her his current address, waiting until she responded before moving on. Each time, she implored him to come home, at least for a visit, and each time he sent back a glib answer and most of his earnings.

The creak of the door interrupted his thoughts and he jumped to his feet, hat clutched in his hand. An older woman advanced into the room and Frank knew he was looking at the young woman's mother. The same blue eyes, creased now by age, glanced at him before again studying the floorboards. The golden hair was peppered with gray and the smile was tight-lipped but he had no doubt. He'd just been bowled over by the minister's daughter.

He bit his lower lip at the irony. The other salesmen might

find the virtuous daughter of a minister intriguing game but he'd always been more cautious, flirting only with women who couldn't go running home to papa. He didn't want to end up shackled to some woman just because he'd let his eyes and hands roam.

The reverend's wife offered him a chair and he sat down across from her. Her expression softened a bit when she smiled at him, and emboldened by that approval, he launched into his sales pitch, bringing out each item with a practiced hand. She nodded, listening carefully, before finally settling on several bolts of sturdy cloth.

He gathered up the rest of his merchandise and slid it back into his case. She pulled a small purse out of her pocket and slowly counted out the coins before handing the stack to him.

He nudged the coins with his thumb as he checked the amount. "You've paid me too much." He held out several of them.

She shook her head, hiding her hands in her skirt as if he'd thrust the money at her. "No, keep it." She lifted her head and gave him a candid look. "Perhaps you could use the extra to call your mother. I'm sure she must worry about you."

"She does. But I'm a grown man now." He bent down and picked up the half-empty case.

"You're never too grown-up for a mother's love," the woman said softly.

He was suddenly aware of the homey aromas around him. The fresh scent of lemon mingled with that of a stew, reminding him of long-ago days when he'd rush in the front door, calling for his mother. She would come out of the kitchen and throw her arms around him in a hug, asking about his day at school....

He brushed the memories aside. He was twenty-one, a man in every sense of the word. His hat still in his hand, he paused at the open doorway and bent at the waist, sweeping the woman a low bow. "Thank you so much for your purchase," he said, "and for your advice," he couldn't resist adding.

She blinked at the implied criticism and he instantly felt sorry.

She'd only meant to be kind, he told himself, and quickly straightened, a contrite smile on his lips. "Perhaps I will call Mom. I might even visit."

He was rewarded by a smile that took years from her worn face. Whistling, he tossed on his hat and headed down the steps, sparing only a brief thought for the lovely daughter who'd first opened the door.

Dusk had fallen while he was inside and he leaned his head back to take full advantage of the remaining sun. When he turned onto the road, he almost bumped into the slight figure that suddenly appeared in front of him.

"Quick, over here." She grabbed his hand and pulled him down the lane, into a clump of bushes. He stumbled over a fallen branch, landing ungracefully at her feet.

She giggled and sat down on the log. "Oh, I've never had a man literally fall at my feet before."

He didn't speak, his eyes wide as he gazed at her, trying to capture her image in his mind. In later years, he decided, he'd remember her like this. I'll tell my children and my grandchildren about the most beautiful woman I ever met. They won't believe me because they won't be able to see her like this, with the dusky light revealing her golden beauty. They wouldn't understand how her smile could be serene while her eyes twinkled. Light and darkness, innocence and mystery.

She dragged him away from his thoughts with an embarrassed laugh. "I don't think you should look at me like that. I'm not sure it's proper."

He jumped up, his eyes wild. She was an innocent, a babe. He knew better than to be in a secluded setting with a young girl. He didn't even know her name.

She reached out and touched his fingers lightly. Her smile was gone and in her seriousness, she looked more beautiful than ever. "Please, sit back down. I shouldn't have said that. I'm sorry."

He wanted to take her in his arms until her eyes held their delicious sparkle again. He was surprised by the mixed feelings she aroused in him. He'd slept with his first woman only a week after leaving home, a neglected wife eager to fill her bed with any able-bodied man. He had listened to women moan about their men, holding those same women in the quiet of their houses, letting them ramble so he could reap the benefits of their sorrow.

But this was the first time he'd truly wanted to comfort, to protect a woman from whatever problems could cloud her life.

"They're probably worried about where you are," he finally said. "You should go home."

The smile returned. "So you can speak, after all. I thought you could since you're a salesman but I was beginning to wonder."

His own lips curved upward at her infectious tone. "You should go home," he repeated as much for his own sake as for hers. But he sat down on the log next to her, careful to keep a safe distance between them. His fingers tingled with a desire to see if her skin felt as silky as it looked.

"No, it's all right." At his questioning glance, she grinned. "My parents trust me and let me have my own way. The townspeople would tell you I'm a bit spoiled."

She leaned back. He was fascinated by her long, white neck exposed by the soft summer dress. Several loose curls danced around her face and her hands fluttered with each word.

"Have you ever heard of Abraham and Sarah?"

He frowned, trying to follow her lightning change of topic. "I'm not from around here."

"They're in the Bible, silly," she said.

He dug in the dim recesses of his mind. Church on Sundays had been a regular part of his growing-up years, walking the few blocks with his mother and two sisters. Their dad always stayed home to read his paper in peace and quiet.

"An old couple who wanted a baby?" he ventured.

She nodded. "My parents see themselves as Abraham and Sarah. They had decided it was God's will that they never have children. And then, just like Abraham and Sarah, they found out I was on the way."

"They must've been very excited."

"They were. Mother was sick a lot but they were so happy, she didn't care. She couldn't go anywhere with my father, even to church. She sewed clothes for me, lovely clothes for this precious baby she was expecting."

Frank watched the changing expressions on her face. She spoke about babies and birth as if they were the most natural things in the world. Maybe she's right, he thought, touched by her candor.

"And here you are," he breathed when she stopped, vowing to start praying again. If God could create a vision like the one sitting next to him...

"I almost wasn't."

Frank caught her hand at that horrible possibility, staring at the sight of her delicate fingers against his much larger palm. She smiled at him and he was ensnared in the spell of her eyes. Sapphires, he told himself, even though he'd never seen the actual gems. Her eyes must look like sapphires. Bright blue rimmed with dark lashes.

She tugged her fingers out of his tight hold and folded her hands in her lap. "My mother suffered complications just before I was born. She told the doctor and my father that if a choice had to be made between her and the baby, then the baby must live. Father argued with her but she wouldn't listen. Finally, he gave in, hoping a miracle would happen."

"And a miracle did." He felt his own faith rekindling at her simple story.

"That's what my parents believe. I still think it's because my father can speak to God so easily, or maybe God finds it easier to understand a minister's requests."

She laughed at his look of surprise, a throaty trill that spun cobwebs down his spine. "Oh, you mustn't mind what I say. Really, I do believe in God but living with people who praise God whenever you walk into a room can be tiring."

She wrapped her arms around her bent knees and rested her head on her arms, her face turned away from him. A delicate pink ear was visible among the disorder of her curls and he clutched his hands in his lap. When a light breeze brought the fresh scent of her soap to him, he closed his eyes. *Help me, God,* he prayed for the first time in years. *She's too young, too innocent. She doesn't know what her mere presence does to a man.*

He opened his eyes and saw her sitting up, watching him with a mixture of longing and worry.

"You won't go away, will you?"

I'm going right now. I'm catching the next train and riding as far away from you as I can.

But the words didn't form on his lips. Looking into her eyes, he knew he couldn't say them.

"Your parents won't let us meet," he said instead, both relief and regret in his tone.

She rose gracefully to her feet and smoothed down her skirt. "Don't worry about my parents. Come to church on Sunday and don't be late." She paused, studying his rumpled clothes. "Do you have another suit?"

"Yes," he lied. Sunday. He had three days in which to buy another suit. If it cost every penny he'd just earned, he would arrive at the church in a new suit.

"Good." She started to walk away. "Then come to the church by 8:00 a.m. The white church, not the brick one."

She was almost gone. "Wait!" he shouted, running after her. "I don't know your name."

"Marian," she called to him. "Marian Cooper."

"Marian," he whispered, walking back to the log. He took off his jacket and rolled it into a pillow. His stomach growled but he pushed his hunger aside. A small price to pay to see her again. He curled up against the suddenly cool summer breeze and whispered her name over and over.

He spent the next three days knocking on doors in nearby

towns. On Saturday he went back to the storekeeper whose wares he carried, received his pay, then asked about a suit. The old man was pleased with his profit and offered Frank a discount on a ready-made suit. He directed him to the tailor's house on the outskirts of town and by nightfall, Frank owned another outfit.

He slipped into an empty freight car and watched the stars through the open door. Sleep eluded him. One part of him hoped the feelings she'd aroused in him would be extinguished by the real presence of her, and another part wondered how he would live if she'd forgotten him or, worse, been toying with him.

What if she *had* only been using him to while away a few summer hours? What if she snubbed him when he arrived at the church, her adorable little nose in the air as she walked haughtily past him? He groaned and punched his bag into a pillow of sorts. He stretched out his long form and, resting his head on the crumpled bag, willed himself to sleep.

By the time the train pulled into the village of Winston, he was a bundle of nerves. Each time he'd drifted off, her face invaded his vision. He could see again the soft curve of her cheek, the gentle sweep of her lashes, the rosebud perfection of her lips. Clenching his teeth to stop another moan, he grabbed the small bag with a sweaty hand and swung himself down from the freight car. The train's whistle sounded in his ears as it chugged down the tracks, leaving him alone in the dark countryside.

He found an empty barn near the edge of town and crawled into a corner, his eyes heavy with exhaustion and his heart aching with worry. Stripping off his jacket and shoes, he lay down and closed his eyes, begging for at least a few hours' sleep to release him from his anxiety.

He was up with the dawn, only slightly rested from his hours in the barn. He gobbled down the sandwich he'd bought the day before and dressed carefully in the new suit. The tailor had assured him he looked extremely well-dressed; he hoped the little man was right. He dusted off his shoes with a handkerchief. Using a bit of broken glass he found in another corner of the barn for a reflection, he styled his hair carefully. Satisfied he looked his best, considering the facilities he had to use, he hid his bag under some dusty tools and headed down the road to town.

Winston, Missouri, woke up early on a Sunday. He could smell Sunday dinners already cooking. Children sat on porch swings, their hair brushed and pulled back from scrubbed faces. Their feet swung in shiny dress shoes. They waved at him and he waved back, his mood lightened by their friendliness.

As he neared the center of town, church bells rang out. People were filing into the brick church; remembering her directions, he joined the throng at the white frame church only a few steps from her home.

He chose a pew in the middle of the right side. He bent his head, unable to look around now that he was finally there. He chastised himself for being seven different kinds of fool for even being in the same village again.

Just as he'd decided to bolt out the door and run for the nearest train station, the organist started to play. Hymnbooks rustled, and his neighbor handed him her open book with a pleasant smile. He returned her smile, nodding in thanks, then froze as he saw Marian.

She was sitting across the aisle in the front pew with her mother. A dark-blue hat rested on top of her curls, enhancing their luminous glow. Her dress was in the same sedate blue and while the high collar hid her neck from sight, he could imagine its slender beauty under the protective material.

She stood with the rest of the congregation and shifted slightly. He got quietly to his feet, his eyes still on her face. A hint of a smile lifted the corner of her mouth and a moment later she was singing lustily. The blood rushed to his head and he could hardly breathe.

He felt relieved when they bowed their heads for the prayer. By the time he sat down again, his breathing was normal. He kept his eyes on Reverend Cooper's face, wanting to know this man who was Marian's father, but he could find no trace of the enchanting woman–child in the man admonishing his flock to always choose the right path.

After the final prayer, the congregation was ushered out. Marian and her mother left first and he watched them walk up the aisle. Not by a single movement did she acknowledge his presence.

Eyes narrowed, he followed the others up the aisle. She had given him her answer. He had spent his hard-earned money on a suit he could ill afford, all for a spoiled country girl who only wanted a bit of amusement.

The noontime sun blinded him as he walked outside, and he shielded his eyes with one hand. "Bright, isn't it?" said the friendly woman next to him and he nodded.

As he turned to speak to her, his mouth suddenly went dry. Marian stood on the steps, her hand lightly resting on her father's arm. She greeted each person who came out of the building, her voice low and melodious. Pushed by the people behind him and hindered by the woman in front, Frank had no choice but to stop.

Reverend Cooper held out a hand. "Welcome, my son. I don't believe we've met."

Frank swallowed, dragging his eyes away from Marian. The reverend still held out his hand and Frank belatedly remembered his manners. "Frank Robertson, sir. I was passing through and thought I'd stay for a while."

"Ah, so our fair town has lured yet another visitor." Reverend Cooper's smile was one of proud ownership. "Many a person has decided to settle in Winston after stopping for only a night."

He glanced around, as if searching for someone, and then tapped Marian on the arm. When she finished her conversation with an older woman, she turned to her father, still without meeting Frank's eyes. "My dear, I can't find your mother."

"She went home to finish dinner. She knew I wouldn't mind taking her place with you."

Her father nodded and turned back to Frank. "My daughter,

Mr. Robertson. Marian, this is Frank Robertson, a visitor to our community."

Marian slid her warm hand into his cold one and smiled. "Welcome, Mr. Robertson. I'm glad you could come today."

The warmth from her fingers remained after she released his hand. He didn't think he'd imagined that slight emphasis on the word *you*. Aware of her father, he pressed his lips together and swung back to the older man.

He searched his memory, trying to recall what his mother would say when she greeted their minister. "I appreciated your sermon today, sir."

Reverend Cooper beamed. "Thank you, young man. Sometimes it's hard to know how to reach people today. So many choices pulling us in every direction."

Marian wrapped her fingers around her father's arm. "Now, Father, church is over. Mr. Robertson doesn't need to hear about this anymore. After all, what could happen in Winston?"

Her father patted her fingers. "The devil is everywhere, Marian. You have to be on guard at all times."

As he watched Marian, the slow rise and fall of her bodice, the slender ankles and calves he could see under the demure dress, Frank knew that her father was right. The thoughts spinning through his brain had nothing to do with the straight and narrow path.

He cleared his throat. "Well, I should be going, sir. Again, thank you for the warm welcome."

He turned toward Marian, schooling his features into a neutral expression. "And I enjoyed meeting you, Miss Cooper."

Her eyes widened, a beseeching look in their depths. He hesitated, unsure what she was asking. How could he see her again without prompting her father's concern?

The movement was barely noticeable, just a flicker of her fingers. Her father frowned, then leaned his head toward her, his thick gray eyebrows raised in question. "Marian?"

She raised herself on tiptoe so she could whisper in her father's ear. The soft cotton dress tightened around her slender form. Frank jammed his right hand into his pocket and flexed his fingers.

"Of course, my dear." Reverend Cooper clapped Frank on the arm, his relationship to Marian now evident from the sparkle in his eyes. "My daughter has reminded me of my manners. If you'd honor us by coming to dinner, we'd be very pleased. I have to greet the rest of my congregation, but then we'll take you home for some of my wife's delicious cooking."

Frank accepted the invitation and stood at the side of the steps, wondering if he'd caught some sort of summer madness. People stopped to greet him, their faces wreathed in welcoming smiles, and he answered them carefully, always aware of Marian only a few feet away. Several of the women were his former customers and he waited for one of them to denounce him as a traveling salesman, not worth the dirt under their feet.

But they didn't see the door-to-door salesman today. Instead, they favored him with their most charming smiles, one daring young woman even rubbing her hip against his as she sauntered down the steps.

She tossed him a saucy look over her shoulder and he grinned. She had obviously paid scant attention to the reverend's words that morning. Frank watched her sway down the walkway, her hips inviting him to spend some time with her. He had no doubt of her intentions.

"So, Mr. Robertson, are you ready?" The reverend tugged the church door to be sure it had locked securely. He joined Frank at the bottom of the steps.

With a last glance at the young woman, Frank made his decision. "Yes, sir. You're sure this won't be an inconvenience for your wife?"

"Of course not. She always plans for some company each Sunday."

The young woman stood poised at the gate, her hand resting on the latch. Frank shrugged, shaking his head at her smile. She spun around and stood toward the village, her black curls bouncing in the sun.

"I wonder what's the matter with Flossie." Reverend Cooper clicked the gate shut and turned toward his home.

"She's not happy about something," Marian agreed, a smug inflection in her voice.

Startled, Frank looked at her but the reverend hid her from view. Was she as innocent as she seemed? She did know a lot about the birth of babies. Did she also know as much about how they came to be, what happened between a man and a woman?

His neck grew hot. Her father was talking about the run of warm weather they'd been enjoying and Frank immediately commented on how good the fields looked.

"And what line of work keeps you traveling so much?" Reverend Cooper asked as they neared the house.

Frank hesitated. Many of the people he met saw traveling salesmen as little more than hobos, slamming doors in their faces and ordering them off their property. The women at church hadn't connected the dashing young salesman with the man they'd met on the church steps. Reverend Cooper professed to love all people, but would that love extend to the man walking next to him, even if he was wearing a new suit?

He couldn't take the chance. "I've worked with my father in his store back in Iowa," he offered, staying close to the truth without betraying his current occupation. "I've always been good with words."

A soft snort from the other side of the reverend almost proved his undoing. He could feel his cheeks flush and he stared at the ground. How could she turn him into this blithering fool in only a few short days?

Her father didn't seem to notice anything amiss. He rubbed his chin with one gnarled hand, reminding Frank that this man had waited a long time for his child.

His footsteps lagged as they neared the house and then he

straightened his shoulders. I might not live in a fine place, he thought, but I have as much right to walk into his home as anyone. His natural confidence returned; he greeted Marian's mother with a smile and a low bow.

The older woman frowned and Frank realized his error. She bit her lip, glancing at her husband from under lowered lashes. When he introduced Frank to her, she shook his hand gravely, giving everyone the impression that she'd just met the young man.

Relieved that he wouldn't be discovered yet and aware that he could be doing the minister a grave disservice, Frank followed Marian and her father into the parlor. Reverend Cooper excused himself at the door, murmuring that he needed to jot down an idea before it left him. Alone with Marian, Frank sank into the soft seat of a tapestry chair and clutched the brim of his hat, studying the carpet.

"That was nicely done," Marian said.

He lifted his head. "What do you mean?"

"My mother. I think you've charmed her. She sets a lot of store by the manners one has."

"She recognized me."

"Mother?" Marian shook her head. "No, you were a traveling salesman the other day. Today, you're a handsome churchgoing young man."

As Frank started to contradict her, Reverend Cooper hurried into the room, apologizing for his urgent departure. "But when an idea comes, I have to capture it as quickly as possible, else it leaves this feebled old brain of mine," he said with a half smile.

Marian sat in a corner of the room, the picture of demure womanhood. When Mrs. Cooper announced that dinner was ready, she let her father escort her into the dining room. Frank held her mother's chair and Marian favored him with a warm look from under thick lashes before resuming her modest demeanor.

The food was simple but plentiful. He complimented Mrs. Cooper on her cooking and had the pleasure of seeing soft color flood her wrinkled cheeks. Reverend Cooper talked about the many advantages of their small village, punctuating each comment with a jab of his fork in the air. Marian ate with her head down, the flash of her dimple showing her humor at the conversation.

He'd begun to relax, even enjoy himself, when the reverend suddenly asked, "You don't have a wife somewhere, do you?"

Chapter 2

Reverend Cooper's question startled him, coming in the middle of a diatribe on city life, and he almost dropped the forkful of mashed potatoes that was halfway to his mouth. Seeing only curiosity on the man's face, Frank relaxed and shook his head. "No, I've never felt much desire to settle down."

"Ah, the arrogance of young manhood," Reverend Cooper said, his fork again waving in the air as he talked. "Well, let me warn you. Before you know it, you'll be an old man like me, your life almost over. You need to start planning now, so you don't miss any of the important things." He plunked the end of the fork down on the table with a loud clang.

"Now, Father." Marian lightly touched his hand, her head bent toward his graying one. "You mustn't say such things. You're not that old and life definitely hasn't passed you by. You'll give Mr. Robertson an entirely wrong picture of you."

He patted her hand. "You're kind, Marian, always have been. But you're like this young man. Mustn't wait too long or you'll find yourself sitting by the roadside wondering when you got left behind."

Frank could see that her father was in the throes of another sermon. Without conscious thought, only knowing that he had to divert the older man, he blurted, "From everything you've said and what I've seen so far, Winston seems like a good place for a man to settle down. What else can you tell me about the town?"

Marian sent him a startled look, Mrs. Cooper a grateful one. How many times did the reverend spoil a pleasant meal with his moribund conversation? Frank had little time to think about it before Reverend Cooper chuckled. "You decide to stay here, young man, and you'll have all the mothers of single daughters after you. We don't have many bachelors around. They'll see you as an answer to prayer."

Frank laughed, and the reverend began a story about a young man who came to town one day last summer, expressing a desire to settle in Winston. Once the matchmaking mamas and single women discovered his presence, his life ceased to be his own.

"And then he just up and disappeared," the reverend said, sipping at the cup of coffee his wife had poured for him. "We never heard what happened to him, did we, Mother?"

Mrs. Cooper stood up and stacked the dishes. "I suppose he went searching for another quiet town." She added the empty potato dish to her load. "Marian, will you help, please?"

Marian picked up her own dishes, then leaned over Frank's shoulder for his empty plate. The soft curve of her breast brushed against him and his insides coiled with desire. She scooped up several more dishes before following her mother into the kitchen.

He wiped his hands on his pants and raised his head to find Reverend Cooper watching him closely. He pressed his lips together and hoped his feelings weren't reflected in his eyes.

"Mr. Bates, perhaps."

Frank blinked. "I'm sorry, sir, what?" Did the entire family jump from topic to topic without warning?

"Adam Bates, over at the feed store. He was saying the other day that he needed another hand. His son married a girl he met on the east coast and they're moving back there to be with her family. Can't say I blame them. It's hard on a young woman to be away from her family. But it leaves Adam in a bind."

Reverend Cooper nodded several times. "Yes, Adam Bates. You stay the night and I'll take you over to see him first thing in the morning."

Marian paused in the doorway, a flicker of alarm in her eyes. "Who's going where, Father?"

"I was saying that Adam Bates needs another hand. Young Frank, here, might be just the man." He dug into the piece of pie she set before him with the same intensity he'd given to his sermon. "I invited Frank to stay the night, Mother."

The thought of sleeping in the same house with Marian only a few feet away was almost more than he could take. The apple pie tasted like sawdust and he couldn't look at any of them as he mechanically chewed and swallowed the flaky pastry, his eyes on his plate.

After dinner, he accompanied Reverend Cooper to the parlor while the women finished clearing the table. The older man withdrew behind his Bible. Frank sat on the edge of the sofa, his fingers silently drumming on the armrest. Did he want a permanent job working in a feed store? Wouldn't have to be forever, he told himself. There was nothing to tie him to this town.

When the women came into the room, Mrs. Cooper brought out some sewing and settled in a corner. Marian wandered over to the narrow window. She pulled back the heavy drapes.

"Mother is famous for her garden," Marian said.

Her father lowered his Bible. "Mother does work wonders with her flowers. Marian, take Frank for a turn around the garden."

They walked out of the parlor and down the back hall. Once outside, he took a deep breath.

"They're not *that* bad," Marian said.

"I felt like I was sitting on pins and needles all through dinner," he confessed.

"You were nervous?"

"With good reason. Your father just kept me on my toes. He's a very sharp man, Marian. I didn't know what he was going to ask me next."

She led the way into the little garden area. They were behind the house, away from the parlor windows.

She stopped near a rose bush, idly touching one of the pink petals, her back to him. "Did you mean that about staying, Frank? Are you really going to interview for a job?"

She had left her hat in the house. The soft breeze ruffled her loose curls. Her skin seemed to reflect the bright colors of the flowers, and his breath caught in his throat. She was so beautiful.

He had to get away so he could think clearly. He stumbled onto the path and started walking in the opposite direction. When she called out his name in a dismayed voice, he didn't stop, breaking into a run as he left the path and entered an unplowed field. He finally slowed near a clump of trees, leaning his head against the nearest one, gulping in the fresh air.

Still trying to catch his breath, he heard her footsteps behind him. "Frank, what's the matter with you?" she asked in a breathless voice.

He bit his lip, unable to face her; he didn't move until he felt a timid touch on his arm.

"Frank, please, what's the matter?"

He turned then and saw his confusion mirrored in her eyes. With a strangled sob, he put his arms around her, pulling her close. Her arms slowly crept around his neck. When she lifted her face, he kissed her.

She tasted of cinnamon apples and sunshine. His eyes closed and he probed her lips with his tongue, wanting to taste more of her.

Her hands pushed at his chest. "Please, Frank…"

Fear sounded in her voice. Cursing himself for forgetting that she was an innocent, he raised his head. "Marian," he said thickly.

She traced the side of his cheek with her fingertips. "Why did you kiss me like that?"

He almost chuckled at the childlike wonder in her question. He rested his forehead against her silken curls. "Because you drive me mad."

"I do?"

A hint of womanly pride edged into her voice. He bent down, gently nipping her nose with his lips. "Yes. Does that please you?"

She giggled. "I've never driven a man mad before."

He pulled away from her until he could gaze into her eyes. "Marian Cooper, you probably drive every man in this town wild."

Her lashes fell but not before he saw the swift gleam of satisfaction in them. "How could I?" she asked softly. "I'm the minister's daughter."

He felt an urge to swat her behind. Instead, he pressed a hard kiss on her lips. "That's exactly why, you little minx. It's enough to drive any normal man crazy."

"I've never wanted to drive a man crazy before."

The implication in her quiet words acted like a tonic on him. He wrapped his arms around her, dragging her off the ground. This time her lips answered his silent pleas and parted under his kisses, letting him taste the fullness of her mouth, her tongue meeting his again and again.

His breath ragged, he slowly lowered her to the ground and knelt beside her, his hands still on her arms. Her mouth was bruised from his kisses and he bent down, gently kissing each swollen lip. "Marian, I'm sorry. I should never have done that."

"Why not?"

"Because you're so young." He dropped his hands and rocked back on his heels, hands lightly clasped behind his back so he wouldn't be tempted to touch her. He wished now that he hadn't been with all those other women, that he could offer her a body as innocent as her own. "I won't be staying, after all. I can't control myself around you."

"Why should you?" she asked in a whisper.

He turned away, jamming his hands in his pockets. "Marian, I'm somebody new and different. I've brought a little variety into your life and when I leave, you'll forget all about me."

She grabbed his sleeve, her touch forceful. "Frank."

He turned again, surprised at the passion in her voice. "Yes, you are different. But I've never kissed a man like I just kissed you, Frank Robertson, or felt any desire to do so. Do you have any idea what the last three days have been like? I didn't know if you'd return. And I wasn't sure what I'd do if you didn't."

She tossed her head, the curls that had been loosened by their kisses fluttering around her face. "I don't want to live without you, Frank. I love you."

He grabbed her wrists. "You can't love me, Marian. You don't know me."

"I know enough." Her lips curved upward and she leaned toward him. "Kiss me, Frank, kiss me and tell me you don't feel something, too."

"That isn't love."

"Kiss me."

Her insistent command pushed him to the brink. He took her by the shoulders, dragged her against him, his blood pounding as his chest collided with her soft breasts. She murmured against his lips and the action sent him into a frenzy of longing. They sank to the ground, his hands searching for the buttons on her dress, only half-aware of her hands tugging his shirt out of his waistband.

Her skin felt cool. She stiffened when his fingers slid over her breast and he hesitated until she arched against his hand. Her fingernails began a delicate dance under his shirt, trailing patterns over the bare skin of his back until he could hardly breathe.

"Marian..."

She pressed her fingers over his lips. "Don't say anything, Frank. Just love me, please."

Her hand found its way to his thigh, moving slowly upward.

She hesitated at the front of his trousers. He caught his breath, waiting. Her fingers were light, sending tremors through his entire body. His body threatened to explode under her caresses and he forced himself to slow down, to savor each glorious moment.

He touched one peaked nipple with his fingers and heard her answering moan. When she shifted, he slid his hand under her skirt, edging the sturdy material up until he felt the soft skin of her thigh above her stockings. She ducked her head against his shoulder and he nuzzled her with his chin until she lifted her head and he could reach her lips again.

His fingers skimmed her leg, the skin heating beneath his hand. "Oh, Frank," she breathed in wonder.

No woman had blossomed under his hands like she did. The others had been eager for him, willing to open their bodies to relieve a temporary boredom, to find a new experience. But Marian had never been with a man before; he knew that as surely as he knew he was embarking on an unparalleled adventure of his own.

His fingers stilled, his conscience awakened by the knowledge that she was a virgin. As if drugged, he lifted his head and surveyed her with heavy-lidded eyes. "Marian, we need to go back to your house."

Her hands clutched him around the waist. "Why? Did I do something wrong?"

He heard anguish in her voice and quickly kissed her lips. "No, darling, no. But this isn't right."

"I love you, Frank."

His heart turned over at the words but he wouldn't take her virginity in the middle of a field. She deserved candlelight and flowers, a soft bed, privacy.

And another man… His conscience jabbed him again. Who are you, anyway? A traveling salesman who'll go off and leave her after your own passion is sated.

The cold water of reality doused the remnants of his passion. He slid away from her, tucking in his shirt and climbing to his feet.

"Frank?"

He reached out a hand without looking at her. "Marian, we have to go. I don't need your father coming after me with a shotgun."

She sprang to her feet. From the corner of his eye, he could see her smoothing down her skirt, brushing away grass and leaves that had attached themselves during their aborted lovemaking. "I'll bet if Flossie were here, you wouldn't have stopped."

He gripped her shoulders. "Don't compare yourself to Flossie," he snapped. Her eyes were a deep midnight blue, the passion only slightly masked by her anger.

Her eyes narrowed. "So, you did notice Flossie."

"Marian..."

She swung out of his hold. "She's been with every man in town, Frank. Do you want to be another in her long list?"

She looked so brave, with her chin in the air, her eyes narrowed. And so young. His anger melted away, swallowed by his chuckle at her defiant manner.

"No, Marian, I don't. But that's exactly why you shouldn't compare yourself to her. She's not fit to be in the same room with you."

Mollified, she let her chin drop a fraction. "Then why did you stop?"

A wave of tenderness washed over him. "You're too young—"

"I am not!" She took his hand and held it to her breast. "I'm a woman, Frank."

His passion threatened to engulf his common sense again and he shifted away. "Marian, I should never have come out here with you. This was wrong. You *are* too young and I won't take advantage of your innocence this way."

"I'm not too young, Frank. I will never feel like this about another man. I know that and nothing you can say will change it."

Her fingers were fumbling with her buttons. He swore, swiftly closing the gapping material himself. Tears glistened on her lashes. He barely stopped himself from bending down and kissing them away. "Marian, you're so beautiful and young. One day you'll meet a man who will make you forget all about me, except as some long-ago memory from a summer's day."

"Stop it." She pushed his hands away, then planted her hands on her hips. "Stop talking about me as if I were a child! And stop *treating* me like one." She caressed his cheek. "Frank, believe me. I'm old enough to listen to my own heart. I love you."

His hands circled her wrists. "Marian, you don't even know me," he said with increasing desperation. "I don't have any money and I don't have a job."

"Father promised to help you get one. You could settle down here and—"

His quiet voice interrupted her. "I'm not the kind to stay anywhere for very long, Marian."

She stared at him, eyes unblinking, then twisted out of his grasp. "I see." Without looking at him, she smoothed down an imaginary wrinkle on her skirt. "Well, before you go, explain something to me. Why *did* you stop? I was in your arms, willing to be plucked like a ripe pear." He winced at her description but didn't say anything. "Wouldn't your buddies have liked hearing about the minister's daughter and how easily she fell under your spell?"

"Marian, I wouldn't tell anyone else about us."

Spots of color stood out on her cheeks. "Please, Frank, don't add to my embarrassment by lying."

Miserable and ashamed, he didn't speak right away. He *had* bragged about his conquests to the other salesmen. On the trains, late at night, they'd laugh about the lonely women they'd met, sharing stories and sometimes even addresses.

He wrenched his thoughts back to the woman in front of him. Tearstains streaked her face but she still managed to retain her dignity and beauty, standing before him in anger and defiance.

"You never had any intention of settling down, did you? You just let Father talk. Were you planning to catch the next train out of town after you were finished with me?"

"Marian, I never intended any of this to happen."

She stepped away from him, her shoulders hunched protectively. He stretched out one hand and let it fall back to his side without touching her.

How could he tell her about his conflicting emotions? He'd never wanted anything except the lure of the road until last week, when she'd opened the door. But what did he have to offer a wife?

A *wife!* Her father's probing questions came back to him. Did he want to get married? Could he marry someone like Marian and be faithful?

His own parents toiled long, silent hours side by side at the family store, tied together through habit. He thought of the Coopers. Mrs. Cooper barely spoke two words without looking at her husband for approval. Reverend Cooper hid behind his Bible.

Head thrown back, he tried to find the answers in the sky above him. A trio of white clouds broke up the monotony of the blue sky, dashing forward in a steady line. A breeze brought Marian's sweet scent toward him.

"Marian…"

She faced him, her eyes bright with unshed tears. "You might see me as a fool, but I'm not. Before you say anything, I suggest you leave this town before people find out what you tried to do with the minister's daughter. And on a Sunday, too!"

He knew then what he had to say. *He* might be the fool but he couldn't walk away from her. No matter where he wandered, he would crave her lips, her body, her very presence. Until he extinguished the fire she'd ignited in him, he would feel no relief.

He caught her hands. "Marian, I'm sorry," he said quickly. "Not for what happened earlier," he added when she twisted to get out of his hold. "For being such an insensitive clod."

She stopped struggling, watching him closely. "What do you mean?"

He kissed the tip of her nose. "The last three days have been hell for me, too."

One corner of her mouth lifted and the dimple played in her

cheek. "I didn't say that. Father would wash my mouth out if I used language like that."

"Then I'd kiss away the bad taste," he murmured, showing her how thoroughly he would do that.

When he raised his head, the color in her cheeks signaled a return to the passion they'd shared earlier, and his resolve to wait for a more romantic place warred with his rapidly growing desire. His resolve won by a tiny fraction.

He touched his forehead to hers. Eyes half-closed, she smiled at him, a slow, languorous smile that threatened the uneasy peace he had gained. "Don't," he groaned.

Her lips drooped into a frown. "What?"

He trailed one finger down her cheek, wrapping a curl around it. "Miss Cooper, you are enough to try the patience of a saint."

"But you aren't a saint," she said with a saucy grin.

He tugged on the curl. "No, and you should remember that."

Her hands slid up his chest and around his neck. "I do," she said in a husky voice.

"Marian, stop it!" He tugged at her wrists, holding her firmly away. "We need to go back to the house. Now."

"But, Frank…"

"No, Marian." He headed in the direction of the house, her hand tucked inside the crook of his arm, warm against his body. "I won't be chased out of town by an angry father. And if we don't return soon, that's exactly what will happen."

In the shadow of a large oak tree, he paused to check their appearance. With an objective eye, he straightened the collar of her dress, smoothed her wild curls behind her ears. He brushed his fingers lightly over her cheeks, wiping away a last tear. She shifted her head and planted a soft kiss on his palm.

His hand seemed to burn at the contact. "Marian, you can't do this."

She nodded. "Once we're home, I'll behave like the decorous young woman my parents expect me to be." She turned to him with shining eyes. "But I could sneak into your room tonight—"

He groaned and seized her hand, almost running down the road with her. "Not another word, Marian. I'll find myself locked up in jail for trifling with you—or worse, tarred and feathered and run out of town on a rail." He drew her back onto the road.

She giggled. "They haven't tarred and feathered anyone since some salesman came into town last spring, trying to sell us all some worthless tonic. Not sure why, though. His tonic made the women want to rip off their clothes—"

"I'm warning you, Marian."

"Oh, I'm sorry."

A quick glance at her showed that she wasn't the least bit sorry. He struggled against a strong urge to spin her around in the road and kiss her until her teasing expression was again replaced with one of desire. The house loomed before them and he rejected the image of her warm in his arms, releasing her hand and slowing to a more sedate pace as they came in view of the windows.

"You will stay, won't you?" she asked, a foot poised above the bottom step of the back porch.

"I'll stay," he promised.

He followed her up the steps, admiring how her skirt clung to the rounded curves of her bottom and the gentle sway of the material as she walked down the hallway. Her parents still sat in the parlor, their positions unchanged.

"Did you enjoy your walk?" her father asked, looking at them over the top of his Bible.

"Yes, Father, we did." Marian sat down with a soft rustle of skirts and picked up a sewing box next to the couch.

"So, what's your opinion of our fair village?"

Frank sat down opposite Marian before replying. "I didn't see much of it, sir, but the weather's very fine."

"You'll discover that this is a most delightful place," Reverend Cooper said. He rested his large Bible on his lap and rubbed his chin. "I was thinking, Frank, that after we see Bates in the morning, we could go by Widow Bartlett's house."

"Widow Bartlett?" Did the reverend want to find him a wife as well as a job?

"She mentioned that she hopes to take in a few boarders. You seem like a respectable young man. I'm sure the two of you can work out a sensible agreement."

From the color that rose in Marian's cheeks, Frank deduced that the widow Bartlett was a young woman. He lifted one eyebrow in question and when Marian glared at him, he had his answer. This town was filled with pitfalls.

And the most dangerous was sitting right across from him.

He excused himself, saying he needed to fetch his bag before supper. When Marian gave him a worried look, he smiled and watched her settle back on the sofa.

Once he'd retrieved his bag from the barn, he considered striding into the night and putting the Cooper family behind him. Even if Marian did cry herself to sleep for a few nights, she would forget him soon enough.

As he hesitated at the edge of the village, the scent of a rose floated toward him and he felt again her arms around his neck, her soft lips pressing against his. With a moan that startled several birds in the tree above him, he turned toward town and the Coopers' house.

Supper was a quiet meal, cold leftovers from lunch served by a silent Mrs. Cooper and a still-glowering Marian. Reverend Cooper kept up a monologue based on his readings of the afternoon. He obviously didn't expect anyone to respond to his observations. Frank found his mind drifting, returning to the conversation with a jerk when Reverend Cooper asked him a pointed question about his family.

"Two sisters, sir, one older, one younger." Frank sipped from his glass, waiting for the next comment.

"Sisters. I have a younger sister and four younger brothers."

Reverend Cooper shook his head with a reminiscent smile. "She never let us intimidate her, though. Like my Marian here." He touched a loose curl on Marian's shoulder, his expression filled with pride.

Frank held back a shudder. This man loved his daughter but more than that, she was a prized possession, if that proprietary look was anything to judge by. The reverend might welcome a passing traveler into his home for a meal, even offer to find him work. All of that would be in keeping with his spiritual calling. But he would not easily give away his only daughter to that same man.

Frank suddenly felt hot and surreptitiously mopped at his forehead. He was relieved when the meal was over, so he could escape to the room under the eaves.

After bidding everyone good-night, he climbed the stairs, shutting the guest-room door with a thankful sigh. It was simply decorated, with the barest of necessities, dominated by a large bed in the middle. He turned back the heavy blanket and sighed happily. Clean sheets! He didn't often have a bed at night. Now and then, he slid between the sheets of a bed with a housewife or a maid left alone in the house but seldom at night and never for very long.

He pushed such images away. Marian was in the room next to him. He could hear her moving around, making her own preparations for sleep. The vision of her smooth skin, naked beneath his hands, made him groan and he stripped off his clothes and crawled into bed, pulling the pillow over his head and ignoring the sounds from the room beside his.

He met Reverend Cooper on the stairs the next morning. "Sleep well, my boy?"

"Yes, thank you." Frank had finally settled into a dreamless sleep, waking only once at the howling of coyotes nearby.

"We'll have breakfast and then I'll take you to see Adam Bates."

The reverend was as good as his word. Adam, the middle-aged, rough-hewn owner of the feed store, studied Frank for a few moments. "If Reverend Cooper vouches for you, you're fine by me," he said, extending his hand. "You can start tomorrow."

"I could start this afternoon," Frank said. He needed hard work, something to keep his mind and his hands busy—to distract him from the minister's daughter.

Adam Bates leaned against the counter and nodded. "Fine, after lunch then."

Widow Bartlett had a room available in her narrow house. She was a tall, slender woman with a weary smile and even wearier eyes. Frank smiled politely when she showed him the common living quarters and he accepted her terms. With the money he made from the feed store, he'd have enough to begin saving.

For what? he asked himself as he carried his bag to his new home. He had thanked the family for their hospitality and promised to be a visitor one day soon. Marian had stood behind her mother, eyes aglow. He'd needed every ounce of control to keep from staring at her.

In his new room, he unpacked his meager belongings, his mind still on his change of plans. He'd never considered his future before. He enjoyed the different towns he visited and the freedom he had to leave them.

He sank down on his new bed. The bedsprings squeaked. The mattress wasn't as soft as the one in the Coopers' guest room, but it was *his* room. He hadn't been in his own place since his departure from his parents' house five years earlier.

The work wasn't hard. Adam Bates kept him until only a thin sliver of the sun was left in the sky. Jamming his hat on his head, Frank walked back to his new home, ready for a hot bath and a long sleep.

He ducked his head under the water and washed the dirt and grime off his body, whistling tunelessly as he did. Marian said she loved him but what could she know of love, young as she was, stuck in this little town? No one could really love someone after such a short time together. The idea was preposterous.

Maybe she was exercising her ability to charm men with nothing more than a smile. Was she practicing on him so she could entice some young man in the village who was her main objective?

Dressed in his slacks and a clean shirt, he went down to the kitchen, hoping his dinner would fill the suddenly painful hollow in his stomach.

Chapter 3

He soon adjusted to the easy pace of the village. Every Sunday, he dressed carefully in his new suit and marched down the road to the white church. While his sole interest in attending lay with the minister's daughter, he found himself paying more attention to her father's sermons every week.

After the service, Marian and her father greeted the congregation while her mother disappeared, presumably to fix the noonday meal. Frank didn't receive another invitation to the house but he didn't mind. He often ate his Sunday meal with his boss and family; it was easier to relax under the roof of the boisterous Bates family.

He'd just started his second week in the village when Marian came into the store with her father. "How are things going?" Reverend Cooper asked.

"Fine, sir." Frank didn't glance toward Marian, afraid that his emotions would show in his eyes. His heart pounded under the canvas apron he wore and he swallowed to relieve the pressure in his throat.

Satisfied that his good deed was still producing positive results, Reverend Cooper sat down on a stool near the front of the store. Mr. Bates took a stool opposite him and soon they were engaged in a lively discussion of politics, the weather and the state of the country.

Dismissed, Frank returned to his work, stacking bags of grain near the back wall. He almost dropped one when he heard Marian's soft voice behind him. "I've missed you."

He swung around, the bag clutched in his hands. "Marian, what are you doing?"

He peered quickly around. Tall sacks of grain separated them from the two men, and he could hear their animated conversation, but it was only a matter of time before her father started looking for her.

"I miss you, Frank."

Her forlorn voice pulled at him. Setting the bag down between them, he framed her face with his hands and tilted it up until he could see her eyes. "I've missed you, too," he whispered. "But we can't meet here."

"Then where? You never come to the house and I can't go to the widow Bartlett's by myself." She sniffed loudly, then let her breath out in a long sigh.

When he chuckled, her eyes flashed. "You think it's funny that we can't meet?"

He bent down and kissed her on the lips. "No, I think your playacting is funny." At the mutinous look in her eyes, he kissed her again, a hard kiss that left them both breathless.

"Frank, what are we going to do?"

When her shining face tipped toward his, he knew he was lost. He wouldn't call it love but he couldn't imagine living without her.

"I don't know yet, but I'll come up with something, Marian." At the scraping sound that signaled the stools were being pushed aside, he nudged her toward the front of the store. "Until then, trust me."

The tremulous look she gave him was full of trust. No one had ever regarded him that way before. His chest swelling with pride, he flung a bag to the top of the pile, her tempting smile urging him on.

That night, he wrote to his mother and told her about his new job and the village. He made only a passing mention of the Coopers, including them in a list of families who'd invited him into their homes. The letter sealed, he lay back on his bed. For the first time since he'd gone on the road, he felt a burning desire to return home, to try again with his father, to see his mother and ask her about his feelings for Marian.

The next Sunday, he saw Marian at the church. When Frank would've walked down the steps, she laid a gloved hand on his arm. He paused, his eyes going from her somber face to that of her father. Reverend Cooper didn't hesitate to offer him an invitation to dinner.

"I appreciate it, sir, but I couldn't impose—"

"Nonsense," Reverend Cooper interrupted with a wave of his hand. "We've been remiss in our duty to you, young man. Only the other day, Mrs. Cooper asked how you were getting on. Come to dinner and set her mind at rest."

"If you insist…"

He didn't look at Marian during the short walk to the house. Once inside the parlor, he sat across from Reverend Cooper and answered his questions about work. "This is a fine town," he assured the older man. "I feel as if I'm already part of the community."

Reverend Cooper beamed. "Wonderful place, Winston. When I left the seminary, I realized immediately that this was where I wanted to raise my family." He reached over and touched Marian's hands. "My family is second only to God, Frank. I hope you feel the same way."

Startled, Frank wondered if the reverend referred to *his* feelings for Marian. After a moment's reflection, he decided the older man was questioning Frank's relationship with his own family.

"I've written my mother about my situation here," he mumbled, glad that in this, at least, he could tell the plain truth.

"Good, good." Reverend Cooper released Marian's hand as Mrs. Cooper announced the meal.

When dinner was over, Frank excused himself, ignoring the frustrated look Marian sent his way. He couldn't sit in the parlor again, not with her father watching him. Even though he was sure the earlier comments were just ordinary conversation, he couldn't shake the nagging feeling that a warning had been implied.

The next Friday, Adam invited him home for dinner. The entire family greeted him, and he recognized several friends of the Bates children already sitting at the table. After a filling meal, he joined the large brood around the piano, letting his tenor mingle with the bright voices of the Bates family. They sang round after round of song. When they broke into "Button Up Your Overcoat," the group roared as Mrs. Bates tugged at his top button before kissing his cheek and sending him home for the night.

Whistling, he pushed open the gate at Widow Bartlett's house. She was gone for the weekend, which meant he had the entire house at his disposal. No new tenants had arrived to rent the other spare rooms and he relished the thought of several hours to himself.

Loosening his tie as he entered his room, he frowned at the sight of a letter on his bed. He tossed his tie over a chair and picked up the envelope. Seeing his mother's firm handwriting, he slit it open, then pulled out the single sheet.

She wanted him to come home. The people he mentioned sounded like good company, she wrote, but wouldn't he rather be with his family?

"We miss you, all of us. Even your father wants you home."

He dropped the letter on the bed and stretched out, his legs crossed at the ankles. Was that true? He couldn't remember anything but arguments with his dad in the years before he left. Everything he'd done had upset his father—his friends, the job he'd pursued, his grades. His mother and older sister had often stepped in to stop the two of them from fighting. He couldn't remember a single relaxing evening such as the one he'd just spent with the Bates family.

Something struck his window and he sat up, frowning. He heard the faint rattle again and crawled off the bed, yanking the curtain aside and peering into the deepening gloom.

"Frank?" A throaty whisper spilled into the open window.

"Marian?" He leaned on the ledge, unable to distinguish her shape from the shadows in the yard.

"Please, Frank, come outside."

She met him at the bottom of the steps and flung her arms around him. "Oh, Frank!"

He disentangled himself from her hold, then led her into the protection of the large oak trees surrounding Mrs. Bartlett's property. Even though his landlady was away, anyone walking by the house would be able to see them. "What are you doing here?"

"It's Father. Oh, Frank!" She flung herself back into his arms. "He says it's time for me to get married and he's already picked out my husband!"

"Get married? Isn't this rather sudden?"

She hiccupped and he could feel her nod. "I turned eighteen on Tuesday and he decided I'm old enough."

Frank leaned back until he could see the outline of her face. He traced her cheek with his thumbs, wiping away the tears. "And who has he selected?" he asked quietly.

"Martin Applethwaite."

Frank frowned, trying to place the name. Was it one of the men who'd come into the feed store? After a moment, he shook his head. "I don't know him."

"You wouldn't." She sniffled and he took out his handkerchief, waiting while she blew her nose. "Father met him when they both attended a special session at the seminary last year, and they've been writing to each other ever since. Mr. Applethwaite wrote that he's coming to visit next month. He's a widower and I don't know if they hatched this plan together or not, but Father's determined that I'll be his next wife."

Her voice rose in a loud wail, and Frank gathered her close to muffle her words. "Marian, surely you can talk to your father. Who knows? Besides, maybe you'll like this Appleton guy."

"Applethwaite," she corrected with another hiccup. "And I don't like him. He's old, Frank, almost forty, and he smells, and he never stops talking. Anyway, I don't *want* to marry him. I want to marry *you*."

Frank's heart pounded. Marian lifted her head. "What's the matter, Frank? Don't you want to marry me? Isn't that why you've stayed in town, so we could get to know each other better?"

"Well, it is. But marriage... Marian, I can't offer a wife very much."

She wiped her eyes with the back of her hand. "That's all right, Frank, I don't need very much. But I refuse to marry someone my father chooses for me."

"He wants you to be happy."

"Why are you agreeing with Father?" Marian stared at him, her eyes almost black in the fading light. "Do you want me to marry another man? I thought you loved me."

Her declaration echoed in his ears. Did he love her? He'd never said the words. But why was he staying in the area?

She struggled to get out of his arms and his hold tightened. "Marian..."

"No, let me go! I thought you'd help me because you cared about me. But I guess I was wrong." She pulled free of his grasp and stepped away, her chest heaving with each angry breath. "I should've realized what was happening when you never came over to the house."

"But, Marian, how could I? What would I say to your father?"

"You could ask permission to court his daughter."

One corner of Frank's mouth twisted into a lopsided grin. "And of course your father would've accepted me with open arms. I'm just the man the reverend Cooper would want for his only child—a salesman who appeared on his doorstep one day."

She stamped her foot. "You're the man I love, Frank Robertson. Isn't that enough?"

Oh, Marian, darling, he wanted to say, you're such a sweet child, with your dreams of romance, flowers, candlelight. At least your father understands marriage requires more than that.

His lips tightened. Would this widower give her the romance she needed? Or was he just looking for a drudge to care for his house?

"Marian, does Applethwaite have any children?"

She nodded against his shirtfront. "Two boys. Father says they're absolute angels."

Frank grimaced. Usually when two boys were described as angels, they were either the exact opposite or dead bores. He couldn't see Marian mothering either of them. No doubt these boys were hellions and the reason their father was going farther afield to find a wife.

"Marian, when is he coming?"

She must have sensed the change in him because when she spoke, her voice sounded stronger. "The end of August. His sister will be visiting him and he's leaving the boys with her."

A sure sign that the boys weren't angels. The man was smart; he didn't plan to ruin his prospects with his friend's daughter by bringing the future stepsons with him.

"All right." He bent down until his face was level with hers. "Dry your eyes and go home. Don't say anything to upset your father but don't agree to the marriage, either."

She nodded and blinked several times. "What will you do, Frank?"

He wasn't sure. But he couldn't stand the idea of her with another man.

Her hand brushed against his cheek. "I do love you, Frank."

He kissed her lips, then turned her toward the road. "Go home and stop worrying about this. Everything will work out."

He watched her walk down the road, her shoulders drooping

and her pace slow. His heart thudded in his chest. Short of marrying her himself, what could he do to save her from Applethwaite or someone else like him?

Disgusted with her father, he climbed the stairs and entered his small bedroom. When he sat down on the bed, a piece of paper rustled under his leg. He stared at the words his mother had written. *Come home.*

Home. He could pack his bags and catch the next train north. By tomorrow night, he could be back with his family, sleeping in his own room, eating his mother's cooking. He could leave the traveling life, go to work for his father.

He leaned against the headboard, hands clasped behind his neck. If he went home with a wife, his father would have to see him as a man. He could rescue Marian and, at the same time, provide himself with a way to convince his father he'd grown up.

The next afternoon, he ran down the street as soon as the feed store closed. He bathed quickly, washing away the smell of grain and smoothing down his thick hair. Dressed in his new suit, he walked over to the Coopers' house, his back straight and his lips clamped together.

Marian answered the door; when she saw him, her hand flew to her throat. "Frank, what are you doing here?"

"I need to see your father, Marian."

Her eyes widened. He tapped one finger against her lips. "Trust me, Marian."

She nodded and led him into the parlor. A few minutes later, her father joined him. "Well, young man, Marian tells me you've requested a few minutes of my time. What would you like to talk about?"

Frank took a deep breath. Now that the moment had arrived, he didn't know what to say. He swallowed more than once before the words came out.

"Sir, I would like to marry your daughter."

The words were soft but their effect was the same as if he'd shouted them. Reverend Cooper advanced on Frank, his normally placid features distorted. Frank took an involuntary step away from the fury in the older man's face, then forced himself to stand still.

"*Marry my daughter?* How dare you? After the hospitality we've shown you, welcoming you into our home, finding you a job. Why, I should throw you from this house!"

Reverend Cooper strode around the room, hands clenched into fists at his sides, body rigid. Afraid to move, Frank watched in awe. He'd been prepared for some anger when Reverend Cooper realized what he wanted but he hadn't been ready for the extent of the older man's rage.

Reverend Cooper stopped by the window, his shoulders heaving. "I suppose my daughter told you about the proposal from Martin Applethwaite," he said without turning around.

"Yes, sir."

"And no doubt you have some romantic idea of saving her from this fate." The man's words were heavy with sarcasm.

"That's not my only reason for proposing."

"No, I'm sure it's not." Reverend Cooper whirled around, his eyes narrowed and his hands still clenched at his sides. "She isn't pregnant, is she?"

Frank gasped and his own eyes narrowed. "No, sir," he snapped. "You insult your daughter by implying she could be."

Cooper's lips were pressed tight. "At least that's one worry I won't have when she goes to Applethwaite."

Frank took a deep breath, trying to restrain his anger. If he could calmly convince this man that he was the right choice for his daughter...

"Sir, Marian doesn't want to marry Applethwaite. She loves me and wants to marry me."

"And you? Do you love her?"

A sneer followed the word *love*. Frank stared at the man, then slowly nodded. "Yes, I do, sir. And I'll do everything in my power to make her happy."

"Happy! Bah!" Reverend Cooper turned back to the windows and placed one hand against the glass. "And what can you offer her? Applethwaite is a respected member of his community, a man already settled with a lovely home and two boys. What do *you* have?"

"I may not have a home yet, but Marian and I don't need much. We'll make our own way."

Reverend Cooper shook his head. "Young love. Do you have any idea how many couples I've counseled after young love disappears? You barely know each other and have little in common. You breeze into town one day, see a girl who catches your eye, and fancy you're in love." He swung around, his hands more relaxed. "I'm doing you a favor, young man. Pack your bags and leave tonight. My daughter will cry for a few days and then, when Applethwaite shows up with his offer, she'll be happy to marry him."

Frank scowled at him. "Is that what you want for your daughter? A marriage without love?"

"I want my daughter to be secure." He waved his hand around the room. "I'm old, Mr. Robertson, and I won't be here forever. With Applethwaite, my daughter will be cared for. She won't have to worry about her next meal."

"I can take of her," Frank said stubbornly.

"How? You live hand-to-mouth. You came into town with all your belongings in one bag. Have you even saved a penny?"

Frank thought of all the money he'd sent to his mother. He would've had a tidy nest egg if he'd kept that money. But his father was stingy, and Frank had assumed he'd have years to start saving for himself.

His pride held him back from saying this. If the reverend had suggested they talk, man to man, about Frank's prospects, his ability to care for Marian, he would've happily explained where his earnings had gone. But he would not let the man reduce him to begging.

"I forbid my daughter to marry you, Robertson." Reverend Cooper's voice was low and gruff. "Leave my house now and get out of town tonight."

As Frank listened, the old man's threat registered deep in his brain. He spun around and slammed out of the room.

He yanked open the front door, which crashed against the entryway wall. Behind him, he could hear Reverend Cooper's furious voice calling for his daughter and wife. A couple stood on the sidewalk in front of the house; Frank brushed past them without an apology.

Once at Widow Bartlett's house, he went over the confrontation again, pacing the long hallway. How dare that man refuse him! Who was he, anyway? Nothing but a small-town minister. And Frank had plenty of prospects. Wasn't his father a respected businessman in Davenport, Iowa? Why, this little village would fit in one street of Frank's hometown.

His breathing more normal, he sank onto a low bench and buried his head in his hands. After the scene in the parlor, he wouldn't be allowed anywhere near Marian. She was probably locked in her room and Reverend Cooper was already informing the community of his edict. With his local influence, he'd be able to destroy Frank's reputation. If Frank didn't leave town tonight…

He *would* leave town. He'd pack up and leave on the next train. And Marian would be with him.

Summer 2004

"I'm going over to see G.G. and Grandpa." Hannah stopped outside the guest room that her brother used during visits to their grandmother. "You coming?"

"I can't." He was digging through his suitcase. "I'm supposed to mow the lawn today."

"Fine. Just don't tell Grandma where I am."

"What's with the secrecy?" He tugged on the worn T-shirt he had unearthed. "And what are you going to tell Grandma when she asks why you're taking her car?"

"I'm not taking her car." She held up a purple bicycle helmet.

"I'm riding Mom's old bike. It's not that far. And the exercise will be good for me."

He followed her into the garage, where a dusty bike leaned against one wall.

Preston pulled the lawn mower out to the driveway. "You could mow for me—get your exercise that way."

"Nice try." She fastened the helmet and hopped on the bike. "I should be back before you finish mowing."

The retirement development was a mile away. The property had once been on the edge of Lincoln but with the resurgence of building in the community, Winter Oaks was now just another part of the sprawling east end.

She parked her bike, then went inside the main building. Tiny cottages dotted the property. One had been Frank and Marian's home when they'd first moved to the community. But after Marian's hip fracture four years earlier, the family had encouraged them to move into the residence lodge, where they would have resources at hand if needed.

"Hi, Hannah." The woman at the front desk gave her a big smile. "They're in the sunroom."

A long room opened onto the back lawn, which separated the more independent living quarters from the lodge. There were bright summer flowers along pathways wide enough for wheelchairs, with several benches tucked among large old oaks. Floor-to-ceiling windows brought the outdoors inside for those who couldn't go out or weren't in an adventurous mood. Little groups of people sat in the sunroom, a few with books or newspapers. Several were gathered around a piano, where one elderly man was playing what Hannah recognized as a musical show tune.

Her great-grandparents sat at the other end of the room, near a table that could be used for family suppers. A newspaper was open on Grandpa Frank's lap. His head was down, his glasses almost slipping from his nose, and Hannah suspected he'd fallen asleep.

Her impression was confirmed by G.G. "Don't wake him."

Marian's smile tightened a few of the wrinkles in her face. "He was reading me the most boring article about the city council's last meeting. Why he thinks I'd be interested in that…" She shook her head in loving exasperation.

Hannah pulled a chair from the table and placed it next to G.G., careful not to wake Frank. "How long will he sleep?" His neck was crooked toward his chest and she didn't want him to be stiff when he woke up.

"About ten minutes. He's been dropping off to sleep like this for the last few weeks. The doctor isn't worried, says it's due to age."

Hannah could hear the worry, though, in G.G.'s voice. And Grandpa Frank was ninety-six. "The staff here will keep track of him, G.G. You said yourself they're very responsible. And he could just be tired. Or he could've bored himself to sleep with that article."

She was rewarded by the soft chuckle that was one of her favorite memories. G.G. and Grandpa Frank had moved into the retirement village before Hannah was born. The short visits Hannah and her brother made to the complex were always full of special treats, movies on the big-screen television and walks through the grounds.

"So, why are you here, Miss Hannah-banana? Not that we aren't happy to see you."

"I think I've outgrown my nickname," Hannah muttered.

G.G. gave another chuckle and patted Hannah's hand. The touch was light and fleeting, like that of a butterfly landing on skin. "Darling, once you have a nickname in this family, it sticks. Do you suppose anyone will ever call me anything besides G.G.? Even your mother uses it now."

Hannah grinned. She'd coined the nickname for her great-grandmother when she was little, trying to put her mouth around the longer name of Great-Grandma Marian. She'd recently learned to recognize her letters and when her mother showed her the name on a birthday card, Hannah had pointed out the two

Gs. From then on, the great-grandchildren and soon the other relatives had started referring to Marian as G.G., distinguishing her from the other grandmothers in the family.

"Do you think you could just call me Miss Hannah instead?" she asked hopefully.

"I'll try. Now, I can see purpose written all over your face."

Hannah cleared her throat. If she didn't want Grandma Anne to ask questions about her whereabouts, she needed to finish her errand and get back quickly. "It's about your party."

G.G. sat back in her wheelchair, her fingers twisting the crocheted lap rug that protected her legs from the air-conditioning drafts. "What party?" Her smile was gone and her eyes were blinking rapidly behind her glasses.

Hannah frowned, worried by G.G.'s agitation. Frank stirred in his sleep, as if aware of his wife's discomfort. "For your seventy-fifth wedding anniversary," Hannah said slowly.

"Who said we were having a party?" She leaned over to pluck at Frank's sleeve, her actions reminding Hannah of a flustered bird. "Frank?"

His eyes opened immediately. He leaned toward his wife, the newspaper sliding to the floor with a rustle. "Marian, what's the matter?"

"Hannah's here." Marian's fingers continued to pluck at his sleeve. "She said we're having a party. You said we *wouldn't* have a party. You told the girls we wouldn't have a party."

Marian's voice had risen. Hannah glanced around the room but they were far enough from the others not to be attracting attention. Yet.

Frank took Marian's fingers in his hand. "Hush, it's all right." His eyes narrowed as he glared at Hannah. "What's this about a party? Your grandmother didn't send you over here, did she?"

Hannah shook her head vigorously. "No, it was my idea, Grandpa. I found some pictures and things and thought you deserved a celebration."

"We don't need a party to remember we've been married seventy-five years." His voice was firmer than she'd heard in her last visits. He leaned forward until he could cradle Marian's still-fluttering hands against his chest, their heads close.

"That's true, Grandpa. But it's just, well—" Her voice trailed off.

"No party. See how it upsets your great-grandmother?"

Hannah knew she should stop but maybe they didn't understand what she was asking. She sat forward, her face only inches from his. G.G.'s face was hidden against Frank's shoulder now. Her breathing was uneven but the fluttering motions had ceased.

"Not a real party," she explained. Maybe it was the idea of a crowd that was bothering her. Or dancing. Now that G.G. was in a wheelchair, maybe she didn't like being reminded of what she could no longer do. "Just a family dinner. Here." She gestured at the table behind them. "A few speeches, some stories about your life together. Cake. That's all."

She shifted until she could look into his eyes. "You've been together seventy-five years, Grandpa. We should celebrate that!"

G.G. was shuddering again. Tiny gasps sputtered against Frank's shirt. "Hannah, no more, please." His voice was sharp. "You need to go now."

Hannah stood up, hesitant to leave after being the unwitting cause of their distress. What had she said? "Grandpa—"

He waved a hand at her, his other hand softly rubbing Marian's back. "She'll be fine. Just leave right now. And no more talk of a party." He mouthed the last word at her.

Hannah nodded and headed toward the entrance, pausing in the doorway. Marian had raised her head from Frank's shoulder. He was softly smoothing her hair from her face. Even standing at a distance, Hannah could sense the love around the two of them, isolating them from the other people in the room.

She pedaled slowly home going over the visit in her mind. Why wouldn't they want to celebrate their anniversary? With so many marriages ending in divorce, staying married was a major feat in itself. And to be married for seventy-five years to the same person, still so full of love...

She parked her bike inside the garage and slipped in the kitchen door. She didn't want to be pushy but somehow, the family needed to recognize their lives together.

Somehow, she'd convince G.G. to have a party.

MARIAN'S STORY

Chapter 4

Winston, Missouri
August 1929

Marian raced into the parlor at the sound of her father's shouting. "Father, what is it?"

He swung around. "You knew what he wanted, didn't you? How dare you?"

The back of his hand struck her cheek. She sank to the floor. Tears sprang to her eyes and she pressed one hand against her throbbing face. "Daddy?"

The door clicked shut behind them. "Joseph, what's going on?" Her mother stood in front of them, her hands on her hips. "The door was open and several people were outside, staring at the house. What are you shouting about?"

"Ask her."

Her mother helped Marian to her feet, exclaiming at the mark on her cheek. She glanced at the man slouched in a chair, then back at Marian. "Well?"

"I don't know, Mother." She felt the greatest desire to throw herself into her mother's arms and cry. Where was Frank? Why was her father so angry? He'd *never* hit her before.

"One of you knows something and I expect an answer."

Marian's eyes widened at the vehemence in her usually quiet mother's voice. "It's Frank," she murmured.

Her mother urged her onto the sofa. "Frank? That boy who works for Bates? What about him?"

"He came to see Father—"

"He asked for your daughter's hand in marriage," her father snapped. "As if he deserved to even walk on the same path as her."

"Daddy, that's not true! Frank's a good man, you know that. Everyone in town likes him. Why, the Bateses think he's wonderful!" *Especially Sarah Bates.* She didn't add how much the younger daughter's compliments had worried her over the past few days.

"And what did you say, Joseph?" Her mother sat down next to her and Marian snuggled in her mother's arms.

"I told him to leave my house and that if he's smart, he'll get out of town."

"Daddy, no!"

Marian sat up but her mother tugged her back down, hands gentle on her arms. "Joseph, why would you do such a thing?"

Her father's chin jutted out as he stared at them. "To protect my only daughter. What would you do, Elizabeth, give them your blessing?"

"I would talk to the young man and let him visit. If they did truly love each other—" she silenced Marian with a pinch on her arm "—I'd accept my daughter's choice."

"You're a fool then." He lumbered to his feet, his actions those of a much older man, and reached for Marian. She shrank against her mother, evading his fingers. He grunted, grabbing her arm, hauling her to her feet.

"You will go to your room, Marian, and stay there. Your mother and I will talk about what's to be done."

"But, Daddy!"

"Go, Marian," her mother said. At the sight of her reassuring smile, Marian shuffled out of the room and up the stairs.

She sat on the edge of her bed. Where *was* Frank? If she could believe her father, he was on his way out of town. But how could he leave her?

A tear trickled down her cheek and she dashed it away angrily. She didn't have time to cry. Her father had banished the only man she could ever love. She jumped up and flung open her bedroom door.

She was halfway down the stairs when her father thundered out of the parlor. "I told you to go to your room, young lady!"

"But, Daddy..."

"And stop that sniveling." Clutching her arm, he dragged her back up the stairs and thrust her into the room with a jerk that sent her tumbling to the floor. Before she could stand up, the key turned in the lock.

She dashed across the room, pounding on the door. "You can't lock me in here! This isn't the dark ages! Daddy!"

"I can't trust you, Marian. I had no idea you were seeing that man behind my back."

She sat on the floor, resting her head against the door, as his footsteps faded away. Now she couldn't stop the tears. Her father had never shouted at her or hit her before. And to lock her in her room...

She didn't know how long she sat there. Brushing away the tears, she crossed the room and knelt by the open window. The sun had set hours before and stars twinkled in the sky above her. A breeze blew across her cheeks, erasing the heat of her crying. Her chin on her palms, she stared sightlessly outside.

"Marian?"

She leaned out the window. "Frank? Where are you?" she whispered.

"I'm in the trees at the edge of your yard. Did your father lock you in your room?"

She nodded, her earlier indignation returning. "He said he couldn't trust me."

She heard his chuckle over the cicadas. "Can he trust you?"

"What do you mean?"

"I'm leaving town, Marian. He threatened me and I've decided I've had enough of Winston. Are you game?"

Her heart lurched. He was leaving. But wait—what else had he said? She leaned farther over the ledge, hanging on to the sill with her fingertips. "What did you say?"

"Do you want to go with me?"

"How can I? My father hates you."

"I'm not asking your father's permission."

She sagged against the window, the implications of his statement suddenly clear. If she left with him, she would forfeit her father's blessing. The whole town would know what she'd done.

And if she didn't? Frank would go away and his pride would keep him away. It wouldn't be long before some other woman convinced him to get married and then he'd be lost to her forever.

"All right, Frank, what do I have to do?"

She heard a long sigh from the shadows and knew he hadn't been certain of her answer. A feeling of power fluttered through her. Initially this man hadn't even wanted to get involved with her. Now he was risking everything.

But he hasn't said anything about marriage, a tiny voice nagged her.

Why else would he take me with him? she told herself. He *had* to be planning marriage.

She listened carefully, barely breathing when he paused, both of them attentive to the voices down the road. He would be back at midnight with a ladder. They'd catch a freight train that usually passed through the edge of town around 1:00 a.m. and be far from Winston hours before daybreak.

Her heart was beating so hard by the time the clock showed midnight that she was afraid her parents would hear. They'd come up the stairs hours earlier, separately. Her father had gone into the guest room next to hers. He was usually a heavy sleeper but his tossing and turning signaled that he was as upset by the night's events as she was. When the iron bed finally stopped squeaking, she swallowed a tiny part of her worry.

A light scrape against the wall of the house announced Frank's arrival. She flew to the window on silent feet, her hands grasping the top of the ladder. His head appeared in the window a few seconds later.

"Ready?" he asked in a throaty whisper.

She nodded, afraid to speak. He took both her bags without a word and headed back down. She followed him, her hands clamped to the side of the ladder, her feet slowly reaching for each rung.

Near the bottom, he grabbed her around the waist and lifted her to the ground, pressing a brief kiss to her lips before releasing her. At the feel of solid ground, she let out a long sigh and realized she'd been holding her breath.

"I need to put the ladder back in the widow's shed, get my bag and then we'll be out of here." He picked up her suitcases, tucking the ladder under his arm. He began walking toward the back of her house.

She tugged at his hand and he stopped. "What, Marian? We don't have much time."

"Are you sure?"

"Sure?"

She could hardly see his eyes in the dark. Clouds covered the few stars that had shone earlier. Only two streetlights illuminated the village, their glow hidden from the parsonage by the huge oak tree.

He put her bags on the ground and slid his free hand around her waist, pulling her into the warmth of his body. "Marian, I want you to go with me. I'm going home, to my family. We'll get married there and start a new life together."

A sigh of relief escaped her lips just before he kissed her. He did want to marry her. He was taking her to meet his family and get married.

She bent down to pick up both of her bags. "Then let's go. We have a train to catch."

They sat in the empty freight train compartment all night while the train rattled its way north. He told her about his family, about his two sisters and his mother. She listened, cradled against his chest, his heart thudding steadily under her ear. She wanted the trip to never end.

He didn't mention his father and she finally asked about him as they rolled through another quiet town, the faint pink of dawn visible behind the rooftops. "We didn't get along too well," Frank said. "I got tired of being told I was no good and I left."

She folded her fingers around his hand. "Will he be upset that you're back?"

He linked his fingers with hers. "My mom's last letter said he wanted me home."

"Then it should be a happy homecoming."

He lowered his head and nipped her fingers with his teeth. She giggled and tried to pull out of his grasp but he wouldn't let her. "And when they see my beautiful fiancée, they'll be even happier."

Her eyes wide, she bent her head, meeting his kiss with one of her own. When he moved away from her a long moment later, she could hardly breathe and settled against his chest with a shuddering sigh.

They arrived outside Davenport in the late morning. Frank tossed their bags onto the ground and jumped down first, holding out his arms for her. She laughed and then jumped, her own arms wide. She landed on his chest and they both fell to the ground, rolling over and over and laughing as the train disappeared around the bend.

Near a row of white houses, Frank stopped talking. An older woman was sweeping the porch of a neat house halfway down the block. As they came closer, she dropped the broom, grasping her skirts with both hands while she ran toward them.

Marian held back, watching Frank's reunion with his mother. Tears blurred her vision.

"Oh, Frank, Frank, my darling boy, you've come home." His mother threw her arms around his neck, pulling his head down to hers.

"Ma, you're embarrassing me."

"After all these years, you can stand a little embarrassment." She kissed him again, then pushed him away, still clinging to his shoulders. "You're all grown up, Frank. Look at you."

He grinned. "You didn't think I'd stop growing just because I didn't have your cooking anymore?"

His mother laughed and moved to link her arm with his, but he reached his hand toward Marian. She skipped forward quickly, setting down her bags. "Mom, this is Marian. She's going to marry me as soon as we can make the arrangements."

Mrs. Robertson stepped back from Frank, a hand at her throat. "Marry you? But who is she?"

A tiny shiver went through Marian. His mother's words echoed those of her father.

Frank wrapped his arm around Marian's shoulders. "She's the woman I love," he said in a firm voice.

His arm supporting her, Marian extended her hand. "I'm pleased to meet you, Mrs. Robertson. Frank has told me a lot about you."

"It would've been nice to hear about you," Mrs. Robertson muttered but she shook Marian's hand.

"Frank! Frank! It really is you." A slender young woman, almost as tall as Frank, hurried down the steps.

"Clara!" Frank seized his older sister by the waist and spun her around, her skirt flaring.

A smaller girl clattered down the steps, jerking to a halt in front of the spinning couple. When Clara laughingly pushed out of his arms, Frank smiled at the girl and tweaked one of her pigtails.

"You're not little Rebecca, are you?" he asked.

She stretched herself to her full height. "I'm the tallest girl in my class."

"I bet you are. And one of the prettiest, too, no doubt."

She grinned, revealing a gap in her teeth, and then leaped into Frank's embrace. Her resounding smack on his lips earned her a sharp reprimand from her mother. "Rebecca, in the middle of the street!"

Frank loosened her hold around his neck and set her on the ground. "Now, Mama, they're just happy to see me. *You* kissed me in the street," he reminded her.

"Well, come inside now," she said, a dull red staining her cheeks. She clutched her broom with one hand and decorously held her long skirt with the other, leading the way up the steps.

Marian followed Frank and Rebecca, conscious of Clara beside her. "She sounds meaner than she is," Clara whispered.

Marian gave Frank's older sister a tight little smile. Clara was three years older than Frank, but her comment seemed naive. Mrs. Robertson was not pleased with Frank's announcement about the coming wedding. "I'm sure it's just the shock of seeing Frank again after all these years," Marian said carefully.

"I'm so glad he's home. We've missed him so much."

Clara held the door open for Marian. Ahead, Rebecca chattered with Frank, her small hand clasped in his bigger one. Marian felt a tiny pang at being left out, then reminded herself that it was only right he spend some time getting reacquainted with the family. After all, she was the one marrying him.

The narrow room at the front of the house was smaller than the parlor in Marian's home but furnished in the same somber style. She wondered if Mrs. Robertson or Clara had made the crocheted antimacassar on the back of the horsehair sofa. She hoped it was Clara's doing. She'd never mastered the intricate steps when her mother had tried to teach her. Maybe Clara could show her how to crochet and she could make decorations for her own house.

"Marian, honey, Mama asked you a question."

Her daydreaming brought to an abrupt end, she blinked and smiled at Frank. The slight pucker between his eyes disappeared when he returned her smile. She shifted on the hard seat until she faced Mrs. Robertson. "I'm sorry. I'm a little tired from the trip. What did you ask?"

"Frank said you're getting married here," his mother said. "Why not at your parents' house?"

Marian hesitated, wondering how much Frank had already shared with his mother. Why hadn't she been listening instead of dreaming about her own home? Now his mother would think she was a fool, not worthy of her son.

She straightened her back, smoothing down her skirt with a careful gesture. "My father refused to let me marry Frank. He thought Frank wasn't good enough for me." She paused, letting her words sink in. "Frank couldn't stay in Winston anymore, but we didn't want to be parted. He was sure you wouldn't turn us away, that you wouldn't want to lose him, the way my father lost me."

The older woman's gray eyes met hers, and Marian held her breath, aware that this woman could still cast them out. And then what? Would Frank trade his family for her love?

"You've had a long trip." His mother stood up. "Clara, help me in the kitchen. Your brother and his fiancée must be hungry. We'll start the wedding preparations tomorrow."

Rebecca followed them out of the room. Once they were alone, Frank closed his arms around her and she collapsed against his chest. "Oh, Frank, I'm sorry. I meant to behave and here I've been rude to your mother the first hour we're in her house."

He kissed the top of her head. "You were perfect. She may not act like it, but she appreciates gumption." His kisses roamed down the side of her cheek and ended at the corner of her mouth. "If you'd been someone mousy and quiet, someone she could walk all over, you wouldn't have been worth two minutes of her time." His kiss trapped her words.

"Ahem."

Frank slowly raised his head, and Marian lifted dazed eyes. Clara stood in the doorway, a tray of coffee and sliced cake in her hands. "Mother's right behind me," she warned.

Marian scooted away from Frank and pushed several stray curls behind her ears before folding her hands in her lap. When Mrs. Robertson entered the room, Marian was quietly conversing with Clara about the cake recipe and asking for help with her crocheting instructions. Frank lounged against the fireplace, a cup of coffee in his hand.

"It'll take at least a month for the wedding preparations," Mrs. Robertson said as she sat down.

"A month?" Frank moved away from the mantel and sat across from his mother. "But I thought we'd just have a simple wedding here, in the parlor."

"Even a simple wedding takes time, Frank. We need gowns, flower arrangements, a minister, your license."

A door opened down the hallway. Rebecca bounded to her feet. "It's Daddy! I get to tell him Frank's back!"

The man she pulled into the room was an older version of Frank. He nodded at his son, received a curt nod in return, then stopped in front of Marian, Rebecca still hanging on to his arm.

"Rebecca says you're going to marry this son of mine."

"Yes, sir. It's kind of sudden, but when he asked me, I couldn't say no."

Mr. Robertson smiled at her. "Frank always was a smooth talker." He grinned, one corner of his mouth slanting upward much as Frank's did.

Marian couldn't keep from smiling at him. "But that's not the only reason I'm marrying Frank. I love him."

Mr. Robertson studied her for a moment, then bent down, giving her a quick hug. "Frank, I'd hang on to her if I were you." He crossed the room in two long strides and clapped his son on the shoulder. "Good to have you home, son. We've missed you."

Her eyes moist, Marian blinked. Mr. Robertson perched on

the edge of the sofa, his long legs stretched out in front of him. Mrs. Robertson had been quiet during her husband's arrival but now she hovered over the two men, refilling their coffee cups and urging them to try the cake.

"Mama does love her men," Clara whispered.

Marian nodded, sipping her coffee. His mother had accepted the wedding. But would she accept her new daughter-in-law as easily?

Chapter 5

Davenport, Iowa
August 1929

Supper was a quiet affair. Rebecca chattered until her mother hushed her. Mr. Robertson ate hurriedly, almost shoveling the roast and potatoes into his mouth. He mopped up the gravy with a piece of bread and, once the plate was scraped clean, pushed it away from him before settling back in his chair.

Clara brought in an apple pie, slicing it at the table and serving her father and Frank first. The men matter most in this family, Marian realized. She tucked the thought away. Her parents had always catered to her needs, but their family was unusual. When they were married, taking care of Frank would be her first priority.

After dinner, Mr. Robertson disappeared into a back room. "His study," Rebecca whispered.

Marian glanced down the hallway. She and Frank's sisters were washing the dishes. Mrs. Robertson had gone into the parlor with Frank and she could hear the murmur of their voices through the partially open door. "He smokes a cigar and reads the paper," Clara explained. "We never interrupt him when he's in there."

"Does he do that every night?"

Rebecca and Clara both nodded. "Right after he eats," Clara added. "Sometimes, if we have company, he'll invite the men in. Frank might get to go with him now that he's grown up."

Marian dried the dishes carefully, wondering if this was what men did, even though it wasn't really part of her experience. Her father liked to be left alone when he was working on a sermon but most nights he sat with his wife and daughter in their cozy parlor. And Adam Bates never went off by himself, always spending the evening with his large family playing games or singing around the piano.

After the dishes were done, they joined Frank and his mother in the parlor. Mrs. Robertson had a basket of mending next to her and she was replacing a pocket on one of Rebecca's skirts. She smiled at her daughters, her eyes cold when she looked at Marian. "You can sleep in Rebecca's room while you're here."

"Thank you." Marian smiled at Rebecca. "I hope I won't be in the way."

"Oh, no. I have twin beds, so you'll have your own."

Mrs. Robertson snipped off the end of her thread. "And, Frank, you can have your old room. We haven't changed a thing since you left."

Frank laughed. "Nothing? I was sure Dad would move all my stuff right into the street."

His mother's hands paused over the striped skirt. "Frank, I won't allow you to speak about your father like that. It was hard when you left. I know you were upset because he wouldn't let you work more hours in the store, but you needed to finish your education. He wanted you to have a better life than he did."

Marian sat very still. Frank ran away because his father wanted him to stay in school? Ever since she'd met his father, she had wondered about the few references Frank had made to the man. She had assumed he'd beaten Frank or been cruel in some other way. But if his only sin was wanting his son to have a better life…

His mother rolled up the skirt she'd mended and tucked it into the side of her basket. Then she stood up. "It's time we all went to bed."

"I'd like to talk to Marian for a few minutes," he said.

His mother shook her head. "No, Frank." She held out her hand to Rebecca. "Come along, young lady. You have school tomorrow."

Marian lingered so that she left the room with Frank. His mother waited at the bottom of the staircase, her thin lips pursed. "We're coming, Mom," Frank said, a note of amusement in his voice.

"It's not funny," Marian hissed. "Are we never going to be alone again?"

He squeezed her fingers. "It's only for a month, honey. Besides, we'll be able to find a few private moments."

At the door to Rebecca's room, he slipped his arms around her shoulders and bent his head toward her lips. When she heard his mother gasp behind them, she pushed at his chest. "Frank!"

"A guy can kiss his girl good-night," he growled. His lips moved over hers in a long, slow kiss that drained her of all protest. When he released her, she staggered, then stepped into her new bedroom.

"Good night, sweetheart."

Marian couldn't look at Mrs. Robertson. She was glad when Rebecca skipped into the room and shut the door. "Wow!" the little girl said. "I didn't know my brother could kiss just like Rudolf Valentino."

Marian giggled. "Don't tell Frank that. He'll get so puffed up we won't be able to live with him."

Rebecca plopped down on the edge of her bed. "Marian?"

"Hmm?" Marian opened her small bag and dug through the jumbled contents for her toothbrush.

"What's it like to be in love? I mean, *really* in love, not like in books or movies."

Marian stared at the toiletries she'd grabbed before she left the house and snapped the bag shut. She sat on a narrow wooden chair, tucking her feet around the lower rung. How do I explain this to a ten-year-old? she wondered. I can't very well tell her that you want him to kiss you, that you want to be alone with him in a room and stay for at least a week. Maintaining her virtue on the train had been the hardest thing she'd ever done. She might have run away, but she was determined that no one would be able to say she *had* to get married.

She chewed on her lower lip. "You have to remember that I'm new at this, Rebecca. I've never loved anyone before."

"Did it happen just like that? I mean, did you see him and you fell in love?"

Marian remembered that first moment on the steps, when she'd opened the door, when she'd seen the tall, handsome stranger smiling at her. She had tilted her head back to look up at him and then his smile had disappeared. Something had come into his eyes, something that had touched her deep inside.

"I did, Rebecca. I didn't realize it was love then, but after a while, I knew I couldn't live without your brother in my life."

Rebecca flipped over on her back and sighed. "That's *so* romantic. Mama said you're too young to get married but I think you're just right. I can't *wait* to get married."

Marian counted to ten, afraid she'd make some remark about Mrs. Robertson that would get back to the older woman. A moment later, when she could speak calmly, she answered, "Don't rush it, Rebecca. You're still young. Your sister's older than Frank and she's not married yet."

"Pooh. Clara's never going to get married if she keeps going around with Sam Johnson. She's been going with him since before Frank left and she's *still* not engaged. He keeps telling her he has to wait because of his mother. I'd tell him either to marry me or leave me alone."

"Rebecca, there's probably some other reason."

"No, there isn't." Rebecca sat up, resting her chin on her bent knees. "Clara told me so one night. I could hear her crying, and when I went into her room, she said she loves him and that he *said* he loves her, but his mother doesn't want them to get married yet. Why does his mother have to be involved?"

"Because she's his family," Marian said. If Frank hadn't come after her, would she be sitting in her bedroom crying, hating her father for stepping between them?

She unpacked her nightgown and a cotton dress. They were both rumpled from being crammed in the bag. The dress she was wearing was wrinkled from the train trip, which meant she'd have to ask Mrs. Robertson for an iron in the morning.

"Rebecca, you need to get ready for bed. Your mother won't be happy with me if I let you stay up late on a school night."

"All right." Rebecca rolled off the bed in a fluid motion. Her nightgown and a flowered robe under her arm, she opened the bedroom door and then paused, her hand on the knob. "If Frank came in here while I'm in the bathroom," she whispered, "I wouldn't tell anybody."

Marian shook her head at the impish expression on the girl's face. The Robertsons were going to have their hands full when she was older. "No, Rebecca. I'm going to finish unpacking. I'll use the bathroom after you're done."

"You don't want to see Frank alone?"

Her fingertips tingled at the idea of being alone with Frank but she was afraid to even imagine his mother's reaction if they were caught. Her father's outburst at Frank's proposal would seem mild by comparison. "Not tonight, Rebecca. Now go."

She scampered off, a frustrated look on her face. Marian shook her head again, grinning, as she pulled the rest of her wrinkled clothing out of her bags.

She heard the door open behind her. "That was quick, Rebecca."

"Quick? I thought she'd never leave."

"Frank!"

Marian whirled around. Frank leaned against the door. She backed away from him as he came into the room, his eyes a dark silver. "You shouldn't be in here," she whispered. "Your mother."

"Is downstairs with my father. Rebecca's in the bathroom and I heard her running the tub. Clara is no doubt in her room wishing Sam had come over or at least called." He stepped closer and she took another step backward.

She bumped against the wooden dresser. He twined his fingers around a lock of her hair. "Your hair's so soft," he whispered, his breath warm against her cheek.

"Frank, you shouldn't be in here. Please…"

"I haven't been alone with you for hours. Just one kiss good-night."

"You did kiss me good-night."

One finger tilted up her chin. "Yes, I kissed you good-night. But you didn't kiss me."

"I couldn't! Not with your mother and your sister standing there."

"Now we're alone." His head lowered and his hand cupped the nape of her neck under her hair. He gently tugged her forward and she closed her eyes, parting her lips slightly.

The kiss lasted only a few seconds. When he drew away, she opened her eyes. "Frank?"

His chest was heaving and he didn't meet her gaze. "You're right, I shouldn't be in here." He jammed his hands in his pockets. "Good night, Marian. From now on, we'll say good-night in the hallway, with my mom and sisters around us."

She stared at the closed door. Had she said something wrong? Done something he didn't like? She hadn't meant to complain but his mother made her nervous.

She was in her nightgown when Rebecca came back into the room, her face shiny from her bath. Rebecca got into bed and hiked the covers up to her neck. "You can use the bathroom now."

"Thank you." Marian draped a crumpled dress around her for

a robe. On impulse, she bent down and kissed Rebecca's forehead. "Good night, sweetie."

"G'night," Rebecca mumbled sleepily.

The month passed quickly. Mrs. Robertson made list after list of wedding plans, ignoring Frank's pleas for a small, simple event. "You're the first one to get married," she stated in a no-nonsense voice one night at dinner. "We're not going to have your wedding a matter of speculation."

Marian bit her lip. His mother disapproved of the way they'd arrived at the house, and her hints about inviting Marian's family were getting broader. But Marian refused to send them an invitation. She couldn't risk her father's fury. Until she had a wedding ring on her finger, she wouldn't sleep easy. Her father could still find a way to stop the marriage from taking place and she lived in a state of uneasiness, worried that Frank's mother would invite them against her wishes.

Except for Frank's clandestine visit to the bedroom, they were never alone again. Sometimes Marian wondered if Mrs. Robertson spied on them, showing up in the parlor or on the stairs as soon as they were alone, her lists in her hand. She would click her teeth together and send Frank off on an errand before enlisting Marian's help with some household task.

Frank left each morning with his father. One afternoon, Clara took Marian to the store while Rebecca was in school and Mrs. Robertson was meeting friends for lunch. Marian found it hard to reconcile the quiet young man who was filling an elderly woman's grocery list with the debonair salesman who'd appeared at her house.

"It's not forever," Frank told her that night when she mentioned it. "This is just a stop, on the way to our bigger plans."

She hoped he was right, that her arrival in his life wouldn't some day cause him regret.

She lay in bed that same night and listened to Rebecca's even breathing. A slight breeze rustled the curtains at the open window. A bird called to its mate from the trees outside and a car rumbled to life down the block. She couldn't get used to the noise of the city at night and wished for the quiet of her small village.

And what would you be doing back there? she asked herself. Would you be dusting the bookcase for the hundredth time? Or would you be getting ready for a wedding to Mr. Applethwaite instead of Frank?

She shifted onto her side and rested her cheek on one hand. The soft glow of a streetlight lit up the room. Rebecca's clothes were tossed carelessly on her desk chair; Mrs. Robertson would snap at her when she came in the next morning, upset that she hadn't put her clothes away before going to bed. Moving quietly so she didn't wake the little girl, Marian folded them neatly and placed them near the dresser. At least one of them would still be in the good graces of Frank's mother.

She crawled back into bed. Two more days. Two more days and I'll be married. Calmer now, she smiled as she drifted off to sleep.

Chapter 6

August 1929

Her wedding day dawned bright and clear. Rebecca presented
her with a light blue handkerchief edged in delicate white
lace. "Clara tatted the lace," she said. "I embroidered your new
initials on it. It's for your something blue."

As Clara helped her into the plain white dress she'd sewn
during the long evenings, she blinked back tears at the absence
of her parents. *They made their decision,* she reminded herself.
*They didn't like my choice of husband so they don't need to see
us get married.*

Her heart ached when she walked into the small parlor and
saw the strangers sitting in the chairs. A few faces were familiar
to her from the neighborhood or church but they weren't *her*
family or friends.

Frank stood near the fireplace, a huge grin on his handsome

face. A warm glow filled his eyes as she walked down the make-shift aisle. She had to clutch the bouquet of roses to keep from dropping them. Her whole body felt like a quivering mass of nerves. She was marrying Frank. It didn't matter if they were surrounded by the entire village of Winston or on a desert island. She was giving her heart and her soul to this man.

Afterward, she didn't remember much of the ceremony. Frank introduced her to the guests and they all chatted while Rebecca and Clara served cake. She couldn't stop touching Frank, wiping a cake crumb from his chin, brushing against his arm when he mentioned his job, leaning into him when he told a funny story. His mother watched them with a frown but Marian didn't care. She was Mrs. Frank Robertson and nobody could take that away from her.

Frank had reserved a room for them in the fanciest hotel downtown. When the last guest walked into the afternoon heat, he squeezed her hand. "I guess we'll be going, too," he said with a catch in his voice that endeared him even more to Marian.

"Now?" His mother glanced at the clock. "I thought maybe you'd stay for supper."

"Now, Mother, I don't think we'll miss them tonight," his father said with a big wink at the couple. "They've been anxious to get away all afternoon."

Marian felt her cheeks flush. "Well, heavens," said his mother, fanning her own cheeks. "I never expected to hear such talk in my own parlor."

Marian ducked her head but not before she saw her new father-in-law pat his wife's hand. "We were young once, Millie. Go change, you two."

When they left, they walked downtown, their hands linked together. "It's really true?" Marian asked.

The bellhop had barely closed the door of the room before she was in Frank's arms. She clung to him, her limbs weak from their frenzied kisses. "I love you, Frank, I love you!" she whispered over and over, gasping with every new discovery. When he carried her to the bed, she helped strip their clothes away, a sense of urgency driving her forward. Her fingers flew down his body, memorizing his muscles, his skin, his strength, making him her own. His hands explored each part of her. Marian's insides jangled with excitement and anticipation.

His lips nibbled along her jawline and she reached for him, tugging him closer. She sucked in a breath at the sharp jab of pain and he paused, his hand stroking her hair. "Marian?"

"I—I—" She gulped in air. "I'm okay, Frank. I love you." She did, and if this was what she had to do to make him happy…

He kissed her forehead. "Relax, sweetheart. It's only temporary."

He moved slowly within her. The pain was ebbing, replaced by that sense of urgency again. Soon she was moaning his name, clutching his shoulders, repeating her words of love with each motion.

When he groaned and collapsed beside her, his breathing ragged, a wave of tenderness flowed through her. She brushed a hand through his damp hair.

"I love you." His barely audible words hummed along her skin and her arms tightened around him. They were bound together now, bound by forces stronger than any she'd ever experienced before. Enfolded in his arms, she closed her eyes and slept.

When she woke up dusk had fallen. She raised herself on one elbow and studied Frank's sleeping body. She had never known a man could be so beautiful. She traced the strong contours of his face, the firm jaw, the straight nose, the line of his eyebrows. He opened one eye; a corner of his mouth rose in a lopsided grin. "Hello, Mrs. Robertson," he said sleepily.

"Hello, Mr. Robertson." She boldly let her lips trace the line she'd just drawn along his face, laughing at his sharp gasp until he rolled her under him and brought a gasp to her own lips.

Darkness had come when they next awoke. She sat up in bed, a pillow behind her back and Frank resting comfortably against her stomach. "Do you realize, Frank, we haven't eaten a thing since breakfast?"

"Hmm. We had cake at the wedding."

She pushed at his shoulder. "That doesn't count. I only had that one little bite you fed me." She'd been too excited to put anything else in her stomach.

She slid away from him and out of the bed. "I'm hungry. Is the restaurant still open?"

He squinted at the clock. "We could try."

The hotel understood newlyweds. A table in the corner was set, and the waiter politely ushered them to their seats. He apologized for the slim selection at that hour but Marian was too hungry to care. She smiled at Frank and ignored his shock when she ordered sandwiches, cakes and soup.

"I need my energy," she whispered suggestively. She felt a sense of power surge through her when his eyes dilated.

They moved back to his parents' house the next day. She was sure that everyone knew what they'd been doing all night, and it took an enormous amount of effort to hold her head high. Alone in their hotel room, making love had been the most beautiful experience of her life. Under his mother's critical gaze, she felt as if she needed to take a long bath to cleanse herself.

Frank gave her a quick kiss before they left his room to go down for supper. "It'll be fine."

She nodded, determined to try for his sake to get along with his mother.

His sisters talked constantly during the meal, Rebecca reliving every moment of the wedding and Clara adding insights about the guests. Once Marian felt a pang of guilt at the sadness in Clara's eyes but she pushed it away. Clara didn't need her pity; she needed action. A resolve to help her new sister-in-law find her own happiness took shape while dessert was being served.

Clara left after dinner to visit friends. Rebecca had homework and she vanished up to her room. The two couples sat in the living room, the conversation revolving around the shop and changes that Mr. Robertson planned now that Frank was home.

When the clock chimed nine, Frank stood up and reached down for Marian's hand. A familiar churning began in the pit of her stomach.

"Good night, Mom, Dad," Frank said. He bent down to kiss his mother's cheek.

"Good night," Marian echoed, following him into the hall.

Her foot was on the bottom step when she heard his mother. "I don't like it, I tell you. Rebecca shouldn't hear those noises. She's too young."

Flame burned Marian's cheeks. Inside his room, Frank pulled her against his chest but she pushed him away with her fists. "Frank, no."

"Yes." He brought her closer, trapping her fists between their bodies. "She *wanted* you to hear her. Are you going to let her stop me from doing this?" He kissed the tip of her ear. "Or this?" His lips slid down her throat, to the top of her blouse. "Or this?"

She moaned at the onslaught of sensation from his touch. "No," she agreed, her fingers uncurling and wrapping around his neck. "But we have to be quiet."

"All right." And then his fingers were skimming silently across her skin, his breath whispering along her jaw, his touch saying louder than any words how precious she was to him, how much he cared. She melted into his arms, the world outside their room disappearing.

The next morning, she sat on the bed and watched him knot his tie. "We need our own place," she said.

"We will. As soon as I save enough."

She walked over and smoothed his jacket over his shoulders. "Frank, do you want to walk downstairs every morning, knowing your mother and father heard us making love?"

"I thought we were pretty quiet. At least, I was."

Her skin heated. He'd been tender the night before, but she'd been unable to stay quiet, biting the pillow to stop her moans from being carried throughout the house.

She swallowed at the memory, then narrowed her eyes at his smug grin. "I just don't think I can handle the embarrassment every day. Maybe we should sleep apart until we have our own place. I could move back in with Rebecca." *Your mother would be thrilled,* she added silently.

His eyes widened. She knew she'd never be able to make good on her threat but it was satisfying to see his grin disappear.

"Marian, you wouldn't."

She stood on tiptoe and kissed his chin. "No. But I *would* like our own place. I'll check the paper while you're at work."

She asked Clara about the area while they cleaned the living room. Clara mentioned that a friend of hers had recently vacated a small garage apartment. "I think it's still empty," she added. Marian kissed her cheek and ran all the way over to look at the place.

A few hours later, she was sitting on the front stoop, waiting impatiently for Frank to come home. Sounds of supper preparation could be heard from the kitchen. His mother had made several pointed remarks about not running a boardinghouse but Clara and Rebecca had soothed her by agreeing to cook the evening meal. When Marian finally heard Frank's whistle, she jumped up and raced down the sidewalk to meet him.

"Guess what happened today?" she asked at the same time as he said, "You won't believe what happened."

She stopped and caught his arm. "You go first."

"No, you."

"Frank…" she started, then laughed. "Clara told me about this darling little apartment. I went to see it and talked to the landlady. It's available if we want it, the rent is reasonable, and we can move in right away. She said we can have two days to make a decision but, Frank, it's perfect! We don't need two days."

"You found a place?"

She nodded. "Now you."

"I have a new job."

She stared at him. "A new job? But what—what about—?"

He laughed, pulling her into his arms and swinging her around. "Dad and I agreed he doesn't have enough work to keep me busy. And I didn't want to take money from Mom and the girls. Joe Wilson needed help and he hired me. I already sold a suit and two pairs of shoes today."

She slipped her arm through his. "So we both had a productive day. Come on, Mr. Robertson, let's go have supper and tell your family."

"Tell my parents? Right now?"

She nodded, bubbling over with happiness. Her handsome husband was home, he had a job that would suit his temperament better, he'd see the apartment was perfect for newlyweds...

She pecked him on the cheek, wishing they could run off right then and be alone. "You'll love the apartment. Mrs. Sullivan will be a wonderful landlady and I can fix up the room so it's ours...."

Her voice trailed off at the look on his face. "What's the matter, Frank?"

"Let's not tell them yet. At least about the apartment. Nothing's settled and she'll be upset enough about me not working at the store. And if we don't end up moving..."

Some of her excitement melted away. "I see." She dropped her hand from his arm and moved away a step. "You need to make a choice, Frank Robertson—your mother or me."

"Marian!"

She shook her head, refusing to be moved by the pleading in his tone or the desire in his eyes. She refused to be in the middle like this. She was his wife, and his allegiance should be to her. She'd given up her family for him. She deserved nothing less from her husband.

His chest rose and fell, and she waited silently. He held out his hand to her. "All right, we'll tell Mom. But couldn't we look at the place first? Make sure it suits us both?"

A little ache grew in her stomach at his distrust, but she nodded. He was willing to compromise. She could do the same.

"Now, come on," he said. "Let's eat. I'm starved."

After supper, they helped wash up the dishes, then left by the back door—for a walk, he told his family. After meeting their prospective landlady and being shown the small space, he agreed it would suit their current needs. Marian skipped beside him as they returned to the house, chattering about the changes she'd make.

"And it won't cost much at all," she assured him when he reminded her that they had little money. "I promise. I'll be creative and frugal. You'll see. We'll be fine."

A flicker of apprehension coursed through her when they entered the living room. His mother and Clara were mending while his father read to them. Rebecca lay on her stomach in front of the fire, a sketch pad in front of her.

"You're back." She jumped up and gave them both a big hug. "Where did you go?" Rebecca took Frank's hand, pulling him into the room. He sat down on the sofa and she squeezed in next to him, leaving room for Marian on his other side.

Marian's courage returned when he gave her a slight nudge with his leg. This had been her idea and her find. She should break the news. "We looked at an apartment today," she said quietly.

She glanced at Clara. Her head was bowed over the sock she was darning. Mr. Robertson had his book open in his lap but Marian didn't think he was reading. Frank's mother snipped off a piece of thread and Marian flinched.

"Did you find one?" Rebecca asked.

She turned to his sister with a grateful smile. "We did."

"A nice one," Frank offered. "We can move in anytime."

"I suggest you move now."

The venom in Mrs. Robertson's voice squeezed Marian's heart. Frank laid his hand on hers. "Mom, you don't mean that." Marian could hear the steel in his voice.

"I do." His mother stood up, snapping the shirt she'd been

mending and folding it with quick, angry jerks. "I'm sure you'll both be much happier."

"Now, Mother…"

Mrs. Robertson rounded on her husband. "She doesn't want to be here. Let them go. He's lost to us, anyway, now that they're married."

Marian rose stiffly to her feet, willing her legs to keep her upright. "I'm sorry you feel that way, Mrs. Robertson. We'll leave tonight. And thank you for your hospitality. Once we're settled, I hope you'll visit us and let us repay your kindness."

She walked out of the room, her head held high. She didn't break down when she went into Frank's old room and began tossing clothes and toiletries into their suitcases. She didn't shed a tear when Clara raced up the stairs and thrust a set of bedding into her arms. "We'll see you at church," she whispered. Marian didn't show by so much as a blink that she was embarrassed when Mrs. Sullivan came to her door in a bathrobe and handed them a key.

Not until they were alone in the tiny room did she give her emotions full rein. She flung the bundle of sheets at the wall. "How *dare* she treat me like that!" Her hands balled into fists and she stormed around the room, kicking at the single chair, and pounding on the little dresser.

"Marian!" Frank grabbed her shoulders and jerked her to a stop.

"Your mother hates me, Frank." Her chest heaved with hurt, and she could feel her throat burning. Angry tears erupted from her eyes. She would *not* cry, she told herself. She would not give that woman the satisfaction.

"And her son loves you." Frank brushed his lips over her flushed cheeks. "Marian, we're in our own place now. Maybe a little sooner than we planned but we're here."

His caresses were erasing the anger, replacing it with a shimmering desire. He slid his hands down her arms and pried her fingers apart, bringing her hand to his mouth and gently nibbling each finger. She gasped as need shot through her.

"Frank," she whispered.

"Hmm?"

"I love you."

He raised his head and grinned. "That works out fine for me, Mrs. Robertson. Because I love you, too. And right now, I have a powerful need to show you how much."

Summer 2004

"Did you find any pictures of Grandpa Frank's side of the family?" Preston spun a picture on the end of his finger until Hannah snatched it away from him.

"Don't do that! Do you realize you're touching history here?" She settled the picture on the stack she was sorting on her bed.

Her room was layered with pictures. Photo albums from the back bedroom, boxes of pictures from the attic. Once their grandmother had given in about the attic, Hannah had forced Preston to go back upstairs with her and they'd spent the entire afternoon carting down boxes.

"Grandma won't have a party if G.G. says no," Preston said. He'd wandered over to the window and sat on the padded seat.

"Well, I'm not giving up. Not yet." Even after her visit, she couldn't drop the idea of a party. "Come on, Preston, they've been married for seventy-five years! Shouldn't they celebrate?"

He shrugged. "Maybe. But they don't *have* to. I mean, they know they've been married that long. Why do they need a party?"

Hannah peered at him over the top of the pictures she was holding, caught by the logic of what he was saying, which was remarkably similar to Grandpa Frank's. "Okay," she agreed. "Maybe they don't *need* a party. But it would be good for the rest of us."

"Why?"

She dropped the pictures she was holding on the bed and turned so she could face him better. He wasn't the audience she had to convince but he would do for practice. And sometimes, she hated to admit, he did come up with some good ideas.

"Think about the world, Preston. Who stays married for very long anymore? G.G. and Grandpa Frank are an inspiration, a reminder that people can make a vow before God and family and keep it. Pretty impressive, isn't it?"

"Yeah." He had the cord of her curtain curled around his hand, and the curtain was hiding and then revealing the bright sunshine. "But I still don't see why we need a party or what you're doing with all these pictures."

That part she couldn't really explain, even to herself. She just felt compelled to go through the pictures that had been taken over the generations, to learn more about these two people who'd met all those years ago. Details of their story had been snapped throughout the decades, and each image she found gave her a new understanding of their lives—and their love.

A photo on one of the piles caught her eye and she picked it up. "Here, this is Grandpa Frank and his two sisters. The older one is Clara and the other one's Rebecca."

He studied the picture, then shook his head. "Okay, now I'm getting worried. You have way too much information about them. I mean, I didn't even *know* Grandpa Frank had sisters."

She stared at him. "Did you think he was an only child like G.G.? He had two sisters. Clara was older and married Sam. They moved to the east coast sometime after Grandpa Frank left Davenport, and they had some kids of their own. Grandma used to get Christmas cards from them. Mom probably did, too."

Preston lifted his hands. "I don't need all the details."

"You *would* like to know about Aunt Rebecca." She tapped the picture she was holding. A young girl with pigtails grinned at them, her bright expression a contrast to the more somber expressions of her brother and sister.

"What?" The word was long and drawn out.

"She married a restaurant owner. They stayed in Davenport for a few years and then he decided to move to California. Holly-wood. His restaurant was very popular with movie stars in the forties and fifties. Aunt Becca, as they called her, was the hostess and everyone loved to see her."

He squinted at the picture. "This aunt?"

Hannah nodded. "Yup. Somewhere there's a picture of her all dressed up. She's wearing a full-length fur coat, before everyone said fur was wrong. And she used to wear the highest heels you ever saw."

"Did you meet her?"

Hannah shook her head. "No. Just heard stories about her. Mom and her cousin Marcia were talking once. Aunt Becca died young, probably from lung cancer, only nobody's ever said that to me. She smoked a lot, something else people used to do without knowing how bad it was." G.G. smoked at one time; Hannah knew this from the snapshots, but she'd never seen her smoke.

"Hmm." Preston held the picture in his hand. "Did she have kids?"

Hannah grinned at his interest. "They adopted two boys. I have no idea where they are now. They'd be Grandma's cousins, so maybe she hears from them. One was a general in the army, with a bunch of stars. I'm not sure about the other guy."

"A general?"

She nodded. "Yeah, probably top-secret special clearance and all that other government stuff." Her brother was interested in the various branches of the service. His room was full of books about soldiers and their deeds.

If only there was a book to explain G.G.'s reluctance.

"Maybe I'll ask Grandma about him," Preston was saying.

"You could. She likes to talk about the family."

Preston put the picture back on the stack. "Hey, Hannah, why don't you go to the pool. Go make a fool of yourself over that lifeguard you said was so cute."

"I can do that anytime. I only get two weeks every summer to look at Grandma's stuff." Her mother, Kate, who was a teacher, shared stories whenever she could, but her life was so busy, she barely had time to keep up with her classroom activities during the school year, let alone delve into family history. And in the summer, she liked to travel with their dad.

Preston hopped off the window seat and headed for the door. "Well, I'm going outside. And I might just go to the pool."

"You do that, Preston. Oh, and if the lifeguard on duty is a girl, don't act like *too* much of a fool."

He stuck out his tongue and she laughed.

The door shut behind him and she sank onto the floor, gathering the photo albums closer.

FRANK AND MARIAN'S STORY

Chapter 7

By the time Frank came home for lunch that first day, Marian had succeeded in cleaning and organizing the tiny apartment. A flowered scarf draped over the top of the worn dresser hid most of the scratches. She'd arranged their combs and brushes side by side. Placing their toiletries together had seemed so intimate, and she'd flushed at the idea of being alone with Frank now, for all time.

Their clothes were neatly hung in the wide wardrobe. She had picked a few flowers from the back of the garage, certain that Mrs. Sullivan wouldn't miss them at all. Sitting in a can she'd covered with a piece of tinfoil, they brightened the round table that would serve for their meals.

The door opened and Frank entered, the noon sun silhouetting him in the doorway. "My, this is a pleasant sight for a man. To come into his house and find a pretty woman waiting for him."

He shrugged out of his suit coat. "You are pleased, Frank?" she asked. "We were right to move here?"

He kissed her. "Yes. Now, let's eat the sandwiches I brought home. I have to get back before long."

She showed him the cupboard under the sink where they could store their dry goods. "And we can squeeze an icebox in that corner once we buy one. I don't mind shopping every day until then. I'll have something to do."

She walked back with him after lunch, first carefully locking the apartment door. At the shop, he leaned down to kiss her but she jumped nimbly away. "Too many people, Frank," she murmured.

He laughed and patted her cheek. "I didn't know I'd married such a prude."

She pouted. "We're married now, Frank. We can't be making a scene in public."

A week after their move, she ventured into his father's grocery store. Rebecca and Clara were stocking shelves. Rebecca immediately ran over to Marian, hugging her around the waist.

"Leave her be," Clara said, pushing Rebecca away with an apologetic glance at Marian. "She's only been gone a week."

"Rebecca, go in the back room and sort those boxes that came in." Mr. Robertson's voice was harsh, and Marian's heart sank. She didn't want him angry with her, too.

But his smile was warm when he turned to her. "Settling in all right?"

She nodded. "We want you and Mrs. Robertson to come for supper soon."

"We'll let you have a few more weeks to settle in," he said. "Let me get you some groceries for now."

He wouldn't take her money. "No, Marian. You don't have to tell Frank, though." He gave her a big wink. "Our secret."

That night, Frank dropped into the easy chair Mrs. Sullivan had unearthed in the attic. She'd sent furniture over to the small apartment until Marian had reminded her the place wasn't that big.

"Thank you very much," she'd added. "Your furniture has made the apartment so homey."

She kissed the top of Frank's forehead. "Tired?"

He nodded. "The longest day ever. Not a single customer bought anything, Marian, but I swear everyone in town came to browse. I put shoes on little boys' feet all afternoon and helped three young guys try on suits. Must all be tired of their threadbare outfits and wanted to see what they could look like. I almost told one of 'em to leave but Fred said anyone can come in. Never know who might buy."

He rolled his head and Marian rubbed his neck. He leaned back against her hands with a sigh.

"Sure could've used you when I traveled the roads. Some nights, I could hardly sleep, I was so sore. Trying shoes on people is harder work, though."

She continued to rub his neck. Supper would keep, and he was in a talkative mood. "Frank, what do you want to do? I mean, do you plan to sell shoes and suits your whole life?"

"Not at all. I'm going to have my own business, first one shop and then two, and pretty soon, shops all over the country. Then you and I can just sit and watch the money fall in."

He pulled her around until she was sitting on his lap. "And we're going to make it happen before we're too old to enjoy it."

He kissed her and started to unbutton her dress. "Supper will get cold," she said but her words lacked conviction.

He successfully unfastened the last button and slipped the dress from her shoulders. He nibbled one shoulder, sliding the strap of her slip down to her elbows. "I'm not hungry for food right now."

Her slip was around her waist. He stood up, keeping her close to him, and quickly let the rest of her clothes fall to the floor. His own followed soon after.

Supper was forgotten. The room darkened. The only sounds were the sounds of the night and a wife comforting a tired husband.

She turned on her side and ran her fingers along Frank's face.

She could barely make out his features in the narrow streams of moonlight filtering in. His eyes were closed, his breathing that of a sleeping man. But as her fingers came to his mouth, he gently bit them.

"What about that supper?" he mumbled.

"Not sure what's left of it." She trailed her fingers across his cheek. "I thought you weren't hungry for food."

He pushed her off the bed, giving her bottom a swat. "That was before. Now I'm starving. Bring me some food."

She bowed to him, aware that his eyes were on her naked body. "Of course, dear master."

He rolled over, burrowing his head into the pillow. "Go, before I decide supper can wait again. And I think I'm going to need my nourishment."

She laughed and walked the few steps into the kitchen area. Moments later, they sat in bed, legs crossed, feeding each other and sharing kisses with the food, the room lit by a single lamp.

"What would your mother or my father say if they could see us?" She popped a piece of meat into Frank's mouth. "Here we are, sitting naked in bed, eating supper. We are lost, my darling Frank."

He washed the bite down with a swig of water. "As long as I'm lost with you."

He looked at her, his gaze searching. Suddenly shy, she reached for her robe. His hand stilled her movements.

"What's the matter?"

"I feel funny, sitting here with you, without any clothes on."

He cleared the dishes and food off the bed and pulled her close. "Marian Robertson, don't ever be embarrassed with me. You have a beautiful body. When I first met you, I could hardly sleep. You were all I thought about, your face, your eyes, your skin. And the reality's even more beautiful than I ever imagined."

She trembled under his touch and at his words. Turning to him, she lifted her face and kissed his mouth. That tempting mouth that could say—and do—such exciting things. She rolled onto her back, offering herself to this man who was her husband, urging him on, holding him close.

Eventually they drifted into sleep, and when she woke, she didn't know how much time passed. He slept beside her, one hand curled under his cheek, his dark hair tousled on the pillow. She climbed out of bed and carried the dishes to the table. Coming back, she gazed at him. For a moment she was frightened at the enormity of what they'd done. They had pledged their lives in this marriage and yet, what did they really know about each other?

He shifted, his mouth opening slightly in his sleep. Her heart lurched with love. He loved her and she loved him. She felt complete, willing to trust him with every inch of her body. They'd been right to marry. She turned off the light, tucked the covers around him and crawled into her side of the bed, curling up next to her husband, settling down for the night.

Frank was gone when she woke up. She stretched. The long day loomed ahead. The cleaning of their small home took little time and she only had one meal to cook. After that first lunch, Frank generally stayed at the shop, using the extra minutes to make another sale.

"I need more to do," she told Mrs. Sullivan. The older woman had invited her over for lunch.

"You can use that patch of garden behind the garage." Mrs. Sullivan poured tea into wafer-thin cups. "Then you can have all the flowers you'd like without feeling guilty."

Marian flushed. "I didn't think you'd notice."

Mrs. Sullivan chuckled. "I didn't. Ellie saw you out the window." The young maid had let Marian into the house. "We both thought it was good that the flowers are being enjoyed. You could grow your own vegetables, too. Tools are in the back of the garage."

"Thank you." Working in the dirt would give her a task for part of the day.

Mrs. Sullivan seemed to read her mind. "Gardening won't keep you busy all day, though. Why not come to my committee meeting? Even if you're pregnant, you won't have the baby for a number of months. You'll need something to do during that time."

Marian jumped, her hands resting instinctively on her stomach. A baby?

"We help women who've been deserted or were widowed by the Great War," Mrs. Sullivan continued. "Even after almost fifteen years, some of these women barely make enough to feed and dress their families. We take in donations and mend clothing and try to assist as many of them as possible. Can you sew?"

Marian's head was whirling by the time she went back to her apartment to fix supper. Mrs. Sullivan had talked about child care, feeding and clothing families, teaching tiny children to read and write, working with elderly people, until Marian couldn't think anymore. She didn't want to work yet. She just wanted to be Frank's wife.

Frank was exhausted when he came in. He sat on the top step, enjoying the light breeze, while she finished supper preparations. He was silent as they ate and after several attempts to make conversation, Marian stopped talking. She washed the dishes, then found that he was already asleep in bed.

She turned off the lamp and crawled between the sheets. When she snuggled up to him, kissing his shoulder, she was answered by a gentle snore. Looking at his back in the pale light of the moon, thinking of how lonely she'd felt all day, she felt an urge to cry or shout. Stifling both, she turned over and went to sleep.

A pattern quickly evolved. Frank was often gone when she woke up, slipping out quietly at first light. She joined Mrs. Sullivan on the committee, patching clothes, baking bread and rolls that were taken to families throughout town, watching children while their mothers shopped or rested. Her own housework took only a few minutes each morning, and she discovered that Frank didn't mind what he ate in the evening, so long as it was filling.

She was worried. They hadn't made love in three weeks. She'd hoped the weekends would be better, that he wouldn't be so tired, but he'd started working Saturdays. Working on commission didn't pay much and he was determined to buy their own house.

"If I never see you, what does a house matter?" she asked him one night.

His eyes were dark as he looked at her. "Marian, this is for both of us. I want your father to see that I can provide for you."

"I don't care about that. Don't I matter more than my father?" She'd written to her parents, informing them that she was married. Her mother had replied with a short note, thankful that she was a respectable woman, but disappointed in the manner of the wedding. Her father had not been mentioned at all.

Frank didn't say anything. And when he tried to hug her, she turned away, unwilling to release her hurt feelings.

The little house was quiet during those days. Laughter seldom echoed around the walls and Marian was eager to leave each morning.

One bright September afternoon, she sat on the stoop, trying to catch any breeze that might blow away the unseasonably hot weather. The thick woolen child's dress she was mending would be warm in the upcoming winter, but now its weight added to the heat. She gratefully put the dress aside when Clara came into view.

Clara picked up the tiny dress. "Do you have news for us already?"

Marian laughed and then sobered. Her lonely nights mocked her. "No, my landlady keeps me busy. I do mending for a committee she's on."

"Oh, the Women for Women Group."

Marian nodded. "Well, don't tell Mother," Clara said. "She believes it's unhealthy. All those women need, she says, is a husband."

"I'm sure they'd like to have theirs back," Marian snapped. "Unfortunately, most of them died in the war or disappeared. And there aren't that many men around now. Not that a husband is a woman's answer to happiness."

"Oh?" Clara's eyebrows went up.

"I mean—" Marian stopped in consternation. "I mean, a woman has to be able to care for herself, not rely on a man…"

"Are you all right?" Clara asked quietly.

Marian paused. How could she tell Frank's unmarried sister the true problem? Even though Clara was older, Marian had more experience.

"Frank doesn't talk to me much," Marian said. "He comes home from work, eats dinner, goes to sleep. He's too tired for anything."

"Anything?" Clara echoed.

Marian couldn't face Clara. She could feel that her skin was probably brick-red. She shifted on the step as a mosquito buzzed past her ear.

"I may not be married, but I do know about men and women," Clara finally said.

Marian turned to her sister-in-law. "I didn't mean to be rude, Clara. It's just that I'm not used to talking about this."

Ellie, Mrs. Sullivan's maid, came out of the house and waved at them. She carried a basket of laundry to the line and began carefully pinning up towels and sheets. Children could be heard running down the alley, home from school. Clara sat silent.

Marian made a decision. She had to tell someone. And maybe Clara had some ideas. "I don't know what to do. I make supper before Frank comes home and I'm waiting when he walks in the door. He sits down, gobbles his food and practically falls into bed. Before I've even cleared the table and washed the dishes, he's asleep. And he wakes up and goes to work before dawn."

"Don't do the dishes."

Marian stared at her sister-in-law. "Leave them on the table?" The one night she'd done that, she had awakened the next morning, appalled at the mess. Her mother had never left the dishes until morning and she was certain Mrs. Robertson was the same sort of housekeeper.

Clara nodded. "What's more important, a clean house or your husband? What would happen if you got up in the morning and did the dishes then? Or got up after Frank went to sleep? Sounds as if your working in the kitchen doesn't bother him or wake him up."

Marian could only frown, trying to readjust a lifetime of teaching. "But, Clara, if I don't do the dishes…"

"What?" Clara interrupted. "Will you be a loose woman if you leave the dishes to go to bed with your husband? I wouldn't say so. And I'm sure if you asked Frank, he'd agree with me."

She couldn't imagine asking Frank. In the early days, they'd discussed so many things but except for his one speech about how much he desired her body, they'd never talked about lovemaking.

Clara changed the subject then, asking about the committee's work. After she'd gone home, Marian continued to sit on the stoop, watching Ellie take down the laundry, shaking each piece before neatly folding it and placing it in the basket. That simple, ordinary act snapped her to attention.

She went into the apartment, the dress in the basket Mrs. Sullivan had provided. She set the table and made a salad and sandwiches. She put tomorrow's breakfast plates in a stack by the sink. After Frank went to sleep, she'd get up and do the supper dishes. Then she'd place the breakfast ones on the table.

Frank flopped onto the bed when he came in the door, his hand over his eyes. Marian bent down and slipped off his shoes, rubbing his feet. His hand dropped to her hair.

"What a day, honey. But I did make two sales so we can pay the rent. I've also got some grocery money for you."

He stretched and sat up, his hand still tangled in her hair. "You are paying Dad for the groceries, aren't you?"

"Of course." And it was true. Except for that first gift, she'd insisted on paying. "I know how you feel about charity."

He held her against him. "It's not just charity, Marian. It's being beholden to them. We can take care of ourselves."

Her evening was not going as planned. She didn't want to discuss his parents. She stood up. "Come on, let's eat supper. The salad will wilt if we let it sit any longer."

He didn't talk as they ate. She kept the silence filled by chatting about Clara's visit and listing several upcoming town activities. He responded with grunts and sighs.

After supper, he closed the curtains and went into the bedroom alcove. He undressed, folding each item of clothing neatly before placing it on a wooden chair near the bed. Just like Ellie folded the laundry, Marian noticed.

She didn't move. She considered Clara's advice and tried to get up from her chair. The dishes waited on the table, taunting her. When she heard the creak of the bed, she put her head down and let the tears come.

Frank was by her side instantly. "Marian, honey, what's the matter?"

The tears flowed faster. He cradled her in his arms, her face pressed against his bare skin. The feel of his chest under her cheek made her sob in sadness and then exasperation. When his hand caressed her neck, she twisted away, putting several feet between them.

"What's the *matter?*" Her voice wobbled, and she swallowed, determined to tell him exactly how she felt. "For the last three weeks, you've come home, eaten your supper and fallen into bed. Have you forgotten you're married? Don't you care about your wife? About me?"

She was shouting, pacing around the room. She brushed at the tears still falling, irritated by her lack of control. The urge to open the door and storm down the steps, into the street, away from these confusing emotions, was overwhelming.

"Marian, I'm tired. I work all day." His voice was patient, like that of a parent consoling a child, which irritated her more.

"Did your father just come home from work and collapse? Or even mine? How do you think we got here? Or your sisters?"

His face creased in angry lines. "What are you talking about? I've never heard you talk like this."

"You haven't heard me talk much at all, Frank. Not about

anything important. I chatter away about mundane events of the day and you pretend to listen while you bolt down your supper. I'm not sure we should even have gotten married. We know hardly anything about each other."

She couldn't breathe. She couldn't stop the angry words. It was as if a huge dam had burst inside her and all the aches and misery of the last few weeks were flooding out, threatening to drown them both. She wanted him to hold her, to dry her tears, to make the hurt go away.

He was zipping his pants, his shirt already buttoned. "What are you doing?" she asked, frightened. When had he put on his clothes?

"I need some air. I'm going for a walk."

He left the room, the door clicking shut behind him. She stared at it, waiting for him to come back. But the door remained firmly closed and the night sounds crowded around her.

She did the dishes, trying to ignore the ugly things she'd said. But her words seemed to tumble around the room, as if they'd taken on a life of their own. She set the table for breakfast, ran a rag over the dustless furniture, straightened the cupboards. When she could stand the empty room no longer, she flung open the door and stepped outside.

And almost tripped over Frank. She stopped inches away from him. He didn't raise his head and she kept still, afraid her voice would crack or those hateful words would come spewing out again.

"Marian, I'm sorry about what I said."

She knelt beside him. Covering his face with kisses, she said, "Frank, I'm so sorry. I was mean. You had a hard day at work and I shouldn't have talked like that."

He gathered her onto his lap, her feet dangling over the side of the steps. "No, honey, I should've been more considerate. You're here alone all day—and then I don't even talk to you at night."

"It's not just the talking," she began shyly.

He kissed her lips and let his mouth trail down the open neck of her blouse. "I've been a fool," he said huskily. "Imagine wanting to sleep more than *this*."

When he began to unbutton her blouse, she moaned. A light came on in the house across the way, and she wriggled in his arms but he held her fast. "We need to go in, Frank. What if Mrs. Sullivan comes out?"

"She'd see that Frank Robertson was making amends for his foolish behavior." He popped the last button out of its hole and pulled the material apart.

The evening breeze whisked over her breasts. "Frank!" She pushed out of his lap and stood up. Then, grinning, she reached down, tugging him to his feet. "Come on. It's late and you need to go to bed." Her hand in his, she led him into their apartment and shut the door.

Chapter 8

A new pattern began. Frank would come home from work and she'd be waiting for him. They would crawl into bed and make love. She would then get up and bring their supper to the bed, where they'd eat and talk about their day's activities. They were becoming friends.

Days turned into weeks. Marian heard talk about trouble in the financial world but she didn't understand much of it. When Frank came home without a sale, Mrs. Sullivan told them not to worry about the rent. Marian didn't. She had a new concern to occupy her time.

She had not had a period for two months. So far, she could fit into all her clothes. However, if she *was* pregnant, she'd only be a few months along. She hadn't experienced any queasiness yet or any of the other symptoms the women at the committee meetings mentioned, but from their talk, she knew each woman was different.

She still hadn't told Frank when he came home early one day, a Thursday in late October. She had decided not to go to Mrs.

Sullivan's house for the regular meeting and was resting on the bed when Frank walked in the door.

She scrambled to her feet, smoothing down her hair. Frank sat at the kitchen table, his hands folded on the wooden surface. His silence worried her. Not since their argument had he been so serious.

"What's the matter, Frank?" She slid into a chair opposite him.

His eyes were dark and hollow. "Marian, the stock market crashed. Businesses are failing all over the country and the banks are closed. You can't get your money out. Not that we have much in there but it's affecting everyone. Joe said not to worry and then closed up shop early. I didn't know what else to do so I came home."

Marian thought of their tiny savings, tucked away in her slip drawer. Every paycheck, Frank peeled off a few bills, enough for their household expenses and a few dollars for savings. He had asked her to open a savings account at the bank, but she hadn't liked someone else having their money. Now she got up and went to the drawer.

He ignored the can she tried to hand him. She finally took off the lid to show him the rolled-up wads of bills.

"I never opened an account, Frank. Don't yell at me, but I didn't want someone else taking care of our money. Not after you worked so hard for it."

He stared at her, then tipped the can over, pouring the bills and coins onto the table. Marian stood there, unsure of his emotions, as he counted the money.

He hugged her around the knees. "I should be mad at you, honey, but you've saved us. We can live on this until things are okay again. Thank goodness you can be so stubborn."

His mood tempted her to tell him about the baby, but a knock sounded at the door. Opening it, she was surprised to see Clara.

"We need Frank. Right now."

No questions were asked as they ran down the street. Marian struggled to keep up with them. When Clara came back for her, Marian motioned her on. "I'll get there. Just hurry." Something awful had happened; she could tell by Clara's face.

People stood on the street corners, talking. Businesses were closed, even though it was only midafternoon. Marian weaved through the crowds, hurrying to the Robertsons' house.

The front door was open and Marian ran in. Rebecca sat in the front parlor, her eyes wide, her arms around her bent knees. Marian heard a commotion down the hall but she couldn't abandon the little girl sitting alone. She sat down next to her.

"Honey, are you all right?"

Rebecca looked around at Marian's words, her eyes unfocused. "Daddy? What's the matter with Daddy?"

Before Marian could say anything, Frank appeared in the doorway. He gestured to her, and Marian left Rebecca, casting a worried glance over her shoulder before turning to Frank.

"I don't understand it all yet, but my father seems to have lost the business and the house."

Marian gasped; she felt her muscles dissolve. Frank caught her as she sank to the floor.

When she opened her eyes, she was lying on the parlor sofa. Rebecca still sat in the same chair. Clara knelt beside Marian, fanning her face. Frank moved closer to her.

"How do you feel? I shouldn't have been so blunt."

Marian shook her head, then regretted the action. The room swam before her eyes. She swallowed, regaining her equilibrium. "Where's your mother?" she asked.

Clara answered, "One of the neighbor ladies is sitting with her. She's asleep now."

Marian looked at Rebecca, and Frank followed her gaze. "She doesn't understand what's happening. Not that any of us do," he added. "She's been like this since he came home. She knows there's a problem but she doesn't know what."

Marian felt a surge of dislike for Frank's mother. She should be comforting her children, not taking to her bed. But then she thought about Frank. How would she respond if something happened to him? Her heart softened a fraction.

The next few days passed in a blur. Mr. Robertson worked at the store, sleeping in the back room. Mrs. Robertson decided to move herself and the girls to her parents' farm, west of town. Their belongings were packed up, and Frank's grandfather arrived in a rumbling truck to take them all away. They left behind an empty house and the few furnishings that were to go to the new owner.

"Strange to think how quickly life can change," Frank mused as they walked back to their small apartment.

Marian held his arm. She had to tell him about the baby but this wasn't the time. He was worried about his family, and his job was precarious. Joe had kept him on, but only because he worked on commission. He lived in daily fear of losing his job.

"They'll be fine. Your grandfather will take care of them." She had liked the gruff older man, seeing a survivor in the weathered face and rough hands.

"Poor Clara." Frank's voice was filled with compassion and she squeezed his arm, loving him even more for the way he cared about his sister. "Now she'll never marry Sam Johnson. Moving out to the country will guarantee she'll end up an old maid."

Marian sighed in agreement.

But they were wrong. The next day, as Marian rested on the bed, Frank at work, there was a knock at the door. Feeling anxious, she answered—to find Sam Johnson standing there.

"You probably think I'm a fool or poor-spirited," he told Marian over the tea she'd made for them. "But I'm neither. I'm all my mother has, and I've had to look after her. However, I don't mean to lose Clara. I want to marry her. Mother agrees we've waited long enough. What I need from you, please, Mrs. Robertson, is her present address."

"Oh, Frank, he was so solemn. And so determined," Marian said that night, as she related the story. "I couldn't say anything except to give him the directions to your grandfather's house. He thanked me, then went off. I felt like I was playing a part in an old-fashioned romance."

Frank stretched out in bed. "Well, I hope this works out for Clara. They'll be living with his mother and she's a hard woman to please."

"Clara should be used to that," Marian replied. With a startled gasp, she covered her mouth with her hand.

Frank chuckled and pulled her hand down. Kissing the palm, he said, "Remember, I lived with my mother, too. I'm sure life wasn't always easy for her. My parents didn't marry for love," he added.

Marian looked at him in astonishment. He nodded. "Their parents were friends. They were expected to marry and they did. I believe they've grown to love each other, though."

Marian snuggled into his arms. "Well, Clara deserves some happiness in life."

As the Christmas season approached, Marian squandered a few of their precious savings on fabric for presents. She sewed every day after Frank was gone, shirts for Frank and his father, a new dress for Rebecca, pillowcases for his mother, a set of sheets for Sam and Clara. They were to be married on New Year's Day, in a small ceremony.

A week before Christmas, Mrs. Sullivan stopped her after their last meeting of the year. "Marian, congratulations. How does Frank feel about the baby?"

Marian wasn't surprised at Mrs. Sullivan's perspicacity. The older woman always seemed to recognize what people needed before the request was even voiced.

And it felt so good to have someone else know her secret. "I haven't told him yet," she confided. "He's so worried. How can I tell him there'll be another mouth to feed?"

"The baby won't be born until spring. By then, things will have settled down. After all, we're beginning a new decade. Tell him tonight." Mrs. Sullivan gave her a hug before she left.

Frank was tired when he came in but happy. He'd sold a pair of shoes, the first sale in days. The money wasn't much, but it clanked reassuringly as she added it to the can.

He sat down in one of the kitchen chairs, waiting while Marian finished the supper preparations. As she set the table, he noticed the fancy china dishes.

"What's this?"

She blushed. "Mrs. Sullivan lent them to me. I have some special news for you."

Dark eyes intent, he watched her closely. She took a deep breath. "Frank, I'm pregnant."

He didn't speak. He sat still for a moment, then leaned forward, scooping mashed potatoes onto his plate. She sat down across from him and mechanically filled her own.

They didn't talk as they ate. The easy camaraderie of the past few weeks was absent. The cutlery clinked against china, echoing in the silent room. Frank ate slowly and methodically, chewing each bite for a long time.

She tried to eat but her stomach kept jumping. Whether that was because of the baby or the continued silence, she wasn't sure. When he pushed his plate away, she sat back in relief. Finally, they would talk.

"Aren't you excited, Frank? Sometime in the spring, we'll have a baby." Now that she was used to the idea, she could envision walking the baby down the street, into the little park two blocks away, playing there while they waited for Frank to come home. Eventually they'd need a bigger place, but for the first year or two, their apartment would be sufficient.

"How far along are you?" he asked gruffly.

She blinked away the visions. "Maybe three months or a bit more."

His chair toppled to the floor as he stood up. *"Three months? When did you find out? Why didn't you tell me at once?"*

She hunched in her chair. "I didn't want to bother you, Frank. First, there was your family's troubles. And then you were so worried about your job. I didn't want you to worry about anything else."

"Not worry? You silly fool." She cringed at his harsh tone. "How are we going to feed a baby? Do you realize what's happening out there? Millions of people have no work, no place to live. I only have a job because of Joe's kindness. He may decide he doesn't have enough business for two salespeople and then where will we be? Mrs. Sullivan doesn't nag us about the rent, but she won't be able to afford that sort of generosity too long, either."

"But, Frank, what can we do? I'm pregnant. We'll have to manage the best we can."

"No, we won't." He paced around the room, his hand clasped behind his back. "I'll talk to a friend of mine. He'll have the name of a doctor who can get rid of it."

His words penetrated the fog that had been surrounding her since his first words. She jumped to her feet, her chair meeting the same fate as his. "You listen to me, Frank Robertson." Her hands cradled her stomach protectively. "I'm going to have this baby. You can run scared the rest of your life, but I'm not. I'll go home if I have to, but I won't visit your doctor. I will not commit a sin for you."

She grabbed her coat from the hook and stomped out of the house, not waiting for his reply.

She walked for hours. The evening was cold and she wrapped her coat more closely around her. A few homes had Christmas decorations, and the irony of arguing about her baby's birth at this time of year wasn't lost on her. She passed families huddled over fires built on the street. She hurried past, her own burdens enough to carry for this night.

Frank was asleep when she came in. She turned out the light, then curled up in a chair, still wearing her coat. A small fire burned in the fireplace and she stared at the flickering flames for hours before she drifted off to sleep.

The baby was not mentioned again. She went along with the pretense, relieved to have the fear of an abortion gone. Frank left for the shop each morning. She sewed her Christmas presents, met with Mrs. Sullivan and her committee, and kept house.

Early Christmas morning, Frank's grandfather picked them up; they were to spend the day at the farm. Marian brought a pie she'd baked, scrimping to save enough ingredients for the sweet pastry.

Rebecca ripped open the paper on her package. "Oh, look, a new dress!" She ran down the hall and soon returned wearing her new outfit.

"You look lovely," Clara said. She'd gushed about her own gift, a set of sheets with embroidered initials.

"You want to model with me?" Frank teased his father. They'd opened their presents while Rebecca was changing.

His father's grin was weak. Marian was glad to see a spark of his former self appearing. "Enough nonsense," Mrs. Robertson said. She carefully folded the paper that had been wrapped around her pillowcases.

"Did you like your present?" Rebecca bounced over, tracing the pattern of roses Marian had embroidered near the hem.

Marian glanced at her mother-in-law. "They're nice," Mrs. Robertson said. Marian was content.

On New Year's Day, the family met together in the farm's living room for Clara's wedding. Marian listened to the vows, remembering her own simple service. "Will you love her, comfort her, honor and keep her?" the minister asked Sam. "In sickness and in health, for richer, for poorer, for better, for worse?"

She stole a look at Frank. He was staring straight ahead, his mouth grim. She clutched her fingers together and swallowed her tears.

Frank started coming home late again. Marian wondered if he was working late, avoiding her by staying out or with another woman. She didn't want to know. Since the night she'd told him about the baby, they didn't speak unless necessary. She was often in bed when he returned and she had perfected the pretense of being asleep. He would quietly slip in, and soon she'd hear his gentle snores.

Near the end of January, the baby moved for the first time. As she felt the sensation of tiny flutters, she stopped, resting her hands on her now-rounded abdomen. A deep peace settled over her.

In February, Mrs. Sullivan took her to a doctor. After his examination, he said, "You're very healthy, Mrs. Robertson. Continue to take care of yourself. You should deliver in early May."

That night, when Frank came home, she waited until he was eating supper before speaking. She had taken to eating earlier, then sitting in her armchair, sewing baby clothes from leftover scraps of material. He would eat his meal alone at the table.

"I saw a doctor today. He says the baby will be born in early May. We'll need to decide if I'm going to stay here or go home to Winston for the delivery."

"Suit yourself," he said curtly.

"Frank, please." She dropped her sewing into the basket. "This is your child, too. Can't you be excited?" She got up and stood next to him. "Put your hand on my stomach. He really moves around. You can feel him." She reached for his hand but he jerked away.

"You know my feelings about this, Marian. This is a rotten time to bring a baby into the world. I can barely support us, let alone another person."

"But babies cost so little! Mrs. Sullivan's promised to help as much as she can. She has a lot of her daughter's baby clothes still here."

"Charity? Is that how you want our child to survive? On charity? We might as well go back to your parents' house if *that's* how we're going to live." He slammed out of the apartment and Marian didn't hear him again until early morning.

She relished her changing shape and altered dresses to fit her larger size. She added to the collection of baby clothes, and Mrs. Sullivan polished the old cradle she had in the attic. Together they planned for the baby that Frank ignored.

One mid-April night, Marian awoke from a deep sleep. Frank wasn't in bed and she turned over. As she did, her stomach knotted. Clutching her middle, she staggered out of bed. The pain was excruciating. Dragging herself down the steps, she stumbled across the yard toward Mrs. Sullivan's house.

She saw the rock but couldn't avoid it. Her arms folded around her stomach to protect the baby, she crashed to the ground.

She lay there, panting. Her legs hurt and her vision was clouded. She cradled her stomach, whispering words of reassurance to the baby. No quivering kick answered her.

Frantic, she tried to stand up but her legs shook. With a desperate cry, one hand holding her stomach, she crawled toward the house.

She fainted twice before she made it as far as the steps. Her entire body hurt and the ache in her abdomen frightened her. She willed herself to think of nothing but reaching the door. She had to get to the hospital. Mrs. Sullivan would arrange it.

Ellie answered her pounding at the door with a shocked cry and hollered for Mrs. Sullivan. Together, the two women bundled Marian into the backseat of the ancient vehicle kept in the garage for emergencies. Marian sank against the cushions. "Please," she whispered, "please, God, let my baby be safe." She hadn't prayed much since she'd left the parsonage. Would He even hear her?

She fainted again before they arrived at the hospital. When she opened her eyes, she was in a hospital room, her stomach feeling incredibly light.

She shifted, and a nurse came out of the darkness. "Mrs. Robertson?" she murmured.

Marian tried to sit up, but she was so tired. "My baby? Where's my baby?"

The nurse took her hand. "Mrs. Robertson, I'm so sorry. The doctor did all he could, but your son didn't make it."

A son. She had a son. With a tiny whimper, she turned her head into the pillow and sobbed. The nurse stood there, holding her hand.

She dropped off to sleep, her pillow saturated with her tears. When she woke up again, light filtered through the blinds into the room. Frank sat in a chair next to her bed.

"Honey? How are you?"

"Frank?" She reached her hand toward him, and then she remembered.

Her baby, her son, was gone. No little arms would slip into the shirts she'd painstakingly sewn. No little feet would wear the booties that Mrs. Sullivan had knitted in the evenings. No little face would light up when she came into the room.

The immensity of her loss threatened to suffocate her. She clutched at her throat, trying to get the air out of her lungs. Frank tried to take her hand, his eyes searching the door for a nurse.

"What is it, Marian? What can I do for you?"

Dry heaves wracked her chest. She had no tears left for her poor child; they'd all soaked her pillow the night before.

A nurse glided into the room, her feet silent in her white shoes, carrying a tiny bundle.

"Would you like to hold your son?"

Frank lifted his arms but Marian waved him away. "No," she said harshly, the word scraping her throat. "He's *my* son."

The nurse gingerly laid the tiny form in her arms. Marian pulled the blanket back and studied the perfect face. His eyes were closed and for a moment, she thought he was only sleeping. She'd suffered a nightmare. Her baby was alive.

But he didn't move. No rise and fall of his chest. Wishing she still had tears, she bent to kiss his smooth, perfect cheek.

A tear dripped onto her hand. Confused, she raised her head and met Frank's anguished eyes.

"I'm so sorry, Marian," he whispered, one finger gently stroking the baby's nose. "I'm so sorry. I never meant for this to happen."

"It wasn't your fault," she managed to tell him. His pain was intense enough to touch. At least I'll never feel the guilt he will, she thought. I never wished you gone, little one.

She kissed the baby's forehead. "I want to call him David. A good strong name to protect him."

"David." His finger edged around the baby's ear, over the little shoulders. "We'll miss you."

Her tears flowed then, spilling onto David's blanket, washing away all the promise that the future had held for this child. Frank put his arm around her, and they held their son together.

When the nurse returned, Frank was reluctant to hand over the baby. "Frank, she needs to take him." Marian touched his hand lightly. Her sorrow left no room for anger. "He's in our hearts now, and that's where we'll have to carry him." She eased the baby from his arms and carefully gave him to the nurse.

"I'm so sorry, Marian, about the past few months." His head was bowed, his hands clasped in his lap.

"I'm too tired now, Frank." She closed her eyes, feeling weak and drained. "I need to rest. Why don't you go home and come back later?"

She felt his kiss on the top of her head, then heard the door shut. Muffling her head in the pillow, she cried, great, wracking sobs that wrenched the soul from her body. When she felt a hand touch her hair, she jerked away, not wanting Frank that close to her.

"Go ahead, cry. You hurt and you need to release the pain." The nurse's voice was soothing, her fingers gentle.

"He was a beautiful boy," the nurse said.

"What will I do? How can I live with his father after this? He didn't want the baby and never even spoke about him." The words poured out of her, rushed by the tears that never seemed to stop.

"You'll find a way." The nurse tucked the wet strands of hair behind her ears. "Women have suffered pain through their children since Eve. Your husband also hurts and you can heal together." She pulled the covers around Marian's shoulders. "You won't forget this little one. But you'll go on, for his memory's sake."

She handed Marian a pill and held a cup of water to her lips. Gratefully, Marian slid into a deep, dreamless sleep.

She was still groggy when Frank returned. He carried a small bouquet of roses, which the nurse set on the window sill. He sat down beside Marian's bed, his hat in his hands.

"Marian, I've been thinking all afternoon. I can't change what happened, but I can make a change for the future. The doctor says it's possible there were complications, and that's why you woke up."

His eyes were on the ground, his voice barely audible. "The doctor doesn't know if the fall caused you to lose the baby or if it was something else. It doesn't matter now. What does matter is that we've lost our son and I will carry the burden of that—of not being with you—for the rest of my life."

A twinge of the love she'd felt for him stirred and tried to come to life. But David's tiny face came back to her and she pushed the feeling away.

"Marian, I don't blame you if you hate me. I turned my back on our marriage, on you. But, please, can you give us another chance? I want to go away from Davenport, leave the bad memories and start fresh."

"To Winston?" She had a strong desire to see her mother, to hear her father quote comforting words from the Bible.

He nodded. "If that's your choice."

They could stay with her parents. She had written them again after Thanksgiving, secure in her marriage and unwilling to continue hurting the two people who'd raised her and loved her. Since then, she had received several letters. They would welcome her back with open arms.

"Jobs are still hard to come by," he was saying, "but not as many people are trying to find work there as in other parts of the country. Your father will help us, Marian."

Tears misted her eyes. "Yes, Frank, I want to go home. Please, take me home."

He moved to her side and put his arms around her. "Honey, no one will ever take the place of David. I'm so sorry he's gone. But we can start over, and this time things will be better. I promise."

She closed her eyes, willing the tears to go away. "I loved that little baby, Frank. Every night, when he moved, I felt so good. I feel empty now."

He pressed his lips against her forehead. "We'll go to Winston, Marian. You can heal there. And there'll be other babies. Babies we'll both love. You'll see."

She couldn't think of other babies. Not with David's face so clear in her mind.

But she would go home to Winston.

Chapter 9

Winston, Missouri
April 1930

"Thank you for bringing her back to us." Mrs. Cooper stopped near Frank, carrying the basket of towels she'd just taken off the line.

Frank looked up from the newspaper article he'd been reading in the back garden. He was glad she had the basket in her arms; her constant pats and hugs were sometimes more than he could handle, especially after a long day at the feed store. He'd slipped outside to enjoy a few minutes of quiet. "You don't need to thank me every day."

"Oh, but I do." She dropped the basket on the ground and took the chair opposite him. "We missed her so much. Her father could barely write his sermons, all that sorrow and guilt weighing on his heart. His actions were what drove her off."

Frank's own guilt weighed on him. "We didn't do right by you, Mrs. Cooper. We should never have stolen away like that. At the very least, we should've told you where we were."

Her eyes teared up, and the sight tore at his heart. Marian would look like this when she was older, a lovely woman with experience and life etched on every inch of her face. How many tears would his wife cry because of him?

He had vowed that their life would be different, that he would pay constant attention to her, that she would hear how much he loved her. The image of her in that hospital bed, her face pale and wan from the loss of their child, would haunt him forever. He would make it up to her, every single day.

He had told her parents about losing the baby, not sure she'd be able to talk about it. Her mother had said she'd speak to Marian. "It's the lot of the women in our family," she had told him, her narrow hands patting him awkwardly on the shoulder. "We seldom can carry a baby to term. That's why Marian is our miracle."

She'd said something similar to Marian, because she'd dismissed all his attempts to talk about future babies. "We won't have any, Frank," she'd muttered once, her tone flat and bitter. "And you needn't feel guilty about David's death. You weren't responsible. My family was."

He had tried to gather her into his arms, but she'd pushed him away. They'd spent the first few nights in separate rooms, Marian in her old room, Frank in the guest room. Her parents had believed it was because of Marian's recent loss, and Frank didn't contradict them. With steady and gentle wooing, he had convinced Marian of his love, and moved into her room.

"Reverend Cooper says you and he are going away for a few days." Mrs. Cooper snapped a towel in front of her and deftly folded it.

Frank nodded. Marian's father wouldn't say where they were going, just that he had a plan for Frank's future.

"He's concerned about you, Frank." She didn't glance up

from her towels. "He thinks you have too much talent to be working in a feed store. That you can do great things, if you put your mind to it."

Frank stared at her in surprise. He had not expected the reverend to ever regard him with favor. Tolerance, perhaps, for his daughter's sake. But the idea that Reverend Cooper thought he could make something of himself...

"I'm humbled, ma'am," he said. "I hope I live up to Reverend Cooper's trust."

She placed the last towel on her pile and stood up. "You will, Frank. Didn't you win your way back into Marian's room? Her father isn't near as stubborn as she is."

His cheeks flushed at her light chuckle. He buried his head in the newspaper again, waiting several minutes before he ventured into the house.

"We saw Brother Grimes," Frank told Marian several days later. They'd returned from their trip and he still couldn't believe his good fortune. He paced around their tiny room as he talked, ducking slightly whenever he came to the pitched roof to one side.

"But why did Father take you to see him?" Marian was unpacking his suitcase. He had offered to do it himself but she'd assured him it was a wife's duty.

She was tucking his clean shirts back into the dresser drawers, her bright curls tumbled around her shoulders. A wife's duty. He was counting on that wifely duty now, that awareness that he was the head of the household.

"I've been accepted into the seminary," he said. "Your father sent my name to Brother Grimes. I had an interview with the board, and they accepted my application."

Her hands stilled. She had her back to him so he couldn't see her expression. He stepped closer, then stopped, waiting for some sort of response.

"You were accepted at the seminary?" Her voice was quiet, a

whisper in the room. Her hands held his shirts, her body frozen as if in a tableau.

He nodded and cleared his throat. "Yes. I start my courses next month. That should give us time to pack and let Mr. Bates find a replacement. If he needs one," he added. He'd never been able to shake the feeling that he only had the job out of respect for Reverend Cooper.

"Next month."

A long moment passed. She finally put down the shirt, closed the dresser drawer with a decisive push, and stepped back. "A month. Well, I suppose I should start sewing some new white shirts for you. Your suit will have to see you through the first term. Will you take the train to Des Moines again?"

He frowned. "You're coming with me, Marian. We already have quarters in the married housing unit."

She turned around slowly. Her lips were curved but he didn't think he'd ever seen a colder smile. "I won't be joining you, Frank. I didn't leave this parsonage to move into another one for life."

A burning ignited within his stomach and spread outward to his hands. He clenched them at his sides. "You married me to escape the parsonage?"

Her trill of laughter grated on him. "Of course not, Frank. I loved you. Leaving here was just a bonus."

Her words were like a bucket of water on the fire of his anger. "You loved me? Are you saying you don't love me now?" What about those sweet words she whispered in the privacy of their bed? Those tender touches? Were they all lies he'd wanted to believe?

"Of course not." She gathered up his pile of dirty clothes. "I would've appreciated some say in the course of our life. That's all. You made this decision without even giving me a hint of what was coming."

He blocked her exit. "Your father gave *me* no hint when he took me away. We can't spend the rest of our lives in your parents' house, Marian. Do you want to settle in Winston? Des Moines is a good-size town, a place with lots to do. And you can make friends in your classes."

Her arms tightened around the clothes. "*My* classes? No, thank you."

"So I go to Des Moines alone? How will that affect my ministry, Marian, if my own wife won't accompany me?"

She shrugged and dodged around him, grabbing the doorknob with her left hand. "I don't know, Frank. I do wish you the best. But I can't go with you."

"Can't or won't?"

"Does it matter? I won't be on that train, and I won't share your married-couple quarters. I can't do it, Frank." She pulled open the door.

"So, will I tell your parents or will you?"

She stopped abruptly, her hand on the knob. "Tell them what?"

"That you aren't going with me. That we're getting a divorce."

She spun around, the door swinging shut with a bang. "A divorce? I didn't say anything about a divorce!"

"If a wife won't go with her husband, then it seems divorce is the only answer. Can't expect a man to live his life in limbo, not married and not single."

"I can't get divorced! It would kill my parents." They'd recovered from her elopement, relieved she was legally married. But a divorce…

"Then what are we going to do, Marian? I've already accepted the position at the seminary. They have an apartment assigned to us."

She brought her hands to her chest, trying to breathe. "I can't do this," she whispered. "I can't live in a parsonage again. Living here was temporary, it was never to be our *life*."

He watched her, unblinking, his mouth in a straight line.

"Frank, please."

"You choose, Marian. I'm going to the seminary. You're my wife, and I want you to go with me. But if you can't… I'll see a lawyer while I'm up there."

How could he trap her like this? *A divorce?* No decent woman was divorced. He wouldn't have a problem finding another wife but what man would marry a divorced woman?

She squeezed her eyes shut, willing her breath to come back, her voice not to shake. "Fine. I'll go with you, Frank."

His arms slid around her shoulders, and he tugged her stiff body against his. "You'll see, Marian, this is the right decision. I have a calling, your father said. I'm good with people. I do well in sales. Bringing people to the Lord is just the ultimate selling job."

She didn't say anything, afraid she'd reveal her true feelings. She would go to the seminary with him but she would have nothing to do with his classes, his colleagues or the duties of a minister's wife.

Chapter 10

The seminary work was difficult. Frank had dropped out of school and studying had always been hard. Now he was in classes with men who'd graduated from high school, many with honors. He struggled with the courses, reading late into the night and during every possible minute of the day.

Marian refused to take the classes offered for wives. "I grew up in a parsonage, Frank. Those classes can't teach me anything I didn't learn from my mother."

"But it looks odd, Marian. You're the only wife not attending the classes."

She favored him with a long, cool stare. "I'm also the only wife who doesn't meekly follow her husband around, waiting for his orders. I'm here, Frank. That's all I can offer you."

"But Brother Grimes said—"

"I'm sick to death of Brother Grimes!" she interrupted. "He's not God, Frank. Now, go on with your studying. I'm going out."

"Another late night?"

"Yes. My friend Jenny's shift isn't over until nine. You don't have to wait up for me."

"I don't like you out so late."

She draped her coat around her shoulders. "Jenny'll keep me safe. She's lived here all her life."

He wanted to say more, demand she stay home. He hadn't met Jenny but she'd become Marian's closest friend since their arrival in Des Moines. He had a feeling they frequented dance halls. He couldn't risk the other couples hearing them fight. The walls were thin and after several loud discussions, he'd noticed furtive looks from their neighbors. He was careful to keep future conversations low and private.

The apartment was empty when he returned from classes the next day. Marian had been asleep when he got up and he'd moved quietly, letting her indulge herself with the extra rest. He had guiltily enjoyed the peaceful atmosphere while he readied himself for class. They seemed to argue every time they talked these days.

The words were blurring on the page when he finally snapped the book closed. Practically midnight, and no sign of Marian. He slid under the covers, leaving one light on for her return.

A thump and a giggle woke him. Marian stood in the middle of the room, her hat tilted sideways, her mouth half-curved in a smile. "Sorry, sweetie, I didn't mean to wake you." She hiccuped and giggled.

"Have you been drinking?" Frank crawled out of bed, his voice a thin whisper.

She pressed her hand against her mouth, muffling her giggle. "A little."

"Marian, it's illegal!"

She fell on the bed, kicking her shoes off. The first one landed on the floor with a loud thud and Frank rushed to catch the second one. Her hat toppled onto the rug and bounced along, ending up under an armchair across the room. He retrieved it and sank down in the chair.

"You are so dull sometimes, Frank. You should come with me, meet my friends. 'Course, I'm not sure they'd like you. You've become so stuffy since we moved here."

She staggered over and climbed into his lap, flinging her arms around his neck. "You want to have some fun, darling Frank? Show me you're not too stuffy?"

He carried her to the bed. "It's late, Marian. I have class in the morning. And you need to sleep. You're going to have a terrible headache when you wake up."

She sniffed, then curled up on her pillow. "All right, I'll go to sleep. But you're gonna be mighty lonely with only your Bible for comfort."

She was asleep in minutes. He undressed her, then tucked the covers around her shoulders. She gave a great sigh and he waited, but she didn't wake up.

The next morning, she groaned when he bent to kiss her goodbye. "What time is it?" she muttered.

"Seven-thirty. I'll make some coffee and toast for you."

She shuddered and burrowed under the covers. "Don't bother. Leave the curtains closed, and I'll take care of everything when I get up."

"We can go out for dinner tonight."

"Don't talk about food." Her voice was muffled by the blankets.

Frowning, he stared at the mound in the bed. "Marian, you aren't pregnant, are you?"

"Pregnant? I hope not! It's probably the ghastly booze I had last night. Now, go to class and let me sleep."

When he came back to the apartment for a quick bite of lunch, she was gone. The covers were jumbled on the bed and the few dishes in the sink showed that she'd managed to eat something, after all. His class load in the afternoon was heavy and he had little time to worry about her. When he was through with his final class, he hurried back to their apartment, determined to keep her home that night.

She was still not back. He tidied the small apartment, then changed his shirt. She dashed into the room just as he was deciding she wouldn't return.

"Sorry I'm late." She gave him a peck on the cheek. "I won't be a minute."

She rushed from their room and down the hall to the community bathroom. When she came back, he stared at her in astonishment.

Her long hair, which she usually wore braided around her head or in a soft bun, was cut short. Instead of the thick mass that only he saw in its glorious release, tiny wisps of hair covered her ears. Bangs barely touched her eyebrows. She looked stunning but the shock was too much.

"What have you done to your hair? Why didn't you talk to me first?"

She gawked at him. "It's *my* hair, Frank. Why should I discuss it with you?"

Anger filled him then. Anger at her refusal to take classes, to participate in any of the seminary activities. Anger at her evenings out, her drinking, her taunts about his studies.

His hand struck out, catching the rack where he'd put the dishes to dry. The plates and cups, silverware, fell to the floor, the sound of breaking glassware echoing around the small room.

Her eyes widened and she backed up. As quickly as his anger had risen, it was gone.

"Marian, I'm sorry, I'm so sorry." He'd never been the kind of man who threw things in a rage.

He lifted his hand to caress her cheek, to assure her he was sorry, that his anger had vanished.

She took another step away from him, moving closer to the

door. "Please don't touch me, Frank. I'm going out. I can't sleep here tonight. I—I—" Her voice caught and when he heard that, his heart ached. "I don't know if I'll be back."

The door closed behind her. Frank stared at it, waiting for her to come back, to accept his apology, to say that she was partly to blame. But the door remained firmly shut.

He sank onto the bed, his face in his hands. What had he done? According to the Bible, the man was to be the head of the household but he didn't think any of the teachers would condone his loss of control. A man was to protect his wife and children, care for them.

And what would he do without Marian? He had threatened divorce in Winston but it had been an idle threat, words he'd thrown out when she'd refused to go with him. He had never intended to make it official.

He sat on the bed, barely conscious of the passing time. Dusk had begun to fall, the sky a dark blue outside the window. His stomach growled, reminding him that he hadn't eaten. Worrying about food when his marriage and possibly his career were both over seemed petty.

He needed to see Brother Grimes. The man had probably gone home, but he had to try. He raced across the campus, stopping at the imposing brick building that housed the administrative offices. A few lights were still on, and he prayed the president would be one of those dedicated souls.

"Ah, Frank, what can I do for you?" The elderly man opened his office door, ushering Frank inside.

"M-my wife left me, sir." Breathless, Frank held his hat in his hands. "We had a fight, and she walked out."

"Sit down." Brother Grimes indicated the two easy chairs; he waited until Frank was seated before sitting down himself. "Now tell me what happened."

Frank poured out the facts of their move to Des Moines, Marian's refusal to take classes, her late nights, her new friends, her drinking. He ended with the haircut.

"She's not the woman I married," he finished. "She's become wild, sir, and I can't control her. If I can't convince my own wife to be a Christian, how can I convince others?"

"Wait a minute, Frank." Brother Grimes stroked his beard, his eyes dark above the white whiskers. "Marian may have done some things that bother you, but she *is* a Christian. She grew up with a strong background, and that doesn't disappear. My suspicion is that she's simply enjoying herself in a big city."

Frank was certain she *was* enjoying herself. And now, with his angry words, he'd sent her back into that city.

"How long have you been here?" Brother Grimes asked.

"Six months."

"And in that period, how often have you been with your wife?"

Frank shifted in his chair. Except for a few minutes grabbed between classes, usually a rush for meals, he hadn't spent any time with Marian. He was so busy studying, it was no wonder she went out at night looking for fun.

Brother Grimes's smile was kind. "A common problem with many of our married couples. And it could be even more of an issue with your wife."

Frank frowned. "What do you mean, sir?"

Brother Grimes hesitated, his thumb rubbing his chin. "What I'm about to say is in the strictest confidence, Frank. I consider Brother Cooper one of my closest friends. We met years ago and I count him as a spiritual giant in his study of the scriptures. That's one of the reasons I was so willing to accept you into the seminary."

Frank ducked his head in acknowledgment of the honor he was receiving. His own knowledge of the scriptures was woefully lacking, as he'd discovered in his classes. His mother had taken him to church, and he'd heard the Bible stories, but the deep meaning behind them had never interested him before.

He sometimes found the comments of his teachers and fellow students confusing. Early in one of his classes, he'd offered the opinion that Jesus had been speaking to the common man, so perhaps His stories were simpler than everyone was making them out to be. The silence that had greeted this statement had convinced him he had much to learn and needed to keep his mouth shut. He was a newcomer in the study of God's word.

He settled into his chair, determined to listen to Brother Grimes and learn any secrets that would aid him in better understanding his wife. He loved Marian; he'd made a commitment to her before God. But most days, he had no idea how to react to her.

"I often disagreed with Brother Cooper's treatment of his wife and daughter, Frank. I don't mean this in disrespect but your father-in-law had many opportunities to travel elsewhere, to leave Winston and share his gifts and talents with other communities. Instead, he chose to sequester himself in that little town, to shelter the women of his family from the rest of the world."

Grimes swiveled around and picked up his large Bible from the ornate book stand behind the desk. "We are not to be tempted by the world, Frank, of that there is no doubt. And yet, there is another temptation that can be as damaging to our souls. That is the temptation to ignore what is going on around us, to forget that we are called to be the leaven, the salt of the earth."

He tapped a passage in the open Bible. "Brother Cooper makes a difference in his community. His time there has been valuable, and he has seen to the spiritual well-being of his flock. Sometimes, though, I wonder if he's been blind to the real will of God. If he has silenced that voice within himself, the voice that tells him what God expects him to do."

Brother Grimes clapped a hand on Frank's shoulder. "You must listen to that voice, Frank. You must hear what is being said to you. Not what others want you to do. What is God's will for you, at this time and in this place?"

He cleared his throat. The lamplight cast a halo around his head, and he appeared much as Frank thought an ancient prophet would have looked. The old man steepled his hands on the desk. "You mustn't forget your wife, Frank. You made a commitment to her that is just as sacred as your commitment to God. She needs you and you need her."

He gave Frank a reassuring smile. "No doubt she'll be back tomorrow. She's a responsible young woman, and those vows you shared are sacred to her. In the meantime, I suggest you do some serious praying about how you can balance your family life and your ministry. Otherwise, you won't succeed at either."

Frank considered those words as he retraced his steps to their apartment. A snowflake drifted down and he glanced at the sky. Snow. He hoped Marian was all right.

He couldn't imagine life without her. Was he hearing God's voice or Brother Cooper's when he'd decided to be a minister? God had sent him to Winston to find Marian; he was certain of that. If being a minister's wife was so difficult for her, maybe he needed to look elsewhere for his career.

Inside the apartment, he was surprised to see Marian sitting on the sofa. Her grin was sheepish.

"I didn't have anywhere to go, Frank. And I didn't even pack a bag."

He gathered her into his arms, rocking her back and forth, inhaling her scent, the softness of her skin. "I'm so sorry, Marian." He kissed the back of her neck. "You have every right to cut your hair." His lips nuzzled her skin and he felt her shiver. He leaned back until he could see her face. "Marian, we have to talk. We need to make a few changes in our life."

"I know." She slid out of his hold. "I'll make some sandwiches. We never did have supper."

They sat at the small table provided with their apartment. Sandwiches between them, he offered grace. "Is this so hard for you?" he asked after the *Amen*.

She kneaded a piece of bread between her fingers, not looking at him. "I grew up in this atmosphere, Frank. Sometimes I thought I'd suffocate. Everyone always watching, expecting things from me that I couldn't provide. When I met you, I was happy to put it behind me. Maybe not forever, but I certainly didn't think I'd be returning to the parsonage so soon."

He had felt that way about his own home, trapped in a family that expected certain things from him. He'd never measured up to his father's expectations. Leaving had been the most freeing experience of his life.

She touched his hand. "This means a lot to you, doesn't it?"

"I can't explain it, Marian. It's not the classes so much as the belief your father has in me. Brother Grimes…" Remembering the old man's words, he wondered if he was in the program for the right reasons. "I just can't quit," he said with a shrug. "Not yet."

Her sigh came from the depths of her being. "All right. But I can't attend the classes. I—" Her voice trailed off. He stayed quiet, determined this time to listen.

She leaned her elbows on the table, her head resting between her hands. "My mother became a different person, Frank, whenever she went out in public. She wasn't the wonderful woman I saw at home, the clever woman who could make me laugh with a quick remark. Did you know my mother was crazy about the theater?"

Frank shook his head. He was pained to realize how little he knew about his mother-in-law.

"Not much scope for her talent in Winston. She was very good at mimicking people. She could grasp a mannerism and you'd figure out right away who she was imitating. But Father said it was sinful, so she was careful not to let him see her do it."

She raised her head and gave him her wide-eyed gaze. "Frank, I can't be that wife who only exists as part of her husband. I don't know what I want to do yet or who I'll be, but I won't disappear into the parsonage, the helpmeet of Frank Robertson. If that's against God's will, I just don't know that I can follow Him anymore."

Frank thought again of his conversation with Brother Grimes, the revelation that his father-in-law had hidden his family away in that small town. He laced their fingers together. "You don't have to go to the classes, Marian. Your support at home is all I need. You're my wife and the others will have to accept you as you are."

"I do love you, Frank. I'm sorry for what I said earlier."

He stood up and held out his hand. "And I love you. More than I ever believed possible."

Their lovemaking that night was gentle, a renewal of their vows. They murmured whispered words of love, of promise, protected from the cold weather by the warmth of their bodies expressing their need in the most primitive and essential way.

Their joy in each other continued. No more late nights with Frank at home studying, Marian out with her friends. Now, while Frank read through his notes and books, Marian curled against his feet with a book of her own. They ate their meals together, laughing around the small table. They joined other couples from down the hall for dinner. Marian's background enabled her to hold her own during the spirited conversations.

"Are you going home for Christmas?" Caroline asked after a light supper early in December. She and her husband, Pete, lived next door and they'd spent several evenings together.

Marian glanced at Frank. "We hadn't discussed the holidays yet."

"We're going to my parents' house," Caroline went on. "It may be our last visit for a while. We're moving to Africa after Pete graduates this spring."

Frank felt Marian freeze. He nudged her leg under the tablecloth. "If we can make the arrangements, we'll be going to Winston for the holidays."

"Africa?" she said when they were alone.

"We're not moving to Africa," he assured her. "There are enough hungry souls in the United States."

"Frank—"

He clasped her body tightly to his, rubbing his hands up and down her back until he felt her begin to soften. "Marian, we make the decisions together." His mouth grazed her neck. "And right now, I think we both know what we want to do."

Her hands slid into his hair. "I'm not sure I understand, Mr. Robertson." Her voice had lost its wary edge and grown husky.

He growled and nipped her earlobe. "Mrs. Robertson, we need to go to bed. Now!"

The Christmas visit to Winston was pleasant. Reverend Cooper was interested in Frank's classes, and Marian and her mother spent hours in the kitchen, laughing and talking as they prepared the holiday meals. Frank watched carefully, noting how different Mrs. Cooper was in the home compared to when she was out in public. And he noted, also, the pleased expression on his father-in-law's face, the subdued Mrs. Cooper next to him at the end of the candlelight Christmas Eve service.

He was reluctant to go to his own family, knowing that visit would not be half as comfortable as the one he'd just enjoyed.

His misgivings were proved right. Tension was high. His parents, grandparents and Rebecca were still squeezed into the small farmhouse. His sister agreed to sleep on the living room couch so he and Marian could have a degree of privacy. Sam and Clara visited for a day, going home that evening rather than crowd the family even more.

His father hadn't found employment and was working around the farm. It had never been prosperous, and as his grandfather had aged, so had the farm. Very little was needed to keep it in order. Frank soon heard that neither man felt the other needed to be there.

The three days were long, and Frank wasn't sorry to pack up and leave. Rebecca was his only regret. She cried, clinging to him as he dropped their bags by the front door.

"You can visit us in Des Moines," Marian promised.

"Are you sure you want her to come?" Frank asked when Rebecca ran off to see if she could ride with them to the depot. "Our apartment barely has enough room for the two of us." He wondered what the neighbors would think of his rambunctious little sister.

"Of course she can come. Life must be boring out here, living with all these adults."

Frank knew she was recalling her own childhood, surrounded by her parents and their friends, older people who had nothing in common with a young girl. He touched his lips to hers. No matter what they did, he thought, her caring spirit would always shine through.

The train was filled with tired holiday travelers. A baby, dressed in a frilly pink outfit, cried and cried, her constant whimpers edging away the bright mood that most of the other passengers had experienced during the Christmas season. Marian curled into Frank's arms, tossing and turning as she tried to get comfortable.

"Not much longer," he whispered, shifting so her hip didn't catch him again in the side.

"How much do you suppose she cries?" Marian asked.

"I don't know." His legs were cramped and he considered walking the aisle to work out the kinks. "Being in this crowd is probably aggravating things."

"I hope our baby doesn't cry that much. I'd go mad."

He forgot about his stiff legs. Lifting her chin with one finger, he gazed into her eyes. "Marian, are you saying—" He couldn't finish the sentence.

She nodded. "That's why the idea of Africa scared me so much. I hadn't been to the doctor yet, so I didn't want to tell you. But I saw my doctor while we were in Winston. The baby will be born in the middle of June."

June. A second chance. "This time, I'll be there. Every day, Marian." He crushed her in his arms, his mouth covering hers in kisses. "A baby. We're going to have a baby."

"Frank—"

"Shh." He couldn't let her worry about anything, he decided. She needed a husband who'd devote his life to her. To their baby.

Is this your answer, God? he prayed silently, the clickety-clack of the train punctuating his words. Are You saying that someone else will have to save souls?

Other ministers had families. Brother Grimes referred to his children often when sharing testimonies of God's love.

He remembered her mother's words, that the women in their family had difficulty carrying a baby to term. But if she had the best medical care, and his complete attention? Surely they could change the odds in their favor. He would do whatever was needed to ensure that this baby was healthy.

He could be the leaven, the salt of the earth, without being in the ministry full-time. His own father had been active in their congregation before the change in his circumstances. He could do the same.

"I'll speak to Brother Grimes as soon as we return." Grimes was the one who'd said that Frank's commitment to his wife was as sacred as his commitment to God. "I'll explain about the baby and withdraw from the seminary."

"Frank, no! I can't be the one to make you give up your calling. Not if this is what you were meant to do."

He kissed away the frown lines on her forehead. "You matter to me, Marian, more than anything else. We'll figure out what we can do together, something that'll be suitable for both of us."

He couldn't stop kissing her. He loved her. And she was carrying his baby.

He felt her relax. A sense of peace flowed through him; he was making the correct choice. His heart had never truly been in the ministry; he knew that not only from his conversation with Brother Grimes, but also from his conversations with Reverend Cooper over the holiday. He didn't have the same fervor, the same desire to spread the Word to the people he met. He'd been determined to succeed because of the men's faith in him but now he saw that wasn't enough. He would always be a devout Christian, even if he wasn't destined to be a minister.

He feathered kisses over Marian's hair. "Nothing is more important than your health," he said.

And that of our baby.

But he didn't say the words out loud. He had asked enough of God for one day.

Summer 2004

"Grandma knows something." Hannah pushed the mower farther into the shed, then waited outside for Preston to fasten the padlock on the door.

"Why do you say that?" They walked around the building and toward the back of the house.

"Because whenever I bring it up, she changes the subject."

Preston slipped off his grass-covered tennis shoes and stepped into a worn pair their mother often threatened to throw away when he wasn't around. "Maybe she doesn't think G.G. should be badgered into a party if she doesn't want one. She must have a good reason, Hannah, not to want a party."

"What good reason?"

"Well, for one thing, she's ninety-three years old. Maybe she's just too tired to have a party."

"G.G. isn't tired. I mean, sure, she probably gets worn out easier than you and me. But you've been over to their place. She's always talking to Grandpa Frank or working on a crossword puzzle or watching TV. I'm not talking about a big, fancy party. Just the family."

"Hello, you two." Anne stood at the kitchen counter, chopping fresh vegetables for supper. "Finish the lawn?"

Preston nodded and climbed onto the stool next to her. "Grandma, Hannah thinks you know why G.G. doesn't want a party."

"Preston!" Hannah hissed.

Their grandmother smiled. "No, it's okay. I can't give you all their reasons, but I can tell you what I think. She's ninety-three, she doesn't like crowds anymore and as she and Dad have said, they don't feel they need a party to remember that they've been married for seventy-five years. They had a big celebration for their sixtieth."

Hannah leaned against the counter. Preston was chomping on a carrot stick, a smug expression on his face. "But being married seventy-five years is a big deal," Hannah insisted, not for the first time. "Just a small celebration... I mean, I know G.G. isn't a big partyer."

"She was quite a partyer in her day," Anne said dryly.

Hannah and Preston stared at her. "G.G.?" Preston asked.

"Yes. I probably shouldn't have said anything. She was a minister's daughter." She slid the chopped vegetables into a pot on the stove. The water hissed and steam rose to the ceiling. "Her father believed my dad would make a good minister, too."

Hannah digested this new information. "Grandpa Frank was going to be a minister?" she asked, realizing how incredulous she sounded.

"Yes, he was studying in Des Moines. He decided that wasn't the direction he wanted to take with his life and they moved here to Lincoln, opening the first shop while I was in high school and later branching into other towns."

"But when did G.G. party if they were at ministers' school?" Preston asked.

Trust him to go for the juicy story, Hannah thought.

"They weren't tied to the seminary." Anne added more vegetables to the pot. "They could go into town whenever they wanted. Not that G.G. was a wild partyer like we think of now. She probably went to help her forget about baby David."

Hannah was digging lettuce and tomatoes out of the fridge and almost missed the last sentence. "Baby David?"

Anne nodded. "My older brother." Her voice had softened.

Hannah shook her head. "But you're the oldest." A picture of the three girls, with Anne in high school, stood on the mantel in the living room. And G.G. and Grandpa Frank had the three class pictures on the wall in their room at Winter Oaks. No boy in sight.

"The oldest living child," Anne corrected.

"How come I've never heard about this?"

"I thought you knew. They didn't keep it secret. He was stillborn."

She set the lid on the soup pot. "Hannah, would you see if any of the green beans are ready for picking?"

"*A baby boy,*" Hannah murmured to herself, walking down the garden rows. They lost a baby boy. That would make a difference in a family's life. Especially in those days, when a man was expected to have a son to carry on his name.

She dropped beans into her bowl and tried to imagine G.G. as a young woman, dressed up, dancing shoes on her feet. What music was popular then? She grinned at the image of her great-grandparents dancing the night away, their arms around each other, their faces alight with laughter and the love she so often saw. It was there, in the way they looked at each other, the way they smiled.

Her bowl full of fresh beans, she marched back to the house. They'd been parents, too, she thought. Raising three daughters after the loss of their son. Three very different daughters, each one adding to their story of love.

ANNE'S STORY

Chapter 11

Lincoln, Iowa
1940–1945

Anne's first clear memories were of warning. Born June 24, 1931, she wasn't even a year old when the Lindbergh baby was kidnapped and found dead two months later. Her parents constantly reminded her not to talk to strangers. When she was six, she and a friend walked downtown to the Lincoln library and came back after dark. The spanking and scolding she received persuaded her to stay close to home and not cause her mother any further worry.

The summer months were different. In May, Frank would rent a small cottage in northern Iowa, near Spirit Lake. The children enjoyed a bohemian life, running around barefoot, their limbs barely covered. Frank would travel to the nearby towns selling vacuum cleaners and accessories. On Sundays, they'd put on dresses and shoes and walk into town to worship at the small community church. Once the cool weather of late August blew in, they'd pack up and return to Lincoln, in time for the start of school.

Most Saturday nights during the summer, Frank and Marian hired a babysitter for the girls and went out to dinner at one of the hotel restaurants. When Anne turned nine, Marian decided to dispense with the sitter, leaving almost six-year-old Margaret and three-and-a-half-year-old Alice in Anne's care.

That first time, Marian had said, "A sitter's a waste of money, Frank. Annie's a big girl now." Her mother's hand lightly brushed Anne's red curls. "You can take care of the girls, can't you, honey?"

"Yes."

Frank didn't look convinced. Alice clung to his leg, her thumb in her mouth. Margaret was nowhere to be seen, no doubt hidden away telling her doll a story.

"Marian, she's little more than a baby herself."

Anne drew herself up to her full height. The tip of her pointed chin reached the middle of his chest. "I'm not a baby, I'm the tallest girl in my class. Anyway, what can happen to us? I'll lock all the doors and we'll play games and read. Don't worry. You and Mom have fun."

He opened his mouth to argue, then snapped it closed. A few minutes later, the front door shut behind them.

Anne played with Alice until the little girl whimpered and rubbed her eyes. Rocking her to sleep, she crooned several of the songs she'd heard her mother sing.

Alice's little hand curved around her finger, and Anne felt a tug of love. Alice nuzzled her soft head against Anne's chest. "I won't ever let anything hurt you," she murmured into Alice's baby-fine curls.

"What did you say to her?" Margaret's piping voice came into the room.

"Shh, she's finally asleep." Anne carefully tucked Alice into bed, then tiptoed out of the room, dragging Margaret along with her.

"What did you say?" Margaret demanded when they were safely out of range.

Anne felt funny confessing the strange wave of protective desire that had swept over her. "That I'll take care of her," she finally muttered.

"Will you take care of me, too?"

Anne knelt down and clasped Margaret to her chest. "Of course, Margaret. We're sisters, aren't we?"

After that first babysitting experience, her mother trusted the girls to stay at the cottage when she went to her book club or a church committee meeting. When she began spending nights out while Frank was away, Anne felt the same overwhelming urge to protect her mother that she'd felt with Alice. Her mother didn't ask her to keep the news to herself but a long-forgotten memory surfaced one afternoon. Anne couldn't risk causing another separation between Frank and Marian.

She'd been little and Alice hadn't been born yet. Her father had stormed into the house, shouting for Marian at the top of his lungs. Margaret and Anne had cowered together in the bedroom, their arms around each other, listening while Frank bellowed and Marian wept. When Frank had slammed out of the house, Marian had rushed into the bedroom, tossing clothes into a suitcase.

They'd ridden the train to Winston and slept at her grandparents' house. Frank had arrived the next day, demanding Marian go back with him. She'd refused. Grandpa Cooper had taken them both into the front parlor. Anne and Margaret sat on stools in the kitchen, watching their grandmother knead bread, all of them trying not to listen to the loud voices from down the hall.

When the voices were silent, Margaret had crawled off her stool and leaned against her grandmother's leg. Anne had rolled a sticky piece of dough over and over on the counter, not stopping even when her parents came into the room. Her breath stuck in her throat. Marian had streaks of tears on her cheeks and Frank's face was flushed but they were holding hands. They'd gone back to Lincoln as a family.

Near the end of her ninth summer, she lay in the hammock

reading, trying to use the last of the evening light before she went inside. Margaret and Alice talked quietly in their bedroom, their thin voices blending with the cicadas and rustling leaves of the trees. Her mother had gone to town earlier and Frank wasn't due back until the next day.

A shadow passed over her book. Annoyed, she marked her place. She'd spent the day with her sisters or doing chores. The girls were supposed to be in bed, and she wanted to enjoy a few minutes by herself. Besides, if Mom came home and found them still awake...

She saw the grim face of her father; her eyes widened. "Where's your mother, Anne?" he asked.

Anne slipped off the hammock, her book falling to the ground. "She—she went into town."

He turned and marched toward his car. Halfway there, he stopped, pinning her with the stare that wouldn't let her lie. "Does she do this often?"

She bit her lip and closed her eyes as she nodded. She didn't open them until she heard his car roar down the road.

Sleep eluded her. She huddled under the covers, suddenly chilled by the slight breeze rustling her curtains. She didn't know how long she lay like that before she heard a car stop in the driveway. A car door slammed shut and she waited for the second one. But there was only silence and then the screen door squeaked.

Sliding from her bed, she cracked open her door and peered out. Her father was stretched out on the davenport, his hat covering his eyes. He seemed more tired than angry.

"You might as well come out," he said quietly.

Anne jumped and closed the door. She scampered across the wooden floor and dove into her bed and under the covers. When the bedroom door opened, she peered out, half-afraid at the sight of her father silhouetted by the living-room lamp.

"Anne, do you know where your mother goes in town?"

She shook her head, unable to talk. She loved her father and had never felt afraid of him, but she couldn't stand to see him hurt. And no matter what she said, she knew he *would* be hurt. Certainly disappointed...

At least she was being truthful. Once she'd asked her mother, using her new role as sitter. "I need a number in case there's an emergency."

Her mother had finished putting on her hat. "You won't have an emergency, Annie, dear," she said. "That's why I can trust you to watch your sisters. Now, give me a kiss and be a good girl."

Now she felt torn. She wasn't sure where her mother was but she had a good idea. Her mother always came home humming dance tunes. Only two places provided dancing in the small town near the lake, and both were at the end of the lake. Somehow, she didn't think her father would like to find out that her mom was going to bars by herself.

She was saved from having to answer by her mother's return. At the sound of the front door closing, her father gave her a distracted kiss and left the room without another word. Anne tiptoed to her door, closing it tight. She got back into bed and pulled the covers completely over her, squeezing her eyes shut.

Sunlight streamed between the open curtains the next morning. Anne peeked out of the window but her father's car was gone. When Margaret and Alice came into her room, she quietly took them into the kitchen and fixed breakfast. She shooed them outside, promising to play with them later if they'd stay away from the house. "Mommy needs to rest," she told them.

Frank didn't come home that night. Alice slept in their mother's room while Anne and Margaret shared a bed. The next day, no one mentioned Frank's arrival and quick departure. Margaret and Anne stayed outside all day, taking a small lunch. They shared a quiet supper with Alice and their mother, Alice chattering to Marian in baby talk and Marian responding in kind. As soon as the table was cleared, Anne and Margaret went into her room, reading and whispering quietly until they fell asleep.

Frank still wasn't back on Sunday. Alice had the sniffles, and their mother decided to keep her home from church, so the two older sisters walked to town together.

Tuesday evening, Margaret and Anne were jumping rope when Frank parked in front of the house. Margaret released her rope and ran to him, flinging her arms around him with a shout. Anne stood nearby, suddenly shy.

He hugged Margaret, then reached out, tugging Anne next to him. "So, how are my two girls?"

They walked toward the house, Margaret chattering about how she could skip a rock three times. Frank's eyes met Anne's, and she turned away, unable to talk to him as if he'd just returned from one of his sales trips.

Marian sat on the davenport, Alice in her arms. In the past few days, Alice had reverted to baby talk and her thumb was seldom out of her mouth. Framed as they were by the window and the soft afternoon light streaming in, they looked like a picture Anne had once seen of Mary and Baby Jesus.

"Hello, Marian," Frank said.

Marian tightened her arms around Alice. Anne wanted to run to her room but her feet felt weighted down with cement. On her father's other side, Margaret's voice faded away.

"Been hearing some unsettling news," Frank continued. "Seems that the war in Europe may affect us after all."

Marian tossed her head. "Oh, Frank, we won't get involved in any war over there. Why should we?"

Frank shrugged, the action dragging Anne's hand up with his. "Just telling you what people are saying. I didn't think you'd heard any news recently."

Her mother's laugh was brittle. "How could I? I don't go anywhere and I don't see anyone."

Frank glanced down at Anne and she gave a tiny nod. Her

mother hadn't left the house since that last disastrous trip into town. She hadn't even gone to her book club, one of her favorite summer activities.

Marian jumped to her feet, almost letting Alice fall. "What a pretty pass to come to, Frank Robertson, when you have our daughters spy on me! Why are you back, anyway?"

Anne could hear the tears under her mother's anger. Frank hurried across the room. "Honey, I had to come back. I can't live without you, you know that."

Marian sniffed, brushing a hand over her cheek. Alice wriggled out of her arms and tottered over to Margaret and Anne.

Frank hugged Marian's shoulders, bringing his head close to hers. Anne led her sisters down the hall and into her bedroom.

They climbed on the bed, listening to the soft rise and fall of their parents' voices. "Is it okay now?" Margaret asked.

Anne nodded, reassured by the steady tone of the voices in the other room, an occasional chuckle from her father. "I suppose it's one of those things married people do."

"I'm never going to fight with my husband," Margaret declared.

Anne laughed. "Oh, Margaret, you're too young to think about a husband." I won't have one, she vowed silently. They're too much work. She didn't fault her mother for wanting fun and some adult company, what with her father gone all the time.

Margaret bristled at her response. "I will, Annie. All girls get married."

Anne patted her shoulder, soothing the ruffled feelings as she often had in the past. "Don't decide yet, Margaret. You're only six."

Alice cuddled against them, her eyelids drooping in sleep. Tucking her under the covers, Margaret and Anne lay down in their clothes, their little sister between them.

They left the lake early that year and didn't come back the next summer. Before they could return, Frank's words came true. The United States did go to war and Frank joined the United States Navy.

Spring 1943

"Frank, you don't have to go." Marian was peeling potatoes for their supper. "You have three children and a wife to support."

"Marian, we're at war. I have to go. If I hadn't enlisted in the navy, I would've been drafted. Who knows what branch I'd be in then? I report to Des Moines tomorrow for my physical."

He put his arms around her as the three girls watched with wide eyes. Anne's heart pounded. Her parents didn't argue much, but raised voices always made her shudder.

Anne stayed up with her mother the next night, waiting for Frank to come home. They chatted about school, the neighbors, the weather. Anything to keep away the silence that left them alone with their thoughts. Her mother finally dozed, one hand flung over the back of the davenport. The fire had died down and the room was cold. Anne unfolded the afghan and covered Marian. Then she added a log to the fire, poking it until flames again filled the fireplace. She curled under a corner of the blanket at the other end of the davenport and closed her eyes.

The soft gray light of dawn had filtered into the room when she opened her eyes. Her father sat on the floor, holding Marian's hand, her mother still asleep.

Frank put his finger to his lips. Embarrassed to see him in such a loverlike position, she slipped into her room and into bed.

When she woke up, she heard her mother crying. She pulled a sweater over her nightgown and hurried into the living room. Alice and Margaret sat together in the easy chair. Her parents were on the davenport, her mother huddled against her father's chest.

Her father gave her a broad smile. "Well, Annie, my girl, you're looking at one of the newest additions to the United States Navy."

"They took you?" she asked.

He nodded. "Don't sound so surprised. Your father's a fine figure of a man, even if he is the old married father of three ornery girls."

Anne grinned at the humor in his voice. But her mother was less amused. "Oh, Frank, this isn't funny!" Tears thickened Marian's voice.

Frank patted her shoulder. "Honey, don't worry. Now that the U.S. is in this war, it'll be over by Christmas. You'll see."

The war didn't end by Christmas but Frank came home. He had trouble shoveling coal and was sent to the Navy Hospital in Idaho. The doctor there detected a heart murmur.

"Probably had it all his life," Marian told Anne, pinning her hat over her curls. She hadn't been able to stop smiling since she'd received the telegram telling them Frank was being discharged. "I know it's unpatriotic, but I'm just so happy he's coming home. The doctor doesn't think he'll die of it but they don't want the responsibility of looking out for a sick man."

She leaned over and kissed Anne's cheek. "Take care of the girls. I'll be back with Daddy as soon as I can."

Frank resumed his traveling, staying away several days at a time. Marian wasn't as upset about his leaving, knowing that he was safe in the heart of the United States. She kept busy with her committees, working with the families who had husbands and sons overseas. The girls prepared packages to be sent to the soldiers and they all endured the enforced rations, determined to do their bit for the war effort.

When Frank was home, he worked in the shed he'd built at the back of their house. People brought him things to repair and he soon gained a reputation as a handyman. He helped wives left alone for the first time in their married lives and he began to feel useful again.

"Not everyone can fight on the front," he told Anne one evening after the war had ended. The town had celebrated with a parade, welcoming home the men and boys who'd survived. Services for the dead or those missing in action had become part of their daily lives, and Anne had been happy to shout and cheer with the rest of the town for the returning soldiers.

Now she listened to her father, polishing the rungs of a rocker he was repairing.

"When I was in the seminary, they used to tell me that not everyone could go to the foreign missions. Some needed to stay here and convert the heathen among us. With so many men gone from Lincoln, I was able to do my part for their families."

Anne stepped back, admiring the smooth surface. "I'm glad you didn't have to go," she said shyly. She knew he'd chafed at being left behind, but she couldn't have borne losing him in the battles overseas.

He put his arm around her. "I did get to watch you grow. Why, you're almost a young woman."

"I start high school this fall."

He set the rocker on the floor. "High school. I never finished high school, Anne. Should have but I ran away. Didn't like my dad's strict ways and thought I could learn more on my own."

Anne was quiet. Her father seldom talked about his childhood and she didn't want him to stop.

"Sounds foolish now but I was determined to make my own way. My father wouldn't let me work more hours in his grocery, said I had to complete my education first. I figured I'd be fine without high school and slipped off one night."

"You ran away?"

"Yep. Not very smart of your dad, Annie. Ended up sleeping in a lot of barns and fields over the next few years. Had some good luck along the way but life was hard. 'Course, if I hadn't run off, I wouldn't have met your mother. And then where would we be?"

He put his tools away, his mind still on that long-ago time. Wiping his hands on a rag, he turned to Anne. "The navy would've helped me finish high school, maybe even go to college. That's why I was so excited about joining up. Now what do I do?"

Anne's mind was racing. "Why not open your own shop, Dad? You could repair appliances, furniture, sell new and used household things. You're good, everyone says so," she told him in a rush.

He paused, the rag still in his hand. "I'm not sure, Annie. That's kind of risky."

"You could do it! Old Mr. Randolph's retiring and he wants to sell his shoe store. The building would be perfect. It's not too big but it's close to town. And he already has display cases built in."

Frank laughed. "Have you been mulling this over for a while?"

Anne nodded solemnly. "Ever since Mr. Randolph told me he was retiring. Think about it, Dad. No more traveling. You'd be home evenings and you'd be your own boss."

"Have you said anything to your mother?"

"No…"

"Don't," he said. "Let's keep it between us for now. I'll visit with Mr. Randolph and see what he has to say."

Anne grabbed his hand, dancing around. He laughed again. "This means that much to you?"

"Not to have you travel? Oh, yes!"

Her mother would be happy, too. The whole house was brighter when Frank was there.

Two weeks later, he came in at dinnertime and winked at Anne. She could hardly contain her grin, keeping her head down so she wouldn't reveal their secret. When everyone was seated at the table, Frank lifted his hands and they quieted.

"I have news. I've leased Mr. Randolph's shop downtown. As of today, you're looking at the owner and manager of Robertson's New, Used and Rebuilt Household Goods."

Marian paused in the act of dishing up the stew. Margaret and Alice gawked at their father, mouths open. Only Anne was composed now that the news was out.

Marian put down the ladle. "Frank? Your own business?"

He nodded, his eyes not leaving Marian's face. "Marian, remember our dream? We were going to open a shop and then have a chain of others around the country. It's taken a while to get going but we're on our way."

Marian added stew to the plate she held in her hand. Anne's heart ached at her mother's continued silence. Why didn't she say something?

"Well, Frank, if this is what you want to do." Marian flicked her napkin and spread it across her lap. "Now that the war's over, you could find other work, but if you're happy to be a handyman all your life…"

"Not a handyman," he interjected. "A businessman."

She shrugged, passing the rolls to Margaret. "I'm your wife, Frank, so I'll support you. But why did you have to keep it secret? Couldn't I have helped with the planning?"

Anne bent over her bowl. The hurt in her mother's voice stabbed her. *She'd* known his plans, *she'd* helped with the decisions. She'd been so excited, she'd never considered her mother.

Except to envision how thrilled she would be to have Frank home all the time.

Marian poured milk into Alice's glass. Frank's spoon was suspended over his bowl.

"I'm sorry, Marian. I wasn't sure you'd be interested. You're so busy all the time…" His voice trailed off, his earlier enthusiasm gone.

The milk jug thumped on the table. "That doesn't mean I don't have time to talk to you!"

Tears glimmered in her mother's eyes. "Don't leave me out, Frank. I'm your wife."

"I'm sorry, sweetheart." He pushed back his chair and crossed quickly to Marian. He pulled her out of her chair and swung her into his arms.

"Frank! Put me down!"

"No." He swung her around again and she leaned her head back, her hair escaping its pins, her mouth curved in a wide smile. "We're in this together, Marian Cooper Robertson. You're the brains and I'm the brawn."

"You're a fool, is what you are, Frank Robertson." She didn't struggle to get away from him, her hands clutching his arms. "Now, put me down before we fall."

He slowed his spinning and set her on the floor, smacking her with a big kiss before letting go. Alice giggled.

"We're in this together, Marian," he said again. "For richer, for poorer. That's what you promised."

Marian laughed and sank into her chair. "I did, didn't I? Who knew what I was agreeing to?" She fanned herself with her hand. Her cheeks were flushed, her eyes shining. "Annie, Mags. Go get that apple pie we baked this afternoon. We can celebrate the new store."

Anne caught Margaret's eyes and shrugged. One minute fighting and crying. The next minute giggling and dancing around the kitchen.

Married people sure were crazy sometimes.

Chapter 12

Spring 1948

"You look beautiful," Alice breathed.

Margaret nodded. "You're gonna be a star, Anne."

Anne stepped off the low stool and moved in front of the mirror. Her red curls were pinned up, and a shiny green band kept her bangs off her face. The short skirt was the same bright green; it accented the white swimsuit that peeked out from her top. She twirled, laughing as the skirt whirled around her.

"Will Daddy get to see you?" Alice asked.

"He promised to take an hour off work," Anne said, tweaking Alice's pigtails. "He said he'd put a sign on the door telling everyone to come to the pool. He thinks he can boost the audience that way."

Alice giggled. "He won't need to boost the audience. Nobody in town will miss your performance."

Anne swallowed hard. She didn't like being the center of attention. If her swim instructor hadn't prevailed upon her to use her talents to dedicate the new swimming pool, she wouldn't be wearing the new suit, butterflies doing a cha-cha in her stomach. A solo performance was different from a synchronized routine with her teammates.

A few minutes later, they walked down the narrow main street of Lincoln, the precious skirt and swimsuit now hidden by a dark raincoat. Alice skipped alongside her sisters, excitement apparent in each happy step. Margaret was more sedate but her pace was faster than normal.

They turned down the street to the town center. At three in the afternoon, the parking lot was crowded and more people were walking in from the side streets. Anne stopped under the shade of a huge elm tree.

"I can't do it," she whispered. She was only sixteen. How could she perform in front of all these people?

Alice frowned at her. Margaret grabbed her hand and jerked her forward. "Yes, you can. You've practiced and practiced until your skin's practically wrinkled for life. Miss Evans said you were the best swimmer of the group. She recommended you!"

At Margaret's sensible words, Anne's fears dissolved. Butterflies still did a cha-cha in her stomach but her sister was right. She knew the routine backward and forward.

She stopped again just before they reached the entrance to the new pool. Dozens of people stood around the cement deck chattering, their faces glowing in the afternoon sun. Most of the community had shut its door for the dedication of the new pool and recreation center.

"I can do this," she murmured under her breath. "I've done the routine dozens of times."

She closed her eyes in a brief prayer.

The music came on and she opened her eyes, seeing only the pool, thinking only of her routine. At the precise beat, she slipped into the cool water and felt the world around her disappear.

The music poured into her very soul and she translated each note into a movement of her hands, her feet, her legs, her entire body. She flowed effortlessly through the steps. The water rippled gently around her, barely disturbed by the twists and turns she'd practiced for hours. The skirt floated around her legs and she could almost imagine that her legs had changed into a mermaid's tail.

The music rose to its final crescendo, and she raised herself half out of the water. She tossed her head back and extended her arms with a flourish, her face pointed toward the blue sky above.

The crowd roared, and she felt her cheeks flush with pride and embarrassment. Now she ducked her head and swam to the edge of the water, where she was greeted by the mayor holding a bouquet of red roses.

He waved toward the crowd. "Thanks to our own Miss Anne Robertson, the Lincoln Memorial Pool is now officially open. Let's give this little lady another hand!"

Her father was in the back of the group. He raised his arms over his head and smiled. She smiled back, and then he disappeared. She would hear his personal congratulations in the privacy of their home.

Friends and neighbors swarmed around her. Her sisters stood to one side. "Mom?" she mouthed. Margaret shook her head.

When the event was officially over, they walked home together, chatting about Anne's routine, the people who'd attended, the fun of having a community pool. When they walked into the house, she saw the lights on in the living room and their mother sat on the davenport.

Marian folded her magazine and placed it in the rack, smiling as she stood up. "So, honey, how did you do?"

"Where *were* you? You know how much this meant to Anne!" Margaret burst out.

"Margaret," their mother warned, "I was speaking to Anne."

Margaret opened her mouth and then closed it again. Withou

another word, she stomped through the living room. A moment later, her bedroom door slammed shut.

Anne and Alice stood frozen to the floor. "Go to your room," Anne said softly to Alice.

"But…"

Anne nudged Alice in the back. "Go."

Alice stayed for another moment, then flounced out of the room. She's taking lessons from Margaret, Anne noticed. Once she was gone, Anne sat down on a chair across from her mother, first arranging her towel on the seat.

She folded her hands in her lap. "You never came to the park, did you?"

"I'm sorry, honey, I shouldn't have gone to the meeting. Those ladies always spend twenty minutes discussing what could've been decided in two. By the time we finished debating the schedule for the next family conference, I'd missed the early bus back from Des Moines. I did mean to be there. I'm sure you were wonderful."

"I've seen you with him."

"What? Who?"

Anne swallowed. She'd never planned to say the words out loud. Thinking them had been bad enough. "I saw you going to the movies the other night. Daddy was still working. You walked right into the movie theater, your arms around each other—"

"What?"

The shout startled Anne into silence. Her mother might raise her voice to Frank but her tone with the girls was usually quiet. Even when she was scolding them, she kept her voice low and even, the words a bit colder when she was disappointed.

Anne's heart pounded under the suit she'd tugged on with such excitement a little while earlier.

"How can you say such an ugly thing?" Marian burst out. Her hands were tightly clasped at her waist. "I love your father! I would never go out with another man."

Anne stared at her mother. Was she protesting too much? "You used to go dancing when we were at the lake."

"I was younger, very foolish and didn't consider how it would look. But I *never* cheated on your father. Several of us wives met for a few hours of fun. That's all it was."

"Daddy left you." Anne voiced her bigger concern, that Frank would leave them.

Marian smiled, a faraway look in her eyes. "We were always leaving each other. Or threatening to leave. We hadn't figured out how to solve our problems together." She reached toward Anne, but Anne ducked away.

Marian gave a rueful shake of her head. "One day, Annie, you'll learn for yourself how tricky married life can be."

Not me, she thought. I'm going to college next year and then getting a job. No man's going to mess up my future.

"I did see you," she insisted.

Her mother shook her head a second time. "I was never with another man, Annie. I shouldn't justify your accusations with answers but I want this resolved." She settled against the back of the davenport. "When did you see me?"

Anne shifted on her cushion. Her mother looked too comfortable.

Could I be wrong? Anne wondered. But she hadn't been alone that night. "Emily saw you, too. Last Tuesday, when we went to the library to study. We walked by the movie theater and Emily said she saw—"

Anne hesitated. The library was nowhere near the downtown movie theater. But her whereabouts weren't the topic of discussion.

"What did Emily see?" Marian prompted.

Anne cleared her throat. "She saw you and another man. When she gasped, I turned around. She didn't say anything, just pointed. Then she said she saw you and another man walking into the theater, your arms around each other."

"Did *you* see me?"

Another pause. "I saw a man and woman duck into lobby. She was wearing a coat like your red one."

Marian nodded. "I see." She edged forward and called down the hall, "Margaret! Would you come here, please?"

Margaret clumped into the room. "What?"

Marian ignored her aggrieved tone. "Would you please tell Annie where we were Tuesday night? When she was studying at the library?"

Anne cringed at the emphasis her mother placed on the last words. Marian was aware she hadn't gone straight to the library that night.

But Marian didn't make any other mention of that. Instead, she smiled at Margaret. "Tell Annie," she urged again.

"We were at school. Mom was helping with our rehearsal for the closing day assembly and talent show."

"It was Tuesday, correct?" Marian prompted.

Margaret nodded. "Yes, Tuesday. The assembly was Thursday and we couldn't practice on Wednesday because of church. Can I go now?"

"Yes. Thank you, Mags."

The room was silent after Margaret's departure. "I'm waiting," Marian finally said.

"I'm sorry." Anne whispered the words.

"Thank you. Now, about your not going to the library Tuesday…"

So much for thinking she was out of the woods. She decided to brazen it out. "Mom, I'm a senior next year. I shouldn't have to tell you everywhere I go."

"Oh?"

"We, well, we, um, *did* go to the library…" She stumbled over the words. "Emily needed to meet a friend before we studied. So we stopped downtown at the malt shop…."

"And then walked by the movie theater, where your friend *just happened* to see your mother with another man."

Marian rested her hand on Anne's wrist. "Anne, honey, you know there's a reason we don't like you wandering around downtown at night."

"The Lindbergh baby kidnapping?" Her mother didn't often refer to that time, and Anne only knew about it from old newspaper stories. But the kidnapping had affected her growing-up years and those of all the children in her generation.

"Mom, nobody's going to kidnap us! Why would they?" Her father was part of the city council and her mother was involved with city and church committees. But they weren't rich. They didn't have anything for ransom.

"Annie, that's not why we don't want you going downtown at night."

"Then what?"

Her mother lowered her chin, her expression stating more clearly than words that she expected better of her daughter. "Nothing but trouble can happen if young women are wandering around town after dark."

"Mom! You can trust me. I'm almost the same age you were when you married Daddy. And I'm going to college in a year."

"I know, dear. And it's not you I worry about. It's your friends. If they are friends," she added quietly.

Anne stared at her mother. "What?"

"Annie, Emily made up that story to protect herself. She was supposed to go to the library, too. Her mother and I talked that evening, about you studying together. Her mother was saying how pleased she was that you and Emily were friends, that she'd been nervous about some of the other girls Emily went around with."

Anne felt disloyal, listening to her mother talk about Emily this way. "She's my *friend*, Mother."

"And she told you a lie about your mother. In other words, she manipulated you—how could you possibly reveal what *she* did? She might repeat the scandal about your mother."

Marian waited a moment. "She's not a very nice friend, Annie."

"Okay, maybe she made a mistake. But I thought I saw you, too!"

"Anne, how many women do you think have coats like mine? It's not that unusual a style."

Anne squeezed her eyes shut. Her mother sounded so plausible. And Emily did know about her parents' earlier arguments and the times they'd separated. The two girls had spent the last few weeks sharing family secrets, whispering in their bedrooms when they should've been studying. Had Emily intended to lie or had she really believed she'd seen Marian? Anne could no longer be sure....

"I'm so sorry, Mama!" She threw herself into Marian's arms, tears flowing down her cheeks.

Marian smoothed her hand along Anne's hair, her touch soothing. Anne couldn't stop crying, all the anxiety of the last few days overwhelming her.

She finally sat up, sniffling until Marian handed her a handkerchief. Anne blew her nose, wadding the hanky in her fist. "I'm sorry, Mama," she repeated.

Marian tucked Anne's hair behind her ears. "I did plan to watch you swim. I was even going to use my position as your mother to push to the front of the crowd. But by the time I got home, I knew I'd be far too late."

She smiled and wiped a last tear from Anne's cheek. "Better now?"

Anne nodded. "You and Daddy aren't going to get a divorce?"

Marian laughed. "Honey, if we've stayed together this long, we can stay together a few more years. There's nothing to worry about." She kissed Anne's cheek. "Now, go wash up for dinner. You don't want your father to see those red eyes."

Anne scurried down the hallway. If her father asked her what was the matter, she'd start crying all over again. She had so wanted Emily to be wrong—but she hadn't believed Emily would lie to her. They were supposed to be best friends.

She flung herself on the bed, tears streaming down her cheeks.

If her father knew she'd even suspected it could be her mother going into that theater, he would be so disappointed in her. She tried to swallow her tears. She couldn't stand the thought of disappointing him.

At supper, Alice chatted about Anne's performance and Marian suggested that maybe later they could enjoy a private family show. "I've seen you practice," she said to Anne. "I would love to see the entire performance." Margaret mentioned an upcoming community play and Frank promised to buy tickets for the entire family. Anne barely spoke, afraid to trust her voice. She still felt shaky.

The younger girls offered to do the dishes without any prompting. Frank settled in his chair with the newspaper; Marian picked up her magazine. Anne opened the closet door and took out her coat.

"I'm going to the library," she announced, glad her voice didn't waver.

Frank lowered his paper. "Be home by nine."

She nodded, kissing the top of his head. She paused at her mother's side. "I'm going to the library," she said. "I have a book to return and I want to find another one."

Her mother smiled. "I trust you, sweetheart."

The words pierced Anne's heart, and she could feel the tears welling up. With a muffled goodbye, she hurried out the door.

The summer passed quickly. She worked at the pool as a lifeguard, glowing at the continued attention her swimming received. Her instructor thought she should apply at one of the tourist attractions down south that featured swimming mermaids, but she was determined to go to college. The first step to breaking out of the small town and seeing the world.

During the next school year, she was more observant of her parents and how they treated each other. She'd never noticed before how often her father touched her mother's shoulder or bent down to whisper something in her ear. The way her mother would glow when Frank came into the room or the girlish giggle that escaped her lips, often after one of those secretive whispers. Sometimes embarrassed by their displays of affection, she nevertheless hoped to find the same sort of love for herself.

But not for many years to come. She had places to go and people to see. Europe. The ocean. New York City.

Love would have to wait.

Chapter 13

Midwest Iowa College
September 1949

"He's looking this way again. Right at you, Anne." Barb giggled.

Anne didn't turn. "You're being ridiculous," she hissed.

"No, she's not." Susan shot a quick glance over her shoulder. "He's been staring at you since we came in. He's really cute. All that dark hair and those broad shoulders."

The registration line moved slowly forward. Anne clutched her purse to her chest, willing herself not to look, even inadvertently, at the next line.

The three girls had been assigned to the same room in the dorm. Anne had been nervous, not sure she could share a room with strangers. But Barb and Susan had already erased her fears, their bubbly personalities pulling her along with them to the beginning-of-the-year activities.

Now they waited to pick up their schedules. The lines were divided by year, which meant the young man watching her was a sophomore.

"He's coming over here, Anne!"

A wave of panic spread over her. "He is not!"

"Hi."

She raised her head and met clear gray eyes. "Hello." His voice was deep, sending a ripple down her spine.

"My name is Richard Sanders."

"Umm." She swallowed. What was her name? "I'm…Anne Robertson. And these are my roommates, Barb Taylor and Susan Campbell."

A tall, lanky boy with a shock of blond hair joined them. "Come on, Richard, let's get out of here."

"In a minute." He smiled at Anne, and her knees threatened to buckle. "See you around?"

She nodded, watching as he loped after his friend.

Barb sighed. "He's a dream, Anne."

"I think we're looking at the future Mrs. Richard Sanders."

Anne's head swiveled back to her friends. "Oh, you are not!" She pressed her hand against the flutter in her stomach. "My dad would die if he thought I was using his money to find a husband. I came here for an education!"

Barb and Susan grinned at each other. "Maybe a husband will be part of your education," Susan said. Barb laughed, and Anne felt a tiny thrill of anticipation.

The week passed without a call from him. Her parents checked in to see if she was getting settled and she babbled on the phone about her roommates, her classes, the weather. She asked about the shop and the new store they'd opened in Des Moines. Anything to avoid mentioning the boy she'd seen in line that first day.

"See?" she said Friday night. "He was just being nice." They were sitting on the floor, painting their toenails.

"He was not," Barb argued. "He'll call."

Anne shrugged, adding pink polish to her little toe. "He won't. Besides, like I said, my dad would *not* be happy if I'm daydreaming over a guy when I should be studying."

"Daydreaming?" Susan asked. "But you're too high-minded to care about anything except your classes. That's what she says, isn't it, Barb?"

Barb's answer was lost in a shout from down the hall. "Robertson, phone!"

Anne froze. "Did she say me?"

Barb pried the nail polish brush out of her hand. "Go on. I bet it's him."

"It's probably Mom or Dad." Her voice sounded normal, and she hoped no one could tell her insides were doing a complicated somersault.

"They already called this week," Susan reminded her. "Go."

"Hello?" she said tentatively into the receiver. Barb and Susan had crowded into the narrow booth with her.

"Hi, is this Anne Robertson?"

It was him. "Yes."

"This is Richard Sanders. You may not remember me, but we met in line when we were picking up our schedules."

She paused. "Oh, yes. I remember. How are you?"

Very cool, Susan mouthed. Anne shifted as much as possible so she couldn't see their faces.

"I'm fine. I was wondering, there's a sing-along in the student center tomorrow night. Would you like to go with me?"

"Tomorrow? Well…" She felt a punch on her back. "Yes, I'd love to."

"Good. I'll pick you up about seven, okay? See you then."

She stood there, the phone in her hand, until Susan took it from her and hung it up. The two girls maneuvered her back down the hall and into their room.

"That was Richard." She couldn't stop smiling. "We're going out tomorrow night."

"Really?" Susan pushed her onto the floor and picked up the nailbrush. "Then we need to make you beautiful. And I don't know if we're going to have enough time."

"What?" She glanced into their laughing faces. Giggling, she pelted Susan on the leg, with a pillow. Barb joined in and they laughingly pummeled each other until they were breathless.

Barb plopped down on the floor. "Okay, that was fun. Now we have serious business. What are you going to wear tomorrow?"

By six-thirty Saturday night, she'd tried on five different blouses, changed her skirt twice and discarded four pairs of shoes. "What do you think?" she asked, standing in the middle of the clothes-strewn room.

"You're *beautiful*." Susan twisted a curl around her finger. "Your hair's so pretty. It's red but not that carroty red. And these curls are gorgeous." She flicked a finger at her own straight fall of dark hair.

"I can thank my mother for the curls but not the color." Anne inspected herself in the mirror, smoothing several curls behind her ears. "Dad says that's the picture he'll always remember, the sun on Mom's golden curls. I don't know how I ended up with red hair."

"Quit fishing for compliments. Richard's going to drop at your feet when he sees you." Barb held out a sweater.

"As long as he doesn't pass out." The somersaults in her stomach hadn't subsided and she only hoped she wouldn't be the one to faint.

When the buzzer sounded, they all jumped. Barb and Susan walked her to the end of the hall, pushing her through the door into the common lounge. "Good luck," Barb whispered. "And have a great time."

He stood by the check-in counter, striding over when he saw her. "You look very pretty," he said.

"So do you," she responded.

She realized what she'd said and felt her skin heat. That was the disadvantage of being a redhead, she thought bitterly. You blushed so easily.

His laugh was as attractive as his voice and it immediately relaxed her. "Thank you. No one ever said I was pretty before."

"Well, first time for everything. Shall we go?"

The evening passed quickly and delightfully. She was a soprano and he sang a deep bass. Twice the leader started a song unfamiliar to Richard and he amused her by singing silly words into her ear, his breath tickling the fine hairs of her neck.

They headed back to the dorm a few minutes before Lights Out. When a breeze suddenly sprang up, she shivered in her sweater, and Richard draped his jacket around her shoulders, his fingers lightly touching her arms.

He halted just outside the glow cast by the dorm light. Anne stood still, hardly able to breathe. Would he kiss her? No one would ever mistake her for a fast woman, but the thought of his lips on hers...

"I had a great time." His voice was husky.

"So did I. Thank you for inviting me." She handed him back his jacket.

Their fingers met. The somersaults were coming in waves, brought on by his eyes gazing at her so intently, the musky smell of his cologne, the uneven stutter of his breath.

"Could we go out again?" His words were a whisper in the shadows.

She nodded, not sure she could trust her voice. He stepped closer, his lips grazing hers, and walked away.

Humming one of the silly songs he'd sung for her, she floated into her room. Susan leaned over the side of her bed. "So?"

Anne sighed. "He is such a gentleman."

"He didn't kiss her," Barb said knowingly.

Anne raised one eyebrow. "He did kiss her!" Susan squealed.

"A tiny one." Anne frowned. "You don't suppose he'll think I'm fast, do you?"

Barb hopped out of bed and hugged her. "No. You're too fragile and delicate to be fast." She giggled. "Oh, I bet you've got a boyfriend now."

She was right. Anne and Richard were inseparable during the next two months. He walked her to class. She waited for him at meals. They were often at the library together, his dark head and her red curls bent over a book. She cheered for him at football games. They walked into town for movies or hot chocolate with friends.

"So, has he asked you yet?" Barb asked one evening in November.

Anne looked up from the book she was reading. Lights Out was in ten minutes, and she was cramming in a few more pages for tomorrow's history test.

"Asked what?"

"Oh, Anne, don't be dense. Has he proposed?"

She frowned at Susan in surprise. "Of course not. We've only been dating for a few months."

Barb and Susan exchanged glances. "Anne, dear, the whole campus expects an announcement any day."

"Lights out!" the housemother shouted.

Anne turned off her desk light and crawled into bed.

"You can't silence us so easily," Barb muttered.

Anne curled up with her pillow. "We're friends, that's all." It wasn't all. There'd been kisses that made her spine tingle. Shared smiles that caused her breath to catch. But she wasn't ready to consider marriage. She had a whole world still to see.

She went home for Thanksgiving, grateful for some time away from the intensity of her friends and their desire to see her married by spring. She liked Richard and she liked spending time with him. But marriage was for the future. The distant future.

Wednesday night she organized receipts at the shop. Her mother did the office work while her father ran the repair department. "Your mom's been training the staff in Des Moines," Frank said, handing her a folder. "I'll be glad when she's working here again."

Stuffing the turkey on Thursday morning she told her mother about her classes. She rolled out pie crust and enthralled her sisters with funny stories. She answered her father's questions about campus activities while they feasted on turkey and stuffing, mashed potatoes, fresh green beans, Waldorf salad, all the special trimmings she remembered from every Thanksgiving they'd celebrated over the years.

"No boyfriends?" her father asked after the meal had been eaten, the dishes carried into the kitchen.

"I'm not there for dating," she said, her stomach giving a guilty lurch.

"I'm glad to hear that." Marian patted Frank's hand. "I don't regret a minute of my life with your father but you don't have to rush into anything. Once you have children, you won't have a chance to see the world."

Anne nodded, determined to slow things down with Richard.

The first weekend in December, he invited her to dinner. They hadn't seen each other much after Thanksgiving; she'd invented excuse after excuse not to be with him. But her imagination had failed her that afternoon and she'd reluctantly accepted his invitation.

As they walked to the single nice restaurant in the small town, he apologized for not having a car.

"I don't mind," she said. "It's a beautiful night."

The sky was filled with stars, and the snow shone bright and clean in the evening light. They crunched through the drifts, the sound of their footsteps accented by the swoosh of snow falling from the branches around them.

They talked quietly. Anne's heart pounded when he took her gloved hand, tucking it in his pocket, his hand curled possessively around hers.

She enjoyed dinner. Richard's views on life were intriguing and he was an attentive listener, focusing on her words, his lips curved in a smile that often made her forget what she was saying.

Leaving the restaurant, Anne turned toward the campus.

"Let's walk to the park." One hand on her elbow, he steered her in the opposite direction.

The small park was set back from the street. Richard led her to the lone bench and dusted off the snow that had gathered on its stone seat.

He waited for her to sit down, then sat at the other end. His face was more serious than she'd ever seen it and he wouldn't meet her eyes.

He picked up her hand, wiggling her fingers back and forth. "Anne, it's only been a few months..." He paused and she waited, her lips suddenly dry. "I just..." Another long pause. "I just knew when I saw you that you were the one."

He slipped an arm around her shoulders, facing her for the first time since they'd sat down. "I don't know how to say this in fancy words. All I know is that I want to spend the rest of my life with you. I—I—" He swallowed. "Will you marry me, Anne Robertson?"

Snowflakes fluttered onto his hair. His eyes were dark in the moonlight. *I'm sorry, Mama,* she thought. I can't let him go. And I can't stop what's happening between us.

She gently reached up with her free hand and traced the shape of his jaw, the curve of his cheek, the straight line of his nose, with her gloved finger.

"Do you think our son will have your nose or mine?" she whispered. "And I do hope he has your hair."

Richard stared at her and then her hand was crushed between them as he kissed her. When they raised their heads for air, she cuddled against his shoulder, her hand running lightly over his jaw.

"So, is that a yes?" he asked after another long kiss.

She straightened her hood. "Of course it is! Do you think I kiss every boy I date?"

His laughter echoed in the glittering night. "From now on you will. Because I'll be the only one you date."

They laughed, kicking snow as they walked home. Anne

stopped partway up the campus hill to make a snowball. As Richard crested the hill, the snowball knocked his cap off. Turning, he raced over to her and pushed her into the snow. When she caught his leg before he could move away he landed next to her.

"Anne, come on! The doors lock in ten minutes!" At Susan's shouted warning, they jumped to their feet and ran the rest of the way, Anne's hand firmly held in his.

Her housemother stood in the doorway, waiting for last-minute arrivals. Richard pulled Anne against his side. "Still sure?" he whispered.

She patted his cheek. "For always."

Barb was already snuggled under the covers when Susan and Anne hurried into the room. "Wouldn't you say there's something different about our Annie?" Susan asked.

Barb peered at Anne. "I saw some unusual behavior tonight," Susan went on. "Richard and Anne rolling around in the snow."

"You two are nuts." Anne draped her wet coat and gloves over the radiator, and steam hissed into the room. "I'm the same as always."

"No, you're not," Barb said. "*Definitely* different."

Barb and Susan continued to tease her as she changed for bed. She sank down on Barb's bunk. "All right, you win. But it has to be our secret."

"Oh, Anne, he asked you!" Barb shrieked.

"Shh." Anne shuddered, expecting the entire dorm to come rushing in.

"So? Tell all," Susan said.

"Well, he asked me at the park."

"The park? But it's freezing out there! Why didn't he ask you at the restaurant?" Barb scooted over so they could settle more comfortably against the wall.

"Anyone can propose in a restaurant." Richard's choice of a quiet snow-covered park was perfect. She would remember that moment all her life.

"Oh, Annie, we're so happy!" Barb threw both arms around her in a big hug and Susan followed suit. "You'll be a beautiful bride."

"And think of those shoulders in a suit!"

Anne whacked Susan on the arm. "Those are *my* shoulders you're drooling over," she said with a sense of wonder at the thought. The rest of her life with Richard. She was still smiling when she fell asleep.

The news spread quickly through campus. Congratulations greeted them wherever they went. Impromptu holiday parties also brought a special toast for the newly engaged couple. Susan and Barb claimed that they'd kept their mouths shut, but she'd seen the twinkle in their eyes. Not answering a question could be just as revealing. She planned to tell her parents when she went home during the semester break at Christmas, not wanting to use the phone to share such news.

Christmas vacation arrived all too soon. Richard was returning to his family in Chicago, and Anne had to go home to Lincoln.

"I'll call on Christmas Day," Richard promised. "I'll tell my parents, and then we can tell your parents together when I visit after New Year's."

"Okay." She sniffed. They were saying goodbye outside her dorm. His bus left at the same time as her train.

"Hey, don't cry." He wiped a tear from her cheek.

She sniffed and managed a watery smile. "You won't forget me, will you?" Once he was back in the city, would he remember his small-town girlfriend?

"No! I love you." His kiss left her dazed and wobbly. "We'll shop for a ring when I come through Lincoln."

The whole family met her at the train depot. Margaret had grown taller but her hair still flopped in her face. Alice had let her own hair grow longer, the golden curls of her childhood giving way to the sleeker style of a teenager. They all looked dearer to her than ever, especially now that she knew she'd be leaving them soon. She swallowed back more tears and hugged them tight.

"Ouch! You're squishing me."

Anne smiled. Alice sounded like herself. Some things didn't change that much.

They celebrated Christmas with the family, opening presents early in the morning before the traditional waffle brunch. She took over for Marian in the shop, giving her mother a few days' break, and several times almost told her father about Richard. But she couldn't brave his disappointment alone.

She was cautious around her mother. She'd never been able to keep a secret from her. Marian asked about her life at college and after a few tentative replies, Anne realized she could avoid uncomfortable questions by focusing on activities and not people.

"I like my classes," she said. They were mixing the dough for the morning's cinnamon rolls, a treat Marian made each holiday season. "I'm learning a lot of new material."

"You don't study all the time, do you?"

Anne sprinkled flour on the counter. "No, I have friends. In fact, one of them is meeting me here after New Year's so we can go back together."

She held her breath. Marian flipped the dough in the bowl, patting it into shape. "I'm glad you're doing so well," she said. Anne exhaled slowly.

"You have so many more choices than I did." Marian poured the dough onto the counter. "You need to enjoy life. I hope you do get married someday. But don't be in a rush. You can settle down after you've seen more of the world."

Anne swallowed guiltily. Her mother hadn't asked about dates this visit, no doubt still believing Anne's Thanksgiving assertions.

On the day before she was to return to the campus, she drove to the bus station alone. Richard had suggested visiting earlier during the holiday but she wanted to spend only one night with her family and Richard together. She told herself it wasn't because she felt worried about what her mother would say, just that she thought her family would adjust better to her coming marriage if she and Richard left right after they gave them the news.

Rather like ripping off a bandage, she mused. Quick. Less painful. It wasn't the way she should probably be thinking of her marriage but her mother would be hurt that she hadn't confided the news before.

Standing next to the car, she saw Richard hurry out of the building, the wind ruffling his dark hair. He grabbed her in a huge hug. "Miss me?"

"Yes, yes, yes!" She pulled his face down for a long kiss.

"Wow! Remind me to take trips often when we're married. I like this greeting."

She laughed and tugged him over to the car. "Come on. I'm going to show you off." Now that they were together, she couldn't believe she'd ever meant to keep him secret.

Frank was still at the shop when they got to the house. Marian was in the kitchen with the girls, the preparations for supper underway.

"Mom, this is my friend Richard Sanders. Richard, this is my mother, Marian Robertson, and my sisters, Margaret and Alice."

Marian slowly wiped her hands on a dish towel. Margaret and Alice leaned against the counter, their eyes wide. No one had ever brought a boy into the house.

"This is your friend?" Marian finally asked.

Richard chuckled. "I'm more than a friend, Mrs. Robertson."

Marian swiveled from Richard to Anne and back again. "Anne?"

She wished her father was home or that she'd gone to the shop first. Dad was always easier to manage.

She took a deep breath and gradually released it. "We're engaged, Mom."

The dish towel slipped from Marian's hand. "Engaged?"

"Engaged!" Margaret screamed, crossing the room, squeezing Anne in a tight hug. Alice joined them, their faces shining with excitement.

"Anne, may I speak to you?" Her mother was heading toward the hallway. "Alone," she added.

Richard turned to Anne. "I'll be right back." Embarrassment washed through her, and she frowned at her sisters. "You be nice to him while I'm gone."

"Oh, we will," Margaret promised. "We'll show him all your baby pictures."

Anne cringed, but she had bigger worries. Her mother was standing in her parents' bedroom door. "Come in, please."

She trailed Marian into the master bedroom and perched on the edge of a chair. She usually came in here to borrow a pair of earrings or get Marian's help with her hair. The atmosphere tonight was vastly different.

"I thought you weren't even dating. And now you tell us you're engaged?"

Anne bit her lower lip, hands clasped between her knees.

"This wasn't news you could tell your mother before the young man showed up?"

"I—we—" She swallowed past the lump in her throat. On the other side of the closed door, she could hear Margaret and Alice giggling. "We were going to tell you together."

"I see." Marian paced around the room, trailing her fingers over the lace runner on the dresser, straightening the wedding portrait on the nightstand.

She sat down on the bed. "Annie, I'm sure he's a lovely man. But you're too young to get married."

"I'm not, Mama. I'm older than you were when you married Daddy."

Marian bit her lip. "And I was too young."

Anne's head jerked up. "But you and Daddy love each other. You work together, you like the same movies, you—"

"Is that what you're basing this engagement on? You like the same movies?"

"No, I—" Anne paused. How could she explain?

A straightforward answer was best. "I love him, Mom. He makes me laugh, he makes me think. I'm a better person when I'm with him."

She walked across the room and knelt in front of her mother, catching her hands between her own. "Mom, you and Dad gave me the best example of two people in love. You don't always get along, but you always make up. You respect each other, you tease each other. I want that for myself, Mom. And I can find it with Richard."

Her mother sniffed. "Oh, Annie, I hoped you wouldn't get married so young. You have the whole world ahead of you. And once you're married, have babies, it's so difficult to go anywhere."

"I don't want to go anywhere unless Richard's with me," she said simply.

Marian pulled her hand out of Anne's grasp and wiped her eyes. "Oh, honey." She sniffed again, then squared her shoulders. "You know your father's going to grill this young man unmercifully. He never intended for you to come back from that college engaged. And where does Richard live?"

"Chicago. We may not move there but we'll definitely visit his family. So, see, I will get to see more of the world."

"Chicago? Oh, that's so far away." She pushed to her feet. "Now see what you've done. You've turned me into a watering pot, and I still have to meet this young man of yours."

Anne placed her arms around her mother's shoulders. "He'll love you, Mom, just like I do." She pressed a kiss on her mother's hair. "Thank you. You'll see. He's the right man for me."

Frank was quiet during the introductions and then excused himself to wash up for dinner. Marian followed him down the hall, tossing Anne a reassuring look.

Dinner was lively, with the girls asking Richard about his life in Chicago. He captivated them, just as he had Anne.

"Do you have a large family?" Marian asked.

"Two younger brothers and a sister," he said. "My parents probably have as many reservations about our engagement as you do, Mr. and

Mrs. Robertson. But I love your daughter, I have big plans for my future and I'll do everything I can to make her life happy."

Frank leaned back in his chair, his arms folded over his chest. "Easy talk, Richard. I know Lincoln's a far cry from Chicago but that doesn't mean we have any smaller hopes for our daughter. We want her to see the world. We didn't expect her to come back from college her first semester engaged."

Anne didn't back down from her father's disappointed expression. "Neither did I, Dad. But then did you expect to find the love of your life when you knocked on that parsonage door in Winston?"

The room was silent, and she wondered if she'd gone too far. After a moment her father's chuckle echoed around the table. "You do see what you're getting yourself into, don't you, Richard? Her mother's the same way. Feisty and not willing to take a back seat to anyone."

"Taking a back seat—is that what you expect from your womenfolk?" Marian's words dripped with sarcasm.

He raised his eyebrows. "If it was, I'd be frustrated every day of my life." He kissed the back of her hand. "And I'm not."

After dessert, Anne borrowed the car and drove Richard to the one hotel in town. "I like your parents." They stood on the carpet outside the entry doors, hands linked, reluctant to say goodbye.

"I think they like you."

"I've always been able to charm the parents."

She studied him. "How many parents have you charmed? And, more to the point, *whose?*"

He grinned, the lopsided grin that made her stomach tilt. "Oh, not many. My date for the prom and a few other girls over the years."

"Well, my parents are the only ones you'll be charming from now on," she said, echoing the sentiments he'd voiced when he proposed.

They made plans for a June wedding. Letters flowed between her dorm and the house in Lincoln, filled with pictures of wedding gowns and decorations, ideas for flower arrangements and reception menus. Twice she went home for the weekend, trying on the wedding dress her mother was sewing and making final decisions about the ceremony that would herald the beginning of her life with Richard.

The day dawned sunny and warm, a propitious sign, Anne decided. In the small chapel, the flowers sparkled in the afternoon sun that streamed through the stained-glass windows. Frank's grip was tight as he walked her down the aisle. Richard stood at the altar, his smile beckoning. It was bittersweet to let go of her father and her past life and move toward her new life with Richard.

She made her vows in a strong, clear voice, surrounded by family, her sisters standing as attendants, her parents seated in the front row.

Marian introduced Richard's family to the Robertson relatives. Becca had traveled from California to celebrate the wedding of her oldest niece. Clara and Sam had arrived that afternoon from Davenport with their four boys. They'd spent the weekend with Frank's widowed mother, who had sent her good wishes and a set of towels.

Marian smiled and chatted with the close friends who'd been invited. Midway through the reception, she whispered something to Richard and kissed his cheek.

"What did Mom say?" Anne asked him as they danced to the final song.

"I'm family now. And she thanked me for not running off with her daughter." He quirked an eyebrow at her. "Was that an option?"

Anne grinned. "Could've become a family tradition." She'd heard the story over and over from her grandmother. Until her mother's parents had passed away, years earlier, they'd visited the house in Winston every year. The girls had been entranced by the window their mother had used for her elopement.

One day, when the newness of their marriage was a little less sparkly, she would tell him about her parents and the love they had for each other. The love that had begun in a small town, led them to climb down a ladder and onto a train, and into an unknown future.

The love that had brought their oldest daughter here, standing next to the man she would love for the rest of her days.

Summer 2004

"What are you doing?" Preston wandered into her room and plopped down on the floor, scattering papers with his feet.

"Preston!"

"Sorry." He scooped the papers into a pile and picked up the top one. "What are these?"

"Some of Aunt Margaret's writings. I thought I'd read through them, see if I can figure out this mystery."

"What mystery?" He shifted around until he was leaning against her bed. "You mean, why G.G. doesn't want a party? It's not a mystery to anyone but you, Hannah. She'd rather just enjoy her last days in peace."

"Yeah, that's right." Hannah picked up a magazine and started leafing through it. "All of a sudden, she's claiming she's old. Have you ever heard G.G. talk about being old before?"

"Well, yeah, I have. When we got here this summer, she said her joints were hurting, that maybe it was time for her old bones to be carted off."

Hannah stared at him, her finger holding her place in the magazine. "Really? She said that?"

He nodded, then shrugged. "Yeah, but I didn't think anything of it. I mean, she *is* ninety-three."

"Yeah." She bent back over her magazine.

Was she wrong, trying to figure out how to have a party over everyone's objections? Maybe just knowing that her great-grandparents' marriage had survived for that many years was enough. None of the other relatives seemed interested in convincing G.G. and Grandpa Frank that they needed a party.

"So, have you found anything exciting?"

"Not really. Except that Aunt Margaret probably wouldn't want her unpublished writing to be read by anybody else. I did find the newspaper articles about the sale of Grandpa Frank's business, though. Gave a lot of history."

She handed the article to Preston. "Too bad we weren't old enough to take over," he said.

"Yeah," she murmured, surprised again at how their minds ran on the same track. From the first shop, Robertson's Appliances had grown to five stores around the state. Grandpa Frank and G.G. had managed the one in Lincoln, hiring local managers for the other four. Grandma Anne had returned to Lincoln after Grandpa Richard died, taking over the shop there until she'd decided to retire. Grandpa Frank and G.G. had then checked with all the grandchildren before selling the entire chain.

Sometimes Hannah wished she'd been old enough to be part of the decision. She'd loved answering the phones when she was younger. The new owner had said she could work in the Lincoln shop whenever she was available and until this summer, she'd gone in a few afternoons every week.

Preston flopped down on his stomach, feet in the air, and scooped a magazine off the pile near the end of the bed. "Do these all have stories by Aunt Margaret?"

Hannah nodded. "I marked most of them. I also found some letters from G.G. that she wrote while Aunt Margaret was in England. You can see where she got her talent."

She'd started the search hoping to find some answers in her great-aunt's writing. Her English teachers had told the class that most authors included autobiographical information in their writing. She'd hoped that if she read the pages thoroughly, she would pick up some details about G.G. and Grandpa Frank's life.

Preston was absorbed in the story he'd chosen. Margaret's stories usually had a happy ending and she knew that was something the critics had complained about when reviewing her work. But as Aunt Margaret had explained in various interviews, life was too short to be gloomy, too many bad things happened in real life and why shouldn't people escape for a few hours? If her stories weren't "literary" enough for the critics, they could read something else.

If only Hannah could find her own happy ending. One that would satisfy her *and* the rest of her family.

MARGARET'S STORY

Chapter 14

Pepperton, Iowa
Summer 1948

The room smelled damp and musty. The ceiling was high and the available lighting was inadequate, casting dark shadows over the bookcases. As Margaret pushed the door wider, she peered around its heavy oak.

She ventured into the room, letting the door go. A draft caught it, the slam echoing through the shelves. She stood still, waiting for certain reprisal.

A tall, thin young man walked from behind the shelves. Wiping his hands on a dish towel, he studied her silently. She hung her head, wishing her braids would magically separate, providing a curtain of hair to hide behind.

"How did a little thing like you make so much noise?" he asked in a pleasant tone.

She peered up at him. He stood a foot away from her, the towel dangling from his hand. Dark hair sprang from his pale brow and he had deep-set dark eyes. He smiled at her.

"You must be new here," he said. "I don't remember seeing you around before. My name is Andrew Campbell." He turned toward the back of the library as he spoke.

She followed him. She couldn't let him out of her sight; he might disappear. The other librarians had been old women who hissed at her when she made a sound. Mrs. Collins, the librarian the last time they were here, would have banished her from the premises for the noise she'd just made.

But this librarian—Andrew, she breathed softly—he was actually talking to her in the library. His voice was smooth, cultured, she told herself. At the age of thirteen, Margaret Robertson had encountered her first love.

She waited at the edge of the shelves. He'd gone into the room and was washing dishes in a small sink. She was affronted by the sight of him doing such a menial task.

"I'll do that," she said sharply. "You must have more important things to do."

He grinned at her over his shoulder. She had read about hearts beating irregularly but she'd never had it happen to her. Not until now. "Actually, I don't have anything else to do," he said. "Not many people come into the library during the summer. Too busy boating and vacationing. You're my first visitor all day."

She walked over to him, proud of her boldness, and picked up a dish towel.

"You still haven't told me your name." He wiped down the sink, then reached for the towel she was holding.

Their fingers touched, heating her skin and making it hard for her to breathe.

He tossed the towels into a basket under the small table. "I'd like to call you something besides the girl who came into the library and dried dishes."

She swallowed and backed up a step. She couldn't concentrate when she was so close to him. "Margaret Robertson." Her voice was squeaky, and she gulped down another breath. "My parents rented a cottage for the summer," she said, glad she sounded more normal. "We used to come to the lake all the time but this is the first year we've been back since before the war."

"Ah, that's why I haven't heard the name before. So where is this cottage?"

She pointed in the general direction. "About a mile that way. We were too late to find one in town but we're closer to the lake."

He'd moved into the main part of the library and settled on a couch in the reading area, one long leg draped over his knee. Margaret quickly sat down on a chair opposite him.

"Did your father bring you in?"

She shook her head. "I walked. That way, I can stay as long as I like." And right now, she'd be happy to stay all day.

"Well, Margaret Robertson, what can I do for you? Obviously you didn't come to the library to visit with me."

No, but I will. The idea of reading a book instead of talking to him was ludicrous. He was much more interesting than any story she could find.

"Let me sign you up for a library card."

He was walking toward the desk in the corner. Opening the top drawer, he took out a form and a fountain pen. She watched as he gracefully inked her name onto the first line.

When he asked her age, she considered lying. But her mother would have to sign the form. And telling the truth was a big deal with her mom.

She answered his questions in a low voice, hoping she seemed older. When all the lines were filled out, he handed it to her. She stared at his neat handwriting. Maybe she could take this one home and tell him she'd lost it. He'd figure she was careless but she would have something of his to treasure.

He pushed back his chair and stood up. "Now, I suppose you'd like a book. I can let you check out one book on temporary loan, until you return your form." He studied her for a moment. "Horses. I bet you'd like a book on horses."

Horse stories had indeed been her passion, but now she wanted to read about love. Her face heated up at the very thought of asking him for a book about a man and a woman. She let him recommend a story she'd already read twice. Ten minutes later, she told him goodbye and left.

She walked home in a trance. She relived his words to her over and over. Her father was handsome, but Andrew was dashing and debonair. He'd held the door open for her and swept his hand forward in a low bow, wishing her "Godspeed." Her heart had threatened to jump out of her chest. In the late-afternoon light, he'd looked even paler. She'd been tempted to smooth back the dark lock of hair that had fallen over his eyes. Instead, she'd murmured a quick goodbye and raced down the street.

Her life soon settled into a routine. She would arrive at the library midmorning. He would greet her and continue sorting and filing books while she read on the big couch. At lunchtime, she would close her book and take out her tiny packed lunch. He would invite her into the kitchen and they'd eat and chat about books they'd read, favorite authors, stories they wished someone would write. Occasionally people entered the library; he would leave for the few necessary minutes and then return to her side.

"Tell me about your family," he said one day.

Margaret paused midbite. How could she tell this amazing being about her ordinary family? He'd met her mother when Marian had come in for her library card. After that, she'd been content to let Margaret visit the library on her own, trusting Andrew to choose appropriate books for her.

"Well," he prodded, "tell me about the family group that created such a charming young lady."

She choked on her bite of apple. She couldn't resist his ornate flattery. "I have two sisters, one younger and one older," she said when she could speak.

"Ah, the sad, neglected middle child."

Oh, he understands. The dam broke and her words burst out. "Sometimes I don't think anyone even knows when I'm gone." She was certain her mother liked the idea of her spending so much time at the library. Anne had gone back to Lincoln with their father; Marian and Alice preferred to laze around at the lake.

She settled in her chair, eager to bare her soul to this kindred spirit. She told of the months during the war, when her father was away, and then the days when her mother went to the Navy Hospital in Idaho, leaving the three girls alone, with only eleven-year-old Anne in charge. She talked about how hard Anne and her mother had worked in the shop with her father, getting the business established, while she was responsible for Alice.

And she told him funny stories.

"Once, before the war, when we used to come to the lake every summer, Anne decided to go to the movies. She was about seven and she'd made friends with the lady in the next cabin, Mrs. Allen. One day, Anne went up to her and said, 'My mother said I could go to the movies with you if you'd like.' Mrs. Allen agreed and then Anne told Mom, 'Mrs. Allen said she'd take me to the movies if you didn't mind.' And off Anne trotted to the local cinema."

He laughed. She loved to hear it, a deep, rumbling sound that reverberated through the room. "Did they ever catch on?"

Margaret nodded, her lips curved in a smile. Anne had told her the story, mocking her younger self. "Anne had to stay in the cottage for two whole days and couldn't go with Mrs. Allen to any more movies. But she always said seeing *Love Finds Andy Hardy* was worth it. And Dad retells the story every chance he gets."

His laughter brought out more stories. Soon she found herself looking for the humorous aspects of an event so she could tell Andrew.

"You should write these down," he said one afternoon.

"What? The stories I tell you?" She shook her head, her hair flying around her face. "No, I couldn't do that."

"Why not? You have a real flair, Margaret Robertson. See all these books?" He waved his arm toward the shelves. "One day, a book with your name on it will sit there, too."

She giggled, even as a flicker of excitement skittered along her spine. "You're silly, Andrew. I can't write books."

He leaned forward, all traces of humor gone. "Of course you can. Even better than some of the books in here."

She'd nodded, astounded at the intensity in his voice. No one had ever believed in her like that. Listening to him, she knew she could accomplish great things, with his support and encouragement to guide her.

All too soon, summer was over and the Robertsons were packing their bags to go home to Lincoln. Margaret managed to slip away the last day of their visit.

"Andrew, what will I do without you?" Tears trickled down her cheeks and she couldn't eat the sandwich she'd brought.

He passed her a tissue. "You'll write to me. You'll tell me stories about your life and the lives of the people around you. And I'll write back, telling you what I liked and what I didn't."

She brightened. "You'll write to me?"

"Of course. Did you think our friendship was over just because you're leaving? What kind of friend are you?"

"I don't know. I've never really had a friend before." She never knew what to say when she was around girls her own age. It was easier to find friends in a book.

He walked her to the door and gave her a light hug. "Well, now we both have a best friend. Don't forget that. I expect at least one letter a week."

Margaret struggled over her letters to Andrew. She spent hours trying to come up with the best word to describe a woman she saw at the grocery, the way a dog walked down the street. The letters she finally put into the envelopes for Andrew were neatly written, showing no indication of the many pages she'd discarded.

His letters were filled with advice and funny stories of his own. She treasured each page, and the days always seemed brighter when she saw a letter from Andrew on the bureau in the living room.

"Your librarian friend seems to have a lot of time to write," her mother said one afternoon, handing her the latest arrival.

Margaret hugged the letter to her chest. "He likes to write letters. He's a very good student."

Marian smiled and patted her on the head. Like I'm a little girl, Margaret thought resentfully. Andrew would never treat me that way.

"Don't forget to do your homework," Marian said. "I don't want to be called into a teacher's meeting because you haven't been keeping up with your assignments."

Margaret rushed to her room, the angry words she'd wanted to shout at her mother ringing in her head. Her mother had never gone to a teacher's meeting about her! Her grades were good. The teachers liked her. Now Alice…

But the letter beckoned and Margaret forgot her family as she read his words. His friendship carried her through each day, helping her look at the world with bright, eager eyes. He recommended authors and she pored over their books, sending him impassioned letters about her reading. She floated through school, in her element, dreaming of next summer and seeing him again, spinning images of their life together once she was old enough to get married.

One April day, after unseasonably cold weather, the flowers poked cautious heads out of the ground and tiny buds appeared on the trees. A school assembly had included an award for an essay Margaret had written. She couldn't wait to share the good news with Andrew, and she hurried home to start her letter.

An envelope was propped on the bureau in the dining room. The handwriting was different but the return address was as familiar as her own. Puzzled, she carried it to her room before breaking the seal. She dropped her books on the bed and sank down beside them.

At first, she couldn't understand the words. She read them twice and then a third time. Not until then did she begin to comprehend.

"No!" she screamed. She crumpled the letter and tossed it across the room. "No, no, no!"

Her mother ran in. "Margaret, for heaven's sake, what's the matter?"

Margaret lay on the bed, staring at the ceiling. "She's lying. Andrew had her write as a practical joke, to see how I'd react."

"Who's lying? What are you talking about?" Marian picked up the paper and smoothed it out. She scanned the page.

"Oh, Margaret, I'm sorry. I know how much he meant to you."

"Means to me!" Margaret screeched. "He's *not* dead. He can't be. He told me he'd write to me forever, that we'd always be best friends."

"Oh, honey."

Marian sat on the bed and Margaret buried her head in her mother's lap, the tears streaming down her face. "How could he die, Mama? He's too young. You can't die that young. Only old people die."

Marian laid a hand on Margaret's hair. "His mother says he's been sick a long time, that the doctors aren't sure why he survived as long as he did." She smoothed the wild mane. "She thinks your letters gave him a reason for living."

"But he never said anything. He didn't tell me he was even sick."

"Maybe he didn't want to upset you. He cared about you, you know that. And he probably liked having somebody who didn't fuss over him."

Margaret sniffed, the tears rolling down her cheeks. "What am I going to do now? His letters were *my* reason for living."

"Don't talk like that!" Her mother clutched her shoulders, shaking them gently. "Would he want you to give up like this?"

She didn't know. She didn't know anything anymore.

Marian tucked a blanket around her. "Close your eyes and rest, sweetheart. In a little while, I'll bring you a sandwich."

Margaret made a muffled sound. Her mother thought food would help the ache in her stomach, but it wouldn't. She couldn't eat. Not with Andrew gone. And she certainly couldn't eat a sandwich. Just thinking of all the lunches they'd shared, all the lunches they'd never share again, brought her tears to the surface.

She stayed in bed for two days. Her mother ran interference with the rest of the family, keeping them away from Margaret's room. She could hear whispered conversations on the other side of the door but she didn't invite anyone in. She crawled out from the covers to visit the bathroom only when she was sure her sisters were gone. Her mother tempted her with favorite meals and Margaret tried to eat, but every bite tasted like sawdust.

She reread Andrew's letters, remembering his voice and his laugh. She saw again his dark hair and understood now that his pallor hadn't been that of a young man staying inside to read books. He'd been sick. She cried, imagining his courage as he struggled against death, refusing to give in, charming her with his wit and encouraging her with his wisdom.

At night she used to dream of him, dream about life with Andrew as her husband. He'd been a college student, a few years older than her, and she'd felt certain he would wait until she was the right age for marriage. In her dreams she'd created a perfect life, where they'd live in a small house, sharing their love of books.

Now that dream was over.

But he'd had a dream for her, and that didn't have to end. She looked at the snapshot his mother had sent—"So you'll remember my darling boy," she'd written. She felt a bond with this unknown woman, who had lost a son in the prime of his life.

She tucked the picture in her mirror, where she'd see it every day. "Don't worry, Andrew," she said softly, hoping he could hear her words. "Your dream will come true. One day a book of mine will be on that library shelf."

She wrote to his mother, saying how sorry she was about his death and how much Andrew's love of books had meant to her.

She returned to school, to her classes, and spent her free time scribbling down stories. But their content changed from the stories she'd told Andrew during those golden days at the lake. Now she recorded the sadness she saw, writing tales of hopelessness and despair. Alice cried when she read a short story describing a small girl's death from neglect and malnutrition.

"Why are your stories so sad, Mags?" Alice pushed the pages away. "I'll have nightmares."

"Life is grim, Alice. Happy endings are only for babies and for people who bury their heads in the sand."

"Well, give me happy endings! I'm not going to end up like one of your characters. They're always so miserable. Like you," she'd muttered under her breath.

Her teachers met with Marian more than once. Her mother called her into the kitchen after one of these meetings.

"Your teachers are worried about you." Marian sat at the kitchen table, hands folded neatly in front of her. "They feel you're isolated from your classmates, that you're unhappy. They said your grades are still good but your writing isn't. Too much gloom and not enough substance. Even your grammar has deteriorated."

"What if Daddy had died right after you met him?" Margaret asked, her voice solemn, her hands as neatly folded as her mother's.

Marian's whole body stiffened. "I would've died inside," she admitted.

Margaret nodded, a lump in her throat. Her mother's voice throbbed with anguish. For the first time, she felt a kinship that had nothing to do with their shared blood.

"Sometimes I can hardly breathe," she confessed. "And it hurts to swallow." As if eating was wrong, when Andrew would never eat again.

Marian leaned across the table and wrapped her arms around

Margaret's shoulders. "He would want you to go on," she said. "He believed in you and your talent."

Margaret opened her mouth, then shut it. "One day at a time," her mother said. "Try one day at a time."

Her wardrobe gave way to baggy shirts and pants. Her hair hung over her face and she shuffled when she walked. She might have to stay bound to this earth but she didn't have to be happy about it.

Timothy Matthews, a boy in her geometry class, asked her to the movies one fall evening her junior year. She was astonished by his attention. Hopeful that her daughter would cheer up and change her attitude and her clothes, Marian agreed to the date.

Margaret never remembered the movie they saw or where they ate hamburgers afterward. But she always remembered the walk home, writing about it in her first short story that sold.

Her love for Andrew had never reached the physical stage, only a worship from afar. Timothy's nearness and the scent of his cologne caused incredible tremors to go through her. And when he stopped in the shadows of the trees on her lawn, his arm sliding around her neck, his hand drawing her head toward his, she closed her eyes, the better to catalog the experience. His warm breath against her mouth. His tongue brushing her lips. His hand on the back of her head. His shoulders bumping hers...

When his hand slipped over her shoulder and touched the tiny nubs of her newly developing breasts, she shuddered and pushed him away.

"No," she whispered.

"No?" His voice was harsh and she backed off. "Why do you think I asked you out?" His hands were clenched into fists.

"I...thought you liked me." She hated how whimpery her voice was, but she couldn't get enough air to speak any louder.

His sharp crack of laughter hurt her ears and her heart. "I heard you were a good time, under all those dark clothes. The joke's on me, isn't it?"

"What?"

"It's all over school. You're a free spirit—and everyone knows what *that* means. Your poetry—"

"I never... I..." She whirled away from him. Her feet pounded over the grass as she raced to the front porch. She paused long enough to school her features into a semblance of her normal expression. Praying no one was up, she pulled open the front door.

"How was your date?" Her mother looked up from the book she was reading.

"Fine." Maybe she should consider acting instead of writing, she thought, turning toward the hallway.

"Mags, come here, honey."

At the sound of her childhood nickname, she dissolved into tears. "I miss Andrew so much!" He would never have been so coarse, so cruel to her.

"I know, sweetheart, I know." Marian smoothed a hand over her hair. "I promise it'll get easier. You'll never forget him but in time, you'll be able to remember him without hurting so much."

"But it's been more than a year!"

"Grief has no time limit, Margaret. But maybe you could stop focusing on the sad part of your relationship with him." Marian leaned back, framing Margaret's face with her hands. "Think about how fortunate you are to have known Andrew, even for that one summer. And all those letters you have from him. Not many people get to experience such a wonderful relationship."

Margaret sniffed. "It's just that sometimes I feel so alone."

"You're not alone," her mother said. "You have your sisters. Your father and me. We all love you very much. We believe in you, honey. Just as much as Andrew did."

Margaret nodded. "I know it. But—" She gave another sigh. "It's not going to be easy."

Marian linked her arm with Margaret's, leading them both down the hallway. "No one ever said life would be easy. But you're strong enough to make a go of it, Margaret Robertson. You come from good stock."

A corner of Margaret's mouth turned up. "Good stock?"

Her mother nodded and pushed her toward her bedroom door. "The best. How else would your father and I have survived all these years with each other and with you girls?"

She kissed Margaret's cheek. "You'll make it. And one of these days, we're going to see a book on the shelf with your name on it. Just like Andrew said." She grinned. "Make sure you don't tell all our family secrets, though."

Chapter 15

Mrs. Marian Robertson
Lincoln, Iowa
October 1954
Dear Margaret,

Thank you for the lovely anniversary present. A silver tea set from England for our 25th! I will think of you whenever I serve tea from now on. We had a wonderful trip to Chicago. Except for a few visits with Richard's family, we went sightseeing like a couple of country bumpkins. Not that I'd ever say so to your father, but we must get out more! I know my mouth was agape most of the time we were traveling around the city. I've already started a fund for our trip to England—perhaps for our thirtieth anniversary. It will take me that long to save up enough money and to convince your father to leave the shop in someone else's hands.

You're an inspiration to me, Margaret. Saving your money and working those extra jobs for this chance to study abroad. Now that you're gone, I can admit I worried about you going so far away but Anne reminded me that you're very responsible.

I can't wait to see your photographs of London! Your letter brought me right into the scenes, with your clever descriptions of Buckingham Palace, Picadilly Circus, Westminster Abbey. You write so well! When I think of how easily your father can make a sale, I don't wonder at the ease with which you use words. I may see if Tim is interested in your letters for the local paper. (Of course, we would leave out the personal details.)

If you do see the queen, well, it's okay if you curtsey. You're there to absorb and explore the culture. Your professors would say the same thing, no doubt. We may have won our freedom from England years ago but there's something about all that royal fuss that makes you believe in fairy tales and happily-ever-afters. Life may not be like that behind the palace doors but we can dream!

Enjoy your visit, my dear. We're all so proud of our world traveler!

Mom and Dad

Mrs. Marian Robertson
Lincoln, Iowa
November 1954
Dear Margaret,

By now you've probably heard that Timothy Matthews is married. He sent us an invitation but we didn't go!

Oh, Margaret, I forgot about that disastrous date with Timothy Matthews! He's married now, to a quiet girl several years younger than himself. He would like to publish your adventures. He said it could be a regular column. I'll edit out the personal parts of the letters you've sent to me or you can write some specifically for the paper.

Paris in springtime! What a lovely possibility. I'm trying not to be green with envy. I must add to our travel fund. With the third shop opening in Cedar Rapids, we should be able to cover a vacation for your father and me. Your father isn't keen on the long boat trip, however. He feels we should wait until there's regular air travel. I don't think I can wait that long!

Anne mentioned that you've been enjoying your evenings. I assume you write different adventures to your sister! I do hope you're being careful. I want you to be happy, Mags, as happy as I've been with your father. Find the right man and we'll support you one hundred percent. Make sure he's worthy of you. Don't settle for anything but the best.

Enough of the motherly advice. I've discovered why women of the past wrote letters so often. It's a very liberating way of communicating. Is this how you feel when you write? I do have to be careful I don't write pages and pages or else I couldn't afford to send them by air mail.

All our love,
Mom and Dad

Mrs. Marian Robertson
Lincoln, Iowa
December 1954
Dear Margaret,

How strange not to have all my girls home for Christmas! This is part of every family's life as the children grow up but it was so different this year. Anne and Richard came for a few days and then left to visit his family. We were glad to hear you attended church. Made us all seem closer that day. Dad attached your first newspaper article to the back of the cash register in the shop. We both love this statement: "Life goes on ahead of us and life stretches behind us. What we do today will affect generations to come. We can't even fathom how much." I'm excited to read more about our family history in "the old country" and to see photographs of your discoveries in Wales. Mother would tell us stories she'd heard from her grandfather about his childhood. Now you're stepping in those same locations.

I'll add a little family history that's more current. Did you know your father attended seminary for a year? Just before Anne was born. I sometimes wonder if we should've continued, but I like to think we've made a difference in Lincoln. The leaven in the bread, Brother Grimes would have said. He was your father's mentor and a very wise man. I didn't realize how wise at the time.

Your father is definitely an asset to this community, helping young people start their own businesses and being such an active part of the city council. Thank goodness he's so busy! That way he doesn't mind that I have my committees, too. My parents taught me that we should give back to our community and I've been fortunate in that I married a man who feels the same way.

Much love and Happy New Year!
Mom and Dad

Mrs. Marian Robertson
Lincoln, Iowa
January 1955
Dear Margaret,
I'm glad to hear you're back in London.

Lots of news this letter. I'm not sure what your sisters have written but I'll fill you in on their news, too. Anne and Richard are expecting! I'm so excited! I never thought about being a grandmother, even after Anne announced her engagement. But of course this is the next phase for your father and me. That baby will be terribly spoiled. Your father's always been such an easy touch for the children that come into the shop. I have to refill that toy box at least weekly. "One toy per child," I tell him. But he never listens. (And I love him all the more for it, I must confess.)

Alice has moved out. She and Tom Carter eloped. They're living in his parents' basement apartment. We had no idea she was that serious about him, which could be another family trait. My parents didn't realize how I felt about your father, either. But I don't understand why your sister couldn't wait until after they both graduated. I don't mean to complain about her to you, but perhaps you could shed some light on what happened. She isn't pregnant, so I'm not sure of the reason for this sudden marriage.

Your father was devastated and was ready to drag her back home. The house is empty, with all of you gone now. Don't worry about us, though. Enjoy the rest of your trip. We have to trust that Alice will be fine.

Love,
Mom and Dad

Mrs. Marian Robertson
Lincoln, Iowa
March 1955
Dear Margaret,
Your trip to Paris sounds delightful! And how wonderful to have a personal tour guide fluent in French. I can't wait for your article. And the neighbors feel the same way. You're a hit!

Well, you'll be an aunt twice over this year. Alice is expecting. She's told us several times that this was not the reason for their marriage, just a natural consequence. I worry about her, Margaret, so young and already married, with a baby on the way. The school won't let her finish her classes, even though Tom's still allowed to go. I tried to sway the principal but he was adamant about the rules. I'll help her with the classes at home and we'll see if she can at least obtain her high school diploma.

I didn't want to upset your trip with this news, Mags, but I was worried you'd hear variations from some of your friends. Alice visits us each week and we've been having Sunday dinner together after church. Tom is a sweet boy. We want the marriage to be successful and his parents feel the same way. She'll need her sisters, and I know you'll be a support for her when you come home.

Have a lovely last few weeks, dear.

Love,
Mom and Dad

Mrs. Marian Robertson
Lincoln, Iowa
May 1955
Dear Margaret,

Your father and I will meet you at the station in Des Moines. I'll try not to embarrass you when you arrive, but we've been a long time without our darling girl. Will we recognize you or have you acquired a continental air that will separate you from your provincial family and friends?

Just a quick last letter with some news you should know. Alice has moved back home. She and Tom are getting a divorce. He is leaving Lincoln to go to college. She assures us this was a mutual decision. For now, she's going to stay with us and we're going to convert Anne's old room into a nursery. I can help with the baby and I hope she'll attend the junior college for the next two years.

Have a safe trip, sweetheart.

Lots of love,
Mom and Dad

Chapter 16

Lincoln, Iowa
Fall 1959

The pounding woke her up. "Margaret, aren't you teaching today?" her mother called through the closed door.

Groggy, she squinted at the clock on her nightstand. "Omigosh! Thanks, Mom!" She scrambled out of bed, tossed on the clothes she'd laid out the night before, grabbed the slice of toast her mother handed her and raced out to her car.

The students were already seated when she entered the junior college classroom. She brushed her hands against her skirt, wiping off the perspiration. Her first class and she was late.

"Today is a good example of how writing can engulf your life," she said as she walked to the front of the room. The talking stopped, all the students watching her progress. "Last night, I had a wonderful idea for a story and I wrote until the wee hours. Before I knew it, I'd overslept and I had to bolt to make it to class on time. As you can see, my bolting wasn't quite fast enough."

Their laughter calmed her. She was soon engrossed in her topic—the influence of personal history on writers and their work. The bell surprised both her and the students. Fifty minutes passed more quickly when she was the teacher.

She assigned them homework—"write the autobiography of your writing life"—and dismissed them.

She packed up the books and materials she'd brought with her. At a sound from the door behind her, she paused. "Yes?"

"I'm sorry, I don't mean to rush you but I'm teaching a class in here at nine."

She glanced over her shoulder, taking in the well-tailored suit, the polished black shoes, the neat haircut. Her perusal stopped at the unruly reddish-brown beard.

He smiled and she turned away, her cheeks hot. "I must be looking at the famous local writer, Margaret Robertson. So, will I end up in your next story?"

"I'm sorry. I didn't mean to stare."

"How well do you have to know someone before they get star billing?"

She snatched up her briefcase and marched to the door. He leaned against the wall, his long legs crossed at the ankles.

"Oh, much better than this," she couldn't resist saying. "I almost have to live with them first." She could have bitten off her tongue.

His grin widened. "Hmm. Could we start with dinner? Tonight?"

"Dinner? Tonight?" All clever repartee was gone. No one would guess she had published even so much as a grocery list.

"I'm sorry." He lifted his hands. "Don't you eat? I'm afraid I don't understand famous writers."

A tiny semblance of her wits returned. "I do eat. It was the short notice that startled me."

He had the decency to look somewhat abashed. Or what she

supposed would be abashed if she could see more of his face. "I'm assuming no one else has a claim on you. Am I wrong?"

She was tempted to say *yes,* to knock him down a peg, but her whole being was suffused with sudden excitement. When had she last gone on a date? The men who lived in town knew her, had always known her. She might be a local celebrity, a writer with a number of nationally published stories to her name, but she was also the Margaret Robertson who'd wandered about the school in baggy clothes and dreary moods.

This man didn't know that Margaret.

Students filed into the room. She made a quick decision. Life was an adventure; hadn't she learned that on her European trip?

"Tonight would be fine. Seven. Ask the secretary for my address."

She eased past him and out the door.

Halfway down the hallway, she stopped. He hadn't told her his name! She pivoted and smiled when she saw him stick his head out the door. "Alex Martin."

"Thanks."

"But who is he?" Marian had asked a variation of that question ever since Margaret arrived home from her class and mentioned she was going out.

"He teaches at the college," Margaret repeated patiently. "Alice says he just moved here, from someplace in Kansas. She has him for a class on Monday evenings."

"But he could be married." Marian folded the towel she was holding and placed it in the basket. "He could be using you for cheap entertainment."

"I'm not exactly cheap entertainment material." Margaret laughed. "Mom, what about Dad? You ran off with him! I'm just going to dinner."

"Can't a mother watch out for her daughter?"

"Of course, Mom. But I'm giving this a try. Who knows?" she said flippantly. "He could be the one."

Her mother swatted her with a towel. "Just take your time.

You have your whole life ahead of you. You don't have to rush into marriage."

"I'm not rushing," she said. "I'm twenty-five, years older than any of the other marrying females in this family."

"Well, be careful."

"*You* weren't careful, and here you are, enjoying another year of wedded bliss." She leaned forward and kissed her mother's cheek. "You're the reason I keep searching for the right man, Mom. Come help me pick out something to wear tonight." She raised one hand as her mother's mouth opened. "I'm not planning to run off and get married but I do want to look my best."

Fifteen minutes later, she was surprised to hear the doorbell. "I'm not ready! He's early." She couldn't hide the panic in her voice.

"I'll have your father stall him." Marian patted her cheek. "Breathe, dear. He's just a man."

She didn't have a chance to retort before her mother disappeared down the hall.

A minute later, she was back, with Alice following her. "What are you doing here?" Margaret demanded.

Alice lifted an eyebrow. "Hello to you, too. Marcia and I were taking a walk and thought we'd drop in on Grandma and Grandpa."

"Well, help me."

Alice sifted through the clothes. "If we had time, I'd throw most of these out. You have atrocious taste, Margaret." She gave an exaggerated sigh. "Let's see what's the best of this stuff."

She settled on a dark-blue patterned skirt and soft white blouse, with a bright blue cardigan Margaret had bought in Scotland. "And a hint of makeup," Alice insisted. "You have a lot of wasted potential, Margaret."

"Be nice to your sister," Marian said automatically as Alice applied rouge and a touch of face powder.

Alice grinned and stepped back to admire her handiwork. "I am. Now, just be your natural charming self. You have a chance to start something here with someone who doesn't know you at all."

Margaret burst into laughter. "That doesn't exactly give me confidence."

The doorbell rang again, and Margaret sent them another panicked look. Alice pushed her toward the door. "Go, before Dad scares him off."

The introductions were made. Four-year-old Marcia was fascinated by him and stood in the middle of the room, her thumb in her mouth, staring. Margaret understood her reaction. He was better-looking than she remembered, his shoulders broad and his brown eyes deep. It took all her concentration to remember how to walk to his 1954 Chevy.

"Junior college teachers don't drive fancy cars," he explained as he opened her door.

She slipped in, holding her skirt carefully so it wouldn't catch on the door handle. "Part-time junior college teachers don't own cars at all." And what did he think about her still living with her parents?

He chuckled and she relaxed.

The talk was light and easy. The owner of the restaurant led them past the crowd waiting for tables to a quiet one in the corner.

"I stopped to make reservations before I went to your house," Alex whispered in her ear. "Otherwise, we wouldn't be seated for at least an hour."

"Ah, an organized man." His breath tickling her neck had driven her senses to a near-frenzy.

He grinned. "My parents would say I'm a perfectionist. That's why I asked you to vacate the room. I need at least five minutes alone to prepare for my class."

She thought of her own rushed arrival and ducked her head to study the menu. Punctuality was not in her repertoire. It was only thanks to Alice and her mother that she'd been ready on time tonight.

Waiting for coffee after their dishes were cleared away, he leaned his elbows on the table. "You're good at the questions,

Margaret Robertson. Lucky for me, I have nothing to hide. I'm just your ordinary, never-been-married thirty-year-old. Which is a good thing, since your father grilled me while we were waiting."

"Oh, I'm sorry." Her father could be the most gentle of men but let anyone threaten one of his four women, and a fiercely protective beast would emerge.

"Perfectly natural," Alex said. "Three daughters. A beautiful wife. The man must have his hands full."

Margaret grinned. She would definitely share the "beautiful wife" comment. Might make her dad spit nails but her mom would warm to Alex the next time they met.

And she hoped there'd be a next time. He was funny and charming and—

"Hello, Margaret?"

She blinked. "Sorry."

"Were you plotting a story?"

She shook her head. How could she admit she was actually plotting to see him again?

"It's my turn," he said, and she forced herself to pay attention.

"Do you have the happy outlook on life that my secretary assumes you enjoy, based on your stories?"

Margaret choked on the sip of water she'd just taken and almost choked again when he patted her on the back.

"You don't have a happy outlook? Or your stories aren't?"

Without warning, she was telling him about Andrew and the years of sadness she'd suffered. His comments were few and sympathetic and she soon launched into tales of her trip to England before coming to a sudden stop.

He counted on his fingers. "Andrew died when you were fourteen. You graduated when you were almost eighteen and went to England when you were twenty. Either you've left out a few years or you're only twenty-one."

She sipped at her water. "I forgot you teach mathematics. In the last four years, I finished my college degree and wrote for the paper. I sold a book last spring, a novel, after a dozen or so short stories. As a local writer, the college offered me a few creative writing courses. You saw me in action. Or, rather, winding down."

"I *would* like to see you in action."

His voice was quiet and she sent him a suspicious look. Was this a pass?

He laughed. "I meant in the classroom, but now you have me curious."

She blushed. Seeing the crowd milling about in the lobby, she turned back. "Shouldn't we let some other hungry souls eat?"

She waited discreetly by the door as he settled the bill. She pushed at the door but he reached across her before she could do more than nudge it partway. "Don't your dates usually open the door for you?" he asked.

His arm rested over her shoulder and she was finding it hard to catch her breath. "I—that is..." She swallowed and tried again. "Most of the guys I've dated recently have known me forever."

She thought she heard him say, "Lucky them," but he was bending down to unlock her door and she couldn't be certain. Probably just more of her daydreaming.

He backed out of the parking lot and headed in the opposite direction from her house. "Where are we going?"

"My apartment. I don't want this evening to end yet, and I can't talk to you with your parents breathing down our necks."

He didn't want the evening to end. A warmth flowered within her. "But I can't go to your apartment. What will people think?"

He looked at her, all trace of his easygoing smile gone. "Do you care?"

His hair fell over his forehead, a tiny crease between his brow. "No," she said. His right hand touched hers briefly before returning to the steering wheel.

His apartment was on the second floor of a house at the edge of town. A large painting of a rushing sea occupied the wall above the couch, the only item in the room that wasn't neat and orderly. Margaret hated to sit down and rumple the cushions. She stood in the doorway.

"What is it?"

"I don't want to mess anything up."

He laughed, a deep, throaty laugh that made her stomach pitch. His smoldering glances had excited her but this laugh made her want to throw her arms around his neck and hold him close so he'd never leave. His laugh was that of a man who saw much joy in life.

He leaned over the couch and pressed it with his palm, creating a dent in the center of the cushion. With a low bow, he turned. "Milady, your seat."

She curtseyed and started to sit. Halfway down, his hands caught her elbows and she raised her face trustingly for his kiss.

His lips were firm. She closed her eyes, letting him support her weight. After a moment, she pulled her arms away and locked them around his neck. He gathered her closer and she sank into his embrace, her back against the cushions of the couch.

She couldn't breathe. For a moment, she thought about cataloging his kiss, storing the sensations away for a story, but then his tongue invaded her mouth and she forgot everything except his kiss.

His mouth seared a path down her jaw, her cheek, along her neck. His hand crept up her side and she inhaled sharply, her nipple puckering in anticipation.

He removed his hand and she opened her eyes. "No," she said, placing his hand back on her waist.

"Are you sure?" His voice was rough with longing.

"I've never been more sure of anything."

They moved frantically, sliding garments off and onto the floor, hands exploring newly bared skin, lips trailing over shoulders, mouths, cheeks. His beard grazed the tender skin of her breast and she giggled, surprised at the soft, ticklish sensation.

He raised his head, eyes dark with desire. "What's so funny?"

"Nothing, nothing." She curled her fingers into the thick mane of his hair, bringing him closer so she could kiss his mouth. "I didn't realize your beard would tickle, that's all."

"It tickles, does it?" He rubbed his beard back and forth over her nipples until she forgot to laugh and moaned with need.

"Okay, you have to understand." He was stretched on top of her, one hand flung over the back of the couch, the other on the floor. "I really did think we'd just talk when we came up here. I don't usually..." He paused.

She pushed a strand of hair out of his eyes. "I should hope not. And I've never jumped into bed on a first date before, so I suppose that says something, too." She'd jumped into bed twice, both times with men she'd met on her English trip, determined to completely expand her horizons.

He kissed her, a hard kiss that pressed her head into the couch arm. When he released her, she gently smoothed a finger over his cheek. "I told you things tonight I've never told anyone before. And now this." She ran her finger over the straight line of his thick brows, down his nose, over his mustache, around the lips that had driven her crazy. "Alex Martin, if you don't stop leering at me, I'll expect satisfaction all over again."

"That can be arranged." He shifted and nipped her bare shoulder and she knew he was speaking the truth.

She sighed, smiling as his gaze followed her breasts. "Call my parents, would you? Tell them I'm not coming home tonight."

He straightened, half lifting himself off the couch. "What time is it? They're probably wondering where you are."

She pulled his head down until his beard tickled her chin. "I'm grown-up now, Alex. I don't answer to them."

But the mood was broken. He jumped off the couch and pulled on his pants. She lay on the couch, watching, her arms tucked casually behind her head. He threw her blouse and sweater at her.

"Margaret, I love you and thank you for a wonderful evening but you must go home."

She sat up, clutching her clothes. "What did you say?"

"I said you must go home. You may not worry about your reputation but I worry about mine."

"No, Alex, be serious. What else did you say?"

He knelt down, his hands cupping her face. "I said I love you. Those words never came out of my mouth before, honest."

Her tears surprised them both. He snatched a handkerchief from his pocket and gingerly mopped at her cheeks. He helped her into her blouse, fastening the tiny buttons with clumsy fingers. She hiccuped and stepped into her skirt.

"I—I—" She hiccuped again. "Thank you. You didn't have to say that, you know. I was a party to all this."

He frowned, then caught her around the waist, bringing her close. "I didn't just say the words, Margaret. I meant them."

Her tears flowed faster. He tilted back her head and captured them with his lips, his mouth on her cheeks and then her lips, his kiss overwhelming her with tenderness.

They were both breathless when he released her lips, his head bent over hers. "When I walked into that classroom today, I had no idea I was meeting my future wife. But after tonight, sweetheart, I am never letting you out of my life. Ever."

The tears threatened again and she swallowed. "Alex, you'd better get me home soon. Or I'm going to flood your apartment."

His kiss was gentle. "Let's go then. Or I'll keep you here for another reason."

She curled against his side on the ride home, too dazed to speak. She hadn't given him an answer and he hadn't asked for one. When he parked in front of her house, she waited but he didn't repeat his proposal. If his kiss hadn't been so possessive and intense, if her body didn't still bear the imprint of their lovemaking, she'd worry that she'd imagined the entire scene.

She made it to her bedroom door before she heard the call. "Margaret? Margaret, is that you?"

"Yes, Mom, sorry it's so late."

"Did you enjoy yourself?"

A grin spread over Margaret's face. "I did."

"And is he the one?" Her mother's voice was sleepy but Margaret could hear the humor in it.

You knew as soon as you met Dad, didn't you, Mom? You took one look at him and you knew. And thirty years later, you're still looking at each other with love in your eyes.

"I think he is," she whispered to herself.

She wasn't ready to say the words out loud, though, so she wished her mother good-night and received a muffled "good night, dear" in reply.

After that, she spent every available minute with Alex, cooking meals at his apartment, grading papers at his dining-room table, making love in his big bed. A week after their first dinner, he proposed again and she eagerly accepted. He breathed an exaggerated sigh of relief, then tumbled her onto the pillows.

He asked her to announce the engagement and choose a wedding date, but she begged for more time. "Not yet, please. I know and you know, but other people might think we're rushing into marriage."

"Why wait when we know it's right?" he asked, nibbling her earlobe.

She ducked away.

He shoved the papers she'd been trying to grade onto the floor and brought her closer to his body. "If you're worried about what happened with your sister Alice, remember your other sister's happily married. We have a fifty-fifty chance of being successful. And that's just going by your sisters. If we factor in your parents, not to mention mine, our odds are even better. Besides, I'm an optimistic kind of guy myself."

"Yes, but—"

She couldn't focus on her argument, not with his arms encircling her, his lips making their way down her cheeks, over her shoulders. He was insatiable, touching her, caressing her, and she basked in the attention. Sometimes she wondered if that was why she was so enamored with him or if—as she hoped—her feelings went deeper. But he never gave her time to reflect on it.

She pushed against his chest. "Alex, please. I can't think when you're kissing me."

"That's the general idea." He nuzzled her neck.

She squirmed out of his hold and stood up. "Alex, please."

He gazed at her, lust burning in his eyes. "All right. What?" He folded his arms over his chest.

She paced around the room, unable to concentrate now. She did better with a blank sheet of paper, and time to formulate her thoughts.

She turned to face him. "It's silly, Alex, but how can I tell my parents I'm engaged to a man they've met once?"

He reached her in a few quick strides, forcing her to stop her mad dash around the room. He raised her chin up with one long finger. "Margaret, I love you and I love the way you care about your family. But I'm not marrying your parents. I'm marrying *you*. Your opinion is the only one that matters."

She nodded, tracing a finger down the buttons of his shirt. "I know you're right, Alex. It's just that—"

He swallowed her objection with a hard kiss. "It's just nothing. Now, repeat after me. I, Margaret Robertson, love you, Alex Martin, and agree to marry you within the month."

She stared at him. His finger and thumb pinched her chin, forcing her mouth to open and shut like a ventriloquist's doll. "Repeat after me," he said.

She giggled and then said the words, pausing after "marry you."

"Finish the sentence," he ordered.

"Within the month," she whispered.

"Good. Now let's go practice for our wedding night."

Six weeks after their first meeting in the classroom, they stood together in the college chapel and exchanged vows. His parents, two sisters and brother came from Kansas, eager to witness the marriage. Anne and Alice were her attendants, his brother and a fellow teacher assisting Alex. Marian sniffled throughout the short service, Frank's arm around her shoulders. After a buffet dinner at her parents' house, Alex drove them to his apartment.

In bed that night, she ran her fingers through his beard, reveling in the different textures against her skin. "Any regrets?" she asked.

He gave a satisfied groan and rolled over so she was resting on his chest. "Not now and not ever."

"Pretty words, my love." She leaned down to give him a floating kiss. "I'll remind you of them during our first fight."

"We won't ever argue." He rolled over again, trapping her beneath him. "From now on, your stories will reflect our happily-ever-after marriage."

She laughed. "Art imitating life."

"You bet." He framed her face with his hands. Her stomach tensed at the need she saw in his dark eyes. "Now, enough talking, Mrs. Martin. This is our wedding night."

Summer 2004

"Shotgun!" Hannah grabbed the front passenger door handle a fraction of a second before Preston reached it. "I'm the oldest, anyway!"

"How long do you get to do that?" he grumbled, crawling in the back.

"Forever. I'll always be the oldest, won't I, Grandma?"

Anne buckled her seat belt and started the engine. "'Fraid so, Preston. That's the way it works. I'm always the oldest in my generation, too."

"No fair ganging up on a guy."

Laughter echoed through the car. Hannah settled more comfortably in her seat, half turned toward her grandmother, and fiddled with her beaded bracelet.

Her grandmother glanced over when they stopped at a traffic light near Winter Oaks. "No talk of parties tonight, Hannah."

"Fine." When her grandmother used that no-nonsense tone of voice, they all listened.

The table was set at the far end of the sunroom. Grandpa Frank rose from his chair and shuffled over to greet them. Every visit, he seemed older. The idea of not having him around one day brought a pang of sadness.

"Such a gloomy face," he chided, chucking her under the chin. "What's the matter?"

"Nothing." No reason to spoil the evening with thoughts of a future without him.

He gave her the same searching look she'd received from both her mother and grandmother. She wondered if she'd be able to perfect it when she had children of her own. "Well, come along," he said and they followed him across the room.

Anne placed her purse and jacket on a chair in the corner. She leaned down and pressed a light kiss on her mother's cheek. "Hello, Mom."

"Annie, Hannah, Preston." G.G. smiled at the children, her eyes brighter than the last time Hannah had seen her. "I was worried you'd forgotten."

"Of course not." Anne draped G.G.'s napkin over her lap. "Dinner with you is a highlight of our week."

"Well, you need a more exciting life, then." G.G. winked at Hannah.

Hannah grinned.

Supper was served to them, a meat patty with mashed potatoes, salad and green beans. This was the same meal they ate every time they visited for the evening.

"So, Hannah, did you leave a string of broken hearts behind when you came to visit your grandmother?"

Preston snorted. Hannah ignored him and smiled at her great-grandfather. "No, I'm not dating anyone."

"She's a little young," Anne murmured. She raised her eyebrows. "You were never this eager to have any of *us* dating," she said. "If I remember, you almost took Richard's head off for even considering one of your daughters."

"That was because you neglected to tell us you were dating anyone. We met him after you were engaged."

Anne passed the basket of rolls to Preston. "If he'd met you before we were engaged, he might have run away."

"Your father could not have chased Richard away," G.G. said. "He was smitten with you."

Smitten. Hannah wished she had a piece of paper to write that down. It was exactly the word she'd been searching for to describe her grandparents. They were smitten with each other.

"If only Alice had been as fortunate as you and your sister." G.G. dabbed at her lips with her napkin.

No one said anything. Hannah watched the two women and then glanced at Grandpa Frank. He was frowning into the distance.

Anne rubbed his hand where it rested on the table. He shifted his gaze to her and she smiled. "She made her own choices, Dad. We all did. You two provided a warm, supportive home. After that, it was up to us."

"It's hard raising children," he said.

"It is," Anne agreed. "But then you get grandchildren. And great-grandchildren."

She smiled at Preston and Hannah. "Even if they're stubborn and nosy," she added so that only Hannah could hear.

Hannah grinned. Stubborn wasn't a bad trait to have. At least she came by it honestly in *this* family.

ALICE'S STORY

Chapter 17

Lincoln, Iowa
1950–1955

Alice never knew if a memory was really hers or a memory that others had shared with her. Other times, stories were so clear in her mind, she knew she'd experienced the incident herself.

"But, Alice, you were three!" Margaret or Anne would insist.

Alice would shake her head, curls bobbing around her face. "I remember!" she'd insist. Her sisters would sigh and turn away, muttering, "She's so stubborn sometimes."

She had learned to be stubborn. Being the youngest was not easy and if she didn't hold out, she'd be ignored. She had to establish her place in the family. Anne was the boss as the oldest; Margaret always had her books. As the baby, she'd discovered early on that a grin and a coyly tilted head could charm the hardest of hearts.

For years, she shared a room with Margaret, and then, when she was six, a tiny dressing room off the hallway was converted into her bedroom. She didn't want to move there, but her natural stubbornness won through and she didn't say anything about her reluctance.

"I can finally have some privacy," she said in a haughty voice.

Margaret laughed and rumpled her hair. Alice ducked away. She hated when her sisters did that. "Why would a six-year-old need privacy?" Margaret asked.

"Because."

"Well, I need privacy, too." Margaret grinned. "Now we can both be happy."

But Alice wasn't happy. She waited until late that first night before she started to cry, hiding her face in the pillows. She'd never tell them how much she hated being alone at night, unable to hear any family sounds. She'd happily fallen asleep each evening listening to Margaret's breathing. In her new room she could only hear unidentified noises, and huddling under the covers didn't comfort her.

Sleeping in her own room was a clear, distinct memory, one that remained clear and distinct even in adulthood.

But the war years were vague. Her most vivid recollection was of attending the different committee meetings with her mother. They'd wrap bandages, fix up packages to send to soldiers, write letters. She'd scribbled pictures and given them to her mother, knowing they'd go to the soldiers but not sure what that meant.

Frank's absence and the early trips to the lake were memories she had because of stories she'd heard. Margaret and Anne would argue about details, and sometimes Alice wished she could add to the discussion but her images of that time were too dim.

"She's too little to remember anything," Margaret said one night. She was working on a school report about their experiences during the war and asked Anne for assistance.

"I remember Dad being in the navy," Alice offered. "And Mom went after him and we stayed alone for a few days."

Her sisters looked at each other. "I do remember!" She couldn't help stamping her foot. They might both be teenagers now but she wasn't a baby anymore.

"Of course you do, dear." Anne gave her an indulgent smile. "You just have different memories than us. We all do. No one remembers things exactly the same."

"Twins do." She was very interested in twins. A pair had started at school, and all the children were fascinated by the two girls who resembled each other so closely.

"Not even twins can have identical memories." Anne picked up her schoolbooks and headed down the hall to her room. "It's okay, Alice. We're *supposed* to have our own experiences."

One experience Alice had that she'd never shared with her sisters happened the summer she was eleven. They had revived their lake visits, their stays shorter because her sisters had to be at school when the academic year started in early September. Anne lifeguarded at the lake and Margaret was usually hidden somewhere with her books and her writing. Alice wandered around, visiting with nearby families, becoming the neighborhood sweetheart.

"Why don't you invite any of your friends to the house?" Marian asked one evening.

"They're busy," Alice said. She didn't want to explain that she'd rather her friends didn't see the small, cluttered cottage, strewn with books and clothes.

"We like to play outside," she added. "That's why we came here, isn't it? To enjoy the weather?"

Marian lit another cigarette. Her smoking always increased when they were at the lake. "Don't be smart with me, young lady. If you're ashamed to bring your friends here, I won't ask you again." She opened her book, pointedly ignoring Alice.

Alice knelt at her mother's knee. "I'm sorry, Mom. I didn't mean to be rude. But we live in such a tiny cottage and they have big houses."

Marian ran her fingers through Alice's curls. "Then we'll plan a picnic."

Alice agreed and happily issued her invitations. Her friends chattered and laughed about the outing. Alice beamed at being able to reciprocate their hospitality.

She agonized over the menu, finally selecting chicken salad sandwiches, cookies and fruit. She baked the cookies with Anne the night before. Marian promised to make the sandwiches the next morning.

Alice woke early. She'd laid out her clothes the previous night and now she pulled on the yellow-and-white striped blouse, the yellow skirt, her favorite sandals. Running downstairs, she stopped in the kitchen doorway, expecting to see Marian making the sandwiches.

The kitchen was empty. She whirled around, looking for her sandwiches. Bare counters. Angry, she darted down the hall to her parents' bedroom.

The door was ajar. She pushed it wider. There was no one in the room, but from outside the open window, she heard her mother's laugh and then the deeper laugh of a man.

Creeping across the wooden floor, careful not to step on the creaking boards too hard, she peeked over the windowsill. Her mother sat on the back porch railing, a cigarette in one hand. The man, a stranger, sat on a rusty metal chair, his long legs inches from Marian's bare feet.

Alice was rooted to the floor. She couldn't move, she couldn't speak, she could hardly breathe. What was that man doing with her mother? He lazily rose to his feet.

With a rush, all feeling came back to her and she gasped, racing down the hall and out the back door. Her sandals slipped and slid on the dewy grass, the moisture soaking her feet, her heart pounding as she ran and ran until she couldn't move another step.

She collapsed under a tree, her eyes squeezed shut against the sight of her mother and a strange man, alone in the backyard.

She must have fallen asleep. Anne was calling her name and she sat up, rubbing her hands over her face. Her skirt and blouse were rumpled and her cheeks were wet with tears. She jumped to her feet, trying to repair the damage.

"We've been hunting everywhere for you!"

She saw the question in Anne's eyes but she couldn't tell her what she'd seen. "What happened with the picnic?" she whispered. Her lips were dry, and her mouth felt as if she'd swallowed a packet of cotton balls.

"Margaret went to everyone's house and told them you were sick. We're going to reschedule it."

Alice shook her head. "No. No picnic." She couldn't stand the idea of eating a chicken salad sandwich ever again.

"What's the matter with you?" Anne's voice was curious. She couldn't know what Alice had seen.

She swallowed. "I thought I was… well, um…" What would Anne believe? Her older sister was too smart to accept just any excuse. "I thought I was, well…" She lowered her eyes and scuffed her sandal along the dirt. A strap had come loose from her mad run. "I thought I was, um, becoming a woman."

Margaret wasn't the only one who could make up stories. "I didn't want anyone around today. Except I'm not, that is—"

Anne hugged her close. "You silly thing. That's no reason to cancel your picnic. We'll have a talk later. Now we need to get you home. Mother's worried sick."

She let Anne walk her back to the house, her legs moving stiffly because of their cramped position all morning. Marian grabbed her in a fierce hug. "Where did you *go?*" Her voice was tight with worry.

Alice bowed her head, unable to meet her mother's eyes.

"Alice had a misunderstanding about her body today," Anne said, a hint of humor in her voice. "She'll probably be hearing from Mother Nature in the near future."

"Is that what this was all about, Alice?" Marian asked.

Alice remained silent. When Anne excused herself to start supper, she began to follow but her mother called her back.

"Alice, please come here."

She kept walking to the kitchen.

"Alice, now."

She couldn't ignore the command. She stumbled to the davenport, perching on the end farthest from her mother.

She thought of her wonderful picnic, her friends, her father. Rage boiled inside and spilled out of her mouth.

"I saw him, Mama. I saw that man."

Her mother lit a cigarette. "He's a friend of your father's, Alice. He visits whenever he's in town." She took a long drag on her cigarette. The smoke billowed out from her lips and rose to the ceiling.

"Daddy knows him?"

Her mother nodded. "They met when your father was first traveling around here. Rob always stops by to say hello if he's in the area."

"I've never seen him before."

Marian stubbed out her cigarette. "I'm not surprised. You're usually out roaming. And Rob never stays very long. Your father and I do have our own friends, Alice."

"But it was so early…" Her voice trailed off.

"He was leaving town. He had appointments all day yesterday and didn't think it was proper to visit last night, since your father's in Lincoln, at the shop. He came out for a quick cup of coffee before his train left."

Her mother kissed the top of her head. "Trust is a very important commodity in a marriage, Miss Alice. Your father trust me, which is why we can enjoy our summers here at the lake. Even if our cottage is dinky and messy."

Her expression was stern, but Alice caught the twinkle in her mother's blue eyes. "I'm sorry, Mom."

"You should be." Her mother tapped another cigarette out of the pack. "And I'm sorry about your picnic. I intended to mak the sandwiches after Rob left. I wasn't neglecting you, Alice. And I love your father too much, honey, to ever look at another man."

Which is probably why she smokes so much, Alice realized in a burst of grown-up clarity. To fill the empty space when her dad wasn't around.

She gave her mother a heartfelt hug. "I love you, Mom."

"And I love you. Now go change your clothes. You're filthy."

She moved back into Margaret's room when they returned to Lincoln. She told her mother that her room was too small for a bedroom and her mother agreed it would be handy as a sewing room. Margaret's objections were ignored, and Alice was soon safely back with her sister.

She moved again when Anne went off to college. "It's foolish for us to share a room when Anne's room is available," Margaret argued.

Frank sided with Margaret. "You need to be more independent, Alice. We have this nice house, room for all of us. Take advantage of it."

Alice carted her few belongings into the room that was still Anne's. She didn't put away anything Anne had left: the stuffed dog from childhood, the books, the magazines. As long as they filled the shelves, she could imagine Anne in the room.

She slept with the stuffed dog in her arms the night of Anne's wedding. Richard was nice and she wanted Anne to be happy. If only she wasn't leaving Lincoln!

After Margaret left for England, her parents acted as if they were on a second honeymoon, going to dinner and movies, holding hands. Alice suspected they didn't mean to leave her out, but she began to spend more and more time in the room that used to be Anne's and was now officially hers. She sewed bright curtains for the window, embroidered a colorful covering for the bed, bought cheerful pictures for the wall. The room took on a pleasant atmosphere that belied the fear of loneliness in Alice's heart.

Loneliness was the reason for her short-lived marriage.

Running off to marry her best friend in the middle of their senior year in high school had seemed a good idea at the time. No more lonely nights. They would talk about their day, sleep together at night. They'd been so young and foolish.

She didn't completely regret the few months they'd spent together. Her daughter, Marcia, was the most precious gift in her life. The little girl reveled in bright colors, happy stories, the world around her. No matter what else happened, she would never wish her daughter away.

Chapter 18

Lincoln, Iowa
1959

"Why are you moving?" Marian asked the question again.

"Marcia and I need our own space, Mom. And you and Dad should have time together." She checked around the room that had been hers for most of her growing-up years—and then Marcia's.

"But your father and I like having you here. You can't take our granddaughter away! I never see Anne's children at all."

"You saw them at Christmas." Alice added the last of Marcia's clothes to the pile in her arms and headed for the car.

"For four days." Marian struggled with a box of Marcia's toys.

"We're not leaving town, Mom. But Marcia's getting spoiled, having four adults fawning over her." And her four-year-old daughter was learning how to manipulate her grandparents. Alice wanted to break the pattern before it became impossible to do so.

"You'll come by for supper every night?"

Alice dumped the clothes on the back seat and reached for the box, cramming it into the already full trunk. "Not every night. You invite us and we'll come over."

"Just be careful. A single woman in an apartment building... You're asking for trouble, Alice."

She kissed her mother's cheek. "I'll be fine, Mom. I'm going now. I want to unload these things before I have to pick up Marcia."

Her daughter was with her other grandparents. Tom had gone on to university after their divorce and was now in medical school. He saw his daughter on visits home, sent her funny cards and presents, and called the first Sunday of every month. Marcia enjoyed his visits but she never fussed when he left. He was a pleasant man who came to visit her. She accepted the homage as her due.

Alice had barely dropped the last box on the counter when the apartment door opened. "This is much better." Ben Hardcastle tucked the key in his pocket and joined her on the couch. "Sneaking around like we did, I was always worried I'd run into a client."

She melted into his embrace. "No talking. I have one hour before I have to go and get Marcia. And I expect to celebrate my freedom."

He grinned, immediately unbuttoning his shirt. "Then let me oblige you."

She leaned back against the cushions, savoring the sight of him undressing, his long legs emerging from his slacks, the tight muscles of his torso, his black hair tousled from his rough handling of the shirt.

Everything about him excited her. Including the facts that he was her boss—and that he was married. Two reasons she shouldn't be seeing him at all. But ever since the night she worked overtime and he'd bumped against her in his insurance office, she'd been crazed with need. His wife lived across the state, in the house they'd bought just after their marriage.

"She chose to stay there," he explained one afternoon at the office. "I was transferred but she wouldn't leave."

Her sympathy had been aroused.

Alice knew she wasn't his first affair. But the other women had lasted less than a month. They'd been together for almost a year.

"Ready for the bedroom?" He'd finished undressing and was starting on Alice's clothes, untying her tennis shoes, stroking off her socks, his lean fingers playing with the arch of her foot.

"No." She stretched against the arm of the couch, bringing her leg up to his shoulders. He was gorgeous naked. "We're going to christen the couch tonight. We can take care of the bed another time."

Forty minutes later, she whispered, "The couch is suitably christened." She ran her fingers lightly down his back.

"Which means what?"

She grinned. "Which means that whenever I sit on this couch, I'll think about you."

He nipped her nose with his teeth and grinned when she yelped. She rubbed a finger over the injured spot. He grabbed her finger and peppered her nose, her cheeks, her eyebrows with kisses. When he stopped, they were both breathless again.

"I have to get Marcia," she panted.

His hands roamed over her breasts. "You will. You might just be a few minutes later than planned."

She was half an hour late. Marcia's grandparents didn't mind. "She could've stayed the night, Alice," Tom's mom said. "We know how hard it is to move."

Alice nodded, unable to speak. Ben had been hard, she recalled with an inward giggle that immediately had her squirming.

Marcia chattered all the way home. "Gramma and Grampa said I could stay anytime I want," she confided.

"I'm sure they did, honey." She turned into the apartment building's parking lot. "And next year, when you go to kindergarten, you can spend the night once in a while."

"But I want to stay *now*." She kicked her feet against the dashboard.

Alice rested a hand on her legs, holding them still. "When you're five."

She'd made the decision arbitrarily. Now that they'd moved, she was glad she'd held to it with Tom's family; she would be consistent with her own family, too.

Marcia would be a natural deterrent to Ben's sneaking up the stairs from his apartment and into her bed every night. She had explained her conditions when he'd told her an apartment was available in his building.

"I could come up after she's asleep," he said.

"No." She didn't want her daughter tainted by any gossip. "Only when she's at her grandparents'."

She would make him keep to the agreement or move again. Her daughter came first.

She was treading on slippery ground, as her father would say. Sleeping with her boss. Her position in his insurance office should be stimulating enough; she had control of the small office, hiring temps when the workload was heavy, organizing his schedule, keeping up-to-date on the latest company policies.

The thrill of their affair enlivened the routine of paperwork and checking claims. During the day, they were careful to keep their relationship strictly professional. He was aware that his reputation in the business community would suffer if he was caught with the daughter of a leading citizen.

She parked the car. "Come on." She swung Marcia into her arms. "Let's go see your new room."

Chapter 19

A flurry of warm August air announced the opening of the office door. Alice finished typing the last words, her eyes on the woman crossing the carpet. Not a local, she thought, pasting a smile on her face. She would remember a face that serene.

"Good afternoon," she said politely.

"Good afternoon. You must be Alice." The woman raised a hand toward her.

She half rose in her seat and extended a hand. "May I help you? I'm Mr. Hardcastle's assistant."

"I know." The woman beamed, turning around to take in all corners of the office. "I've heard so much about you. If it weren't for you, well—" Her voice broke off and she gave a quick shake of her head.

She touched the collar of her pale yellow suit jacket. "You must think I'm a complete ninny. Gloria Hardcastle, Ben's wife."

Alice blinked. *Ben's wife?* In all their years together, she'd never imagined a woman like this as her competition. Not that they were in any competition. Ben had made it clear from the beginning that his marriage was dead, that he and his wife believed in modern living and hadn't secured a divorce because of the mess they'd have dividing up their property. Alice had accepted his excuses, not wanting to enter into a second marriage, content to live on the fringes with him, enjoying their clandestine nights when Marcia was out of the apartment.

But seeing this woman, his wife... She shook herself out of her trance. "Is Ben expecting you?"

Gloria smiled. "No. I thought I'd surprise him. Bring him some news about Adrian."

"Adrian?"

Gloria's sunny expression vanished. "He never mentioned our son?"

Alice shrugged. "Not to me. But then, he tends to keep his personal life separate from his business."

"Of course." Her eyes were shadowed. "He always did work too hard."

Alice came around the desk. "Why don't you sit down?" She gestured toward one of the soft chairs Ben provided for his clients. "He's investigating a claim right now. I expect him back any minute."

"Thank you." Gloria lowered herself gracefully into the chair, holding her purse on her lap.

Alice hovered, unsure what to do next. What was the proper etiquette for entertaining your lover's wife? "Would you like a cup of coffee? Or some tea?" Marian always served tea during an emotional crisis.

"Tea would be nice. With a splash of milk, if you have it."

"Be right back."

Alice sagged against the cupboard of the small kitchen. A son.

Ben had a son. And a lovely wife who wasn't anything like the woman she'd imagined. This woman exuded friendliness, kindness, concern. And from their short conversation, she could tell that Mrs. Hardcastle had no idea her husband didn't love her and respect her.

Alice poured hot water into a cup and added a tea bag. Rummaging through the cabinet, she found a small measuring cup. Filling it partway with milk, she placed the meager offering on a metal tray and carried it into the front office.

"Nothing too fancy, I'm afraid." She set the tray on the low table between the chairs.

"It's fine." Gloria waved at the desk. "Feel free to finish your work. Please, don't let me interrupt you."

"Thank you."

Alice typed the last few lines on a page, ripped it out, then slid another piece of paper into the machine and made short work of the letter. She carried both documents into the inner office, where she placed them on Ben's desk. She signed the one on top, scanned the room for a moment, then walked back to her own desk.

She was covering her typewriter when the door opened. Another blast of heat came into the room. "You will not believe what that numbskull Overton is claiming," Ben said. "He—"

Alice cut off his next words. "Your wife is here."

If she hadn't still been so stunned, his expression would have been comical. "Gloria?"

"Hi, darling." His wife stood up and approached him, settling her hands on his shoulders, lifting one foot slightly while she kissed his cheek. "I thought I'd surprise you."

"You did." He sent Alice a quick glance over his wife's shoulder.

She crouched down and collected her purse from the bottom desk drawer. "I'll leave you to your reunion."

Opening the door, she paused. "Your letters are on your desk. You'll want to sign them before you go home tonight."

"Alice—"

"Good night." She gave Gloria a genuine smile. "It was a pleasure meeting you, Mrs. Hardcastle."

"And you, Alice."

She'd have to move, she thought, pacing the living room of her apartment. Maybe to one of the new duplexes being built at the edge of town. Tom's child support had kept pace with his increase in earnings as a doctor. She and Marcia could survive for a few months while she searched for a new job.

Leaving Lincoln wasn't an option, not with both sets of Marcia's grandparents still alive and in town. But her daughter would be changing schools at the end of the summer, transferring to the middle school for her fifth-grade year. A new location wouldn't affect her friends or her education.

"Go away," she snapped through the door later that night. Marcia was at Tom's parents'. They hadn't minded the short notice, eager to have another visit before school started.

Alice had needed to be alone. She'd considered calling her mother, but Marian would've figured out instantly that something was wrong. And as much as she was tempted to spill everything, she couldn't. This was her mess. She had to clean it up.

She'd guessed he would come to her door. The letter, his wife's appearance… He didn't do well with changes to his routine.

"Alice, let me in."

She rested her head against the door for a moment, then stood back and yanked it open. "For five minutes," she said firmly.

He tumbled into the room. "Alice, you have to believe me! I had no idea she was coming."

She edged away from his outstretched hands, putting the couch between them. "That doesn't bother me as much as learning you have a son. I've worked for you for seven years. Not once did you mention your child." Or give her a clear impression of his wife. But that was a discussion she would never have with him.

She had known as soon as she saw his wife that their affair was over. She should have ended it long ago. Or forced him to divorce his wife and make an honest woman of her. But it was easier to hide, to play the game. No real emotions were involved that way.

He ran his hand through his hair. The tousled mane didn't thrill her as it usually did. "Alice, I couldn't talk about him. Not to you, not to anyone."

"Why?"

He whirled away from her. "He's in a state hospital, Alice. He's mentally retarded."

She gasped. No wonder he sounded anguished. The injustice would be daunting— Ben with his perfect body, his keen wit, to have a son who wouldn't even be able to carry on a conversation, who would need constant care.

"That's why Gloria wouldn't move with me. She had to stay near him. We agreed that I would work from this office, that we would stay married and not inflict the probability of having another child like him on anyone else."

No wonder he'd been so insistent about using protection. She'd been touched that he was willing to forgo his pleasure by using a condom. They didn't need the complication of a child, he'd said. At the time, she'd believed he was concerned about *her*.

"I know you think I'm a heel, not telling you about him." His words were muffled, his back to her. "I just couldn't live with the knowledge that my only son is a retard. And now she's talking about taking him out of the hospital, finding him a place in one of these new community living centers. She expects me to move back and help with him."

She had frozen at his first words. "A *retard?* That's what you call your son?" He had yet to use his son's name with her.

He spun around. "Don't be righteous with me, Alice Robertson! You've spent the last seven years committing adultery."

"No, no, I haven't." She shook her head. "I'm not married. You are. I made a stupid choice and I've wasted years. But I'm through. You read my letter of resignation?"

His laugh was harsh, destroying any last remnant of feeling she had for him. "Get out of here!" She jerked the door open, pointing toward the hallway.

"Alice, please."

The pleading tone didn't move her. "No, get out. I believed you, that your marriage was dead, your wife was a witch, every one of your horrible lies. All because I didn't want to go to bed alone."

She rubbed a hand over her eyes. Tomorrow she'd have to look for a new place, find a job, come up with an explanation for her daughter. Now she had to survive these last few moments, maintain her dignity and her pride. "Some things are worse than being alone," she said quietly.

She'd never understood this before. But seeing his wife, listening to his callous comments about his son…

He didn't say a word. He walked out of the room, his shoulders stiff, his shoes scuffing the carpet. She shut the door behind him, resisting the urge to slam it.

No more. No more men. I can live by myself, for myself. Steeling herself against the lonely days ahead, she went into her bedroom and started sorting through the clothes she would pack for her new life.

Summer 2004

"Hey, Mom sent me a postcard!" Preston waved it as he came into the house.

"Anything for me?"

He sifted through the rest of the stack. "Nope. Maybe yours will come tomorrow. Or maybe she forgot you." He gave Hannah a devilish grin. "I *am* her favorite."

"Son!" she reminded him. "I'm her favorite daughter."

Preston laughed and ran into the kitchen to bring Grandma the mail.

When she was little, she'd been jealous of Preston, stomping her foot or pouting whenever her mother, Kate, left to take him to one of his activities. Her father had reminded her that he was always at her soccer games because he was the coach. "Somebody has to take your brother to his activities," her father had said. "And since I have to be at your games, your mother does that. Doesn't mean she loves you less. You'll have your turn with her when you're older."

He'd been right. Her mom was traveling with her dad for a few weeks, since they were all out of school, but when she was home, she and Hannah were together a lot, talking about colleges, looking at clothes, working on craft projects. The beaded bracelets they made were a hit at her high school, and Hannah sold every one she brought in.

She sighed. Her mom would be able to unravel the mystery. She could always see into the heart of a problem.

"I could call her," Hannah murmured to herself. "Talk to her for a little bit."

She shut her bedroom door and climbed onto the bed, digging her cell phone out of her pocket. Her mother answered on the second ring.

"Hi, Hannah! Everything okay?"

Tears welled up in Hannah's eyes and she blinked them impatiently away. She wasn't a baby, crying for her mother. Every summer they spent at least two weeks with her grandmother. She'd never been homesick before.

"Yeah, we're fine."

"Mom said you're trying to organize a party for G.G. and Grandpa Frank."

"I was. But nobody wants to have a party. They all say G.G. is too tired. But I don't think that's the real reason."

"Hold on a minute, sweetie."

She waited while her mother spoke to someone. She could hear the roar of the waves and people shouting.

"Are you on the beach?" she asked when her mother came back.

"I am. Your father had some meetings this morning and I couldn't stay cooped up in that hotel another minute. I was regretting that I never took a lifeguarding job at a beach. Pools were fine but the ocean…that would've been fun."

Hannah giggled at the image of her mother sitting in a beach hut or on one of those towers, waiting to rescue someone.

"I was a good lifeguard," Kate sputtered over the line. "Your grandma taught me herself."

"I'm sure you were, Mom. I was just picturing you in a lifeguard outfit."

"Your father is very appreciative of me in a swimsuit."

Hannah shuddered. "Mom! Don't tell me stuff like that."

Her mother chuckled. "Then don't act like your mother's nothing but a dried-up old hag."

"I never said that!"

"Humph. It was implied. Now why did you call?"

Hannah hesitated. Hearing her mother's no-nonsense voice was making her rethink all her efforts.

But her curiosity wouldn't rest. "I wondered if you know why G.G. doesn't want a party."

Silence came over the line. Hannah could imagine her mother's face, her brow creased and her lips slightly parted as she worked out how to answer or not answer the question.

"I think the others might be right. She may be too tired for all the fuss."

The same old excuse everyone was giving her. "But she's never tired," Hannah argued.

"Honey, G.G. isn't a young woman anymore. She needs to take it easy."

"They should celebrate their anniversary," she said stubbornly. "They've been together for ages!"

And with all that talk about them being tired and older, she was afraid they might not have many more years left.

They deserved a party. They had lived their wedding vows, day after day, weathering all kinds of setbacks. Supporting each other and their family together for seventy-five years.

And still smitten with each other.

She didn't say any more about the party to her mother. She ended the conversation after they'd chatted about plans for September and the new school year. Her senior year. She stared around the room. The answer wasn't in the collection of pictures and magazines she had found.

The answer was with G.G. and Grandpa Frank.

KATE'S STORY

Chapter 20

Lincoln, Iowa
1982

"Sometimes you have no choice." Marian poured tea into three cups and served Kate and then Marcia. The two young women added milk to theirs, Marcia dropping in a spoonful of sugar.

"I hate to tell Mom." Marcia sat in the wingback chair, her long legs tucked beneath her. The delicate china wobbled and she carefully set it on the side table. "I can't stop shaking. I still can't believe it's over." Her eyes were red-rimmed. "Owen was so matter-of-fact about it, and here I am, all those years of my life gone."

Kate picked up the cup. She held it to Marcia's lips. "Drink."

Marcia swallowed two sips and pulled back. "What am I going to do?"

"He's such a handsome boy." Marian settled the lap rug around her knees. The afternoon had a slight chill, but Kate could barely remember a time when Grandma didn't have her rug around her legs.

"That sturdy jaw and full lips. And those eyes. A girl would kill for lashes like his."

"Grandma!" Marcia's squeak was close to her normal voice.

Marian shrugged. "He was cute. Still is. Just goes to show that outward appearances can hide secrets."

"I thought we'd be married forever, that I'd grow old with him like you and Grandpa."

"Humph." Marian sipped her tea.

Kate grinned. "She didn't mean you were old, Grandma, just that you and Grandpa have been through a lot—and you're still together."

"We *have* been through a lot." Marian's head fell back, and she stared at the ceiling, her eyes glazing over.

Kate waited, knowing her grandmother was reliving her past. Sometimes she'd resurface and tell them stories, filling in the gaps their mothers had left in their storytelling.

"Your grandfather and I have had our share of troubles." She picked up a cookie from the tea tray and held it between her fingers. Her worn wedding band winked in the afternoon sunlight. "We left each other a time or two." Her lips curved up in a reminiscent smile. "But never for long. And we always came back."

"This is different from an argument, Grandma."

Kate couldn't stand to hear the hurt in her cousin's voice.

"I realize that." Marian put her cup and saucer on the table. She took Marcia's hands in hers. "You have no choice, my dear. This can't be worked out with an apology and some flowers. You have to be strong, honey, watch him leave, and then tell your mother. She'll be upset but when she learns the reason, she'll be fine. She loves you. She wants you to be happy."

"I don't know if I'll ever be." Marcia's lips quivered. "I can't… I can't believe it's over. Seven years of marriage and I turn out to be his best friend."

Marian handed her the cookie she'd been holding, her usual

method of consoling weeping grandchildren. Marcia bit into it, more out of habit than conscious thought.

"You're making the right decision," Kate said softly. They had talked late into the night, tears flowing freely from both. She had brought her to Marian's house for tea, counting on their grand-mother's wisdom and the routine of tea and cookies to give Marcia a sense of normalcy.

"He's moving away." Her words were muffled around the cookie.

Marian nodded. "Good. This town is too small for him to survive once word gets out."

"I just don't understand how he could do this to you!" Kate's voice rose in the indignation she had shown when Marcia had first told her Owen wanted a divorce.

"He didn't know. He hoped I could change him, that maybe he wasn't…gay." Her voice staggered over the word.

Marian passed her a tissue to mop the streaming flow of tears. "If anyone could change a man, it would be you, Marcia."

One corner of Marcia's mouth turned up. "Thank you."

"She's right." Kate smiled at her cousin. Marcia had always been beautiful, inheriting her mother's golden curls instead of her father's red hair. Her skin was clear, without a single freckle or even a pimple, and the summer before she'd entered high school, she'd developed a figure that had every boy drooling.

"Well, I guess that wasn't enough." She wiped her eyes and tossed the tissue into the trash can.

Kate hugged her. "I'm so sorry."

Marcia stood up, her sweater clinging to her curves, her jeans molded to her hips. Kate was comfortable in her own body now, the teenage jealousy of her cousin a thing of the past, but she couldn't prevent a fleeting stab of satisfaction that her cousin's life wasn't picture-perfect.

"Maybe we're not meant to be married," Marcia said.

Kate frowned. "What?"

"You and Max. Me and Owen. Mom." Aunt Alice was dating

yet another successful businessman with no sign of settling down. "Except for Aunt Margaret and Grandma, the women in our family haven't had much luck with love."

"My mom and dad were very happy together."

Marcia swooped down and gave her a big hug. "Oh, I didn't mean to bring up your dad. I'm sorry, Kate, I am."

Kate brushed away the tears clinging to her eyelashes. Even after all this time, she couldn't think of her broad-shouldered father, his eyes alight with laughter, without tearing up. She didn't know if it would ever get easier to accept that he was gone from their lives forever.

"Well, I'm not giving up on happily-ever-after just yet." Kate was proud of how firm her voice sounded.

"I'm putting it on hold for a while." Marcia bent down and kissed Marian's cheek. "Thank you, Grandma, for listening. I'm going to Mom's house, while I still have your courage inside me."

"Do you want me to go with you?" Kate wasn't sure she could handle another emotional scene, but her cousin had been there for her when Max broke off their engagement.

Marcia shook her head. "No. I can do this."

The front door closed softly behind her. "She'll leave, too," Marian said.

Kate swung around to face her grandmother. "No, she won't!"

Marian nodded. "Yes. She won't be able to handle the gossip. At least nurses are always in demand. She can go anywhere."

"It's so unfair. Her family's here, her friends." Kate vaulted to her feet and paced around the room. "I could just kill Owen. He told her he thought he was gay back in high school. He didn't want his father to find out. Poor Marcia." She sighed. "Poor Owen, too."

"She'll survive. You girls will both survive." Marian gathered up the tea things and Kate hurried to her side. "We're strong women, Kate Sanders. Don't forget that. The women in this family have weathered a lot of trials. You and Marcia will make it."

Kate followed her into the kitchen she had visited more times than she could count. As a little girl sitting quietly on the bench against the wall, she'd often listened to family stories—until someone noticed her and sent her out of the room. Now she was adding her own chapters.

"Maybe I *should* give up on men, Grandma." She ran soapy water in the sink and carefully washed a teacup before swishing it in the rinse water.

Marian chuckled. "Really?" She took the cup and dried it with a flowered tea towel Kate had embroidered for her years before.

A warm glow spread through Kate at the ritual. The tea towels were only for drying the good china; Marian had declared all those Christmases ago that they were too pretty, too special, to be used for everyday drying. Kate had bloomed under her attention, her love.

She smiled at her grandmother and rinsed the third teacup. "Really. And since I've already washed the cups, you can't read my tea leaves and predict a tall, dark and handsome man in my future. Women don't need a man to be complete anymore, Grandma. You said yourself we can make it on our own."

Marian deposited the last cup on the rack. "Perhaps. But you'll miss so much." She raised her eyebrows at Kate's sarcastic laugh. "Life is richer when you share it with someone."

She sat down in a kitchen chair, the towel caught between her hands. "I wasn't always so wise about this, Kate. I was stubborn, expected my own way a lot during the early days of our marriage."

Kate sat across from her grandmother. They were alone in the house for another hour, until Grandpa Frank closed the shop. A lot could be shared in an hour.

"My father—your great-grandpa—was strict, a minister in a small town. When your grandpa came along, I assumed he knew all about having a good time. And I had to get out of that little town."

Her eyes had that faraway look again. "I don't know now if I loved your grandfather the way I should have when we married. If I had, I probably wouldn't have been so restless. I thought he should make me happy. I didn't realize I had to find my own path but that we could walk on it together."

She patted Kate's hand and stood up. Kate knew she was going into her bedroom, where she'd freshen her makeup before Frank came home. It was another ritual she'd observed over the years. "Thank goodness your grandpa stayed with me. We may have wasted some of our years together but now…" She kissed Kate's cheek. "Now my greatest wish is that you and your cousin will experience the same happiness I shared with your grandfather."

Chapter 21

Lincoln, Iowa
September 1984

Kate strolled around her friend's neatly furnished living room, pausing at the bookshelf to scan the titles. "Did you finish the book we're reading for book club?"

"No." Nancy's voice came from the small bedroom. "We cannot let Barb pick any more titles. Her choices are always so dreary."

"They're supposed to enlighten us, make us smarter." Kate tapped the velvety leaf of an African violet on the middle shelf. "Schoolteachers like us need that, you know."

A snort of laughter answered her and she smiled. She'd met Nancy two years earlier, just after Marcia's departure from Lincoln. Nancy had been hired on at her elementary school, and they'd quickly discovered a common interest in books. Nancy had formed the book club they attended twice a month. The group was going to dinner tonight and then to a movie based on one of the earlier books they'd discussed.

The doorbell rang. "Would you get that, Kate?" Nancy called from the bedroom. "I'm expecting a package and it was probably delivered to my neighbor."

Kate answered the door and stared at a dark-blue silk tie. Raising her head, she met the amused expression of a tall, slender man.

"Hello."

She opened her mouth but nothing came out. Nancy had a neighbor who looked like *this* and she never mentioned him? She'd have to scold her when they were alone.

For now, she had to get her voice back. She swallowed. "Hello," she squeaked. She made another attempt. "Do you have Nancy's package? She's busy right now, but she asked me to take care of it."

"Nancy's expecting a package?"

She peeked at his hands, then wished she hadn't. Long, slender fingers with well-manicured nails. A gold watch—right side. No ring on his left hand.

And no package anywhere in sight.

She met his amused eyes again. Deep blue, with tiny flecks of brown. She had to tilt her head back to see his face, which was unusual. Except for her brothers, most men she met were either her height or a scant inch or so taller.

"Was it my package, Kate?" Nancy came into the living room, adjusting her necklace as she walked.

"It wasn't a—" Kate began and was interrupted by Nancy's excited flight across the room.

"Ed!" Her normally sedate friend launched herself into the man's arms. "I didn't know you were going to be in town!"

He slid his arms around her waist and spun them both in a slow circle. Kate watched with the first stirrings of jealousy.

"Quick trip. Had to go to Des Moines for business and finished early. Figured I'd run over and see if you were free for dinner."

Nancy wriggled out of his arms and stepped back, her fists on her hips. "You came to Des Moines and you didn't let me know?"

"Spur of the moment, sis, don't get mad."

Sis. Kate blinked. The resemblance was there. The blue eyes, the golden-brown hair. Nancy wasn't tall but she did have a slender build.

She wasn't going to analyze the rush of relief she felt at knowing they were brother and sister. He didn't wear a ring but he was left-handed. Maybe the ring interfered with whatever business he did. The cut and style of his suit plainly said that his job paid well. No scrimping and saving to have a monthly night out on the town.

"Oh, where are my manners?" Nancy dragged her brother over to Kate. "Kate, this is my rotten older brother, Ed Midgorden. Ed, this is Kate Sanders, a colleague and dear friend."

Her hand was engulfed in his. "I'm her only brother," Ed said. "So I am by turns her favorite, her rotten and sometimes her dearest relative." He gave Nancy a wide grin and Kate felt a shiver ripple through her.

"Ignore him, Kate." She frowned. "We have dinner plans, Ed. The book club's meeting and then going to a movie."

"What kind of movie?"

They both grinned at his suspicious tone. "It's a women's group," Kate said. "It's a romance."

"We read the book," Nancy said.

"I'll go to dinner, but then I have to leave." At Nancy's groan, he scooped her into another tight hug. "I could only stay for dinner, anyway, Nance. My plane leaves late tonight. I have to be back in New York for an early meeting tomorrow."

"Fine." She opened the closet and took out her coat, waiting for Ed to assist Kate with hers first. "But we expect you to pay for our dinner."

"Nancy!" Kate protested.

Nancy looped her arm through Ed's and then Kate's. "He can afford it, Kate. And we deserve it. Consider it his civic duty."

The group accepted Ed's presence with no complaints. Kate suspected it had as much to do with his appearance as their friendship with Nancy. He listened to the discussion about the book and upcoming movie with fortitude, only grimacing twice that Kate could see. He steered the conversation in other directions after the food was served.

Now the members were considering the merits of a short list of books, trying to decide which would be next for discussion. Kate voiced her opinion and then sat back. The group's more vocal members would have the final say. She didn't mind. She enjoyed the group for the camaraderie.

"Have you known Nancy long?" he asked a half hour later under cover of the conversation surging around them.

"Two years. When she transferred to our school. She's a very good teacher," she said loyally.

He smiled, a dimple appearing in his right cheek. "She is. The best. From what I understand, she moved to Lincoln where they pay teachers more. Obviously you're also an excellent teacher, which is why they hired you."

She laughed. "You have no idea how I teach. You shouldn't make assumptions."

He brought a hand to his chest. "Thank you for that bit of warning. As a lawyer, I should know better than to take someone at face value."

A lawyer. And a successful one, based on the cut of his clothes, the style of his watch. "My guidance counselor wanted me to go to law school," Kate said. "But I wanted to help kids before they got in trouble, not afterward." She knew it sounded corny but he didn't laugh, just favored her with a pleasant smile.

She was soon telling him about the car accident that had claimed her father's life a few weeks before her college graduation. The decision to move back in with her mom and teach in Illinois until her brothers had finished high school. The relocation to Lincoln, so her mother could help Grandpa Frank with his shop.

"No boyfriends, no husband?" he queried lightly.

She shook her head, astonished at the information he'd gleaned with a few well-chosen questions. "You must be a very good lawyer," she said. "Almost as good as I am at teaching."

She grinned and he grinned back. "I do my best."

Nancy caught the last bit of their conversation. "He's wonderful, Kate. He'll be a partner before he's thirty-five."

"Ah, I'm back in her good graces." He glanced at his watch. "Listen, I hate to leave but I need to get to Des Moines to catch my flight." He rose from the table with that lithe grace Kate had noticed earlier. "Thanks for letting me crash your party. I had a great time."

He pecked Nancy on the cheek. "See you, squirt. Take care of yourself."

The questions started as soon as he left the restaurant. Kate didn't join in. His farewell had included all of them. Why had she expected anything special? He'd visited with her because of the seating, nothing more. Besides, he lived in New York. She lived in Lincoln. She'd tried one long-distance relationship, with no good results.

The phone rang just as she was getting into bed. "Hello?"

"Hi."

The voice was familiar and yet she couldn't place it. "May I help you?" she asked carefully. Her mother had drilled into her at a young age what information could and could not be given over the phone.

The low chuckle alerted her. She sat up abruptly, the phone clenched to her ear. "Is this Ed?" she asked hesitantly.

"Well, that's a blow. I thought you'd recognize my voice right away."

He *had* sounded familiar but she decided not to tell him that and feed his ego. She'd spent several agonizing hours thinking she'd spilled her guts to a polite stranger.

"Are you back in New York?" she asked.

"Yes. How was the movie?"

She talked about plot twists, he asked about characters, she told him how the movie differed from the book. When there was a lull in conversation, she glanced at the clock. "Ed, it's almost one o'clock here! Does that mean it's two o'clock at your end?"

"Must be."

"Then we need to say good-night."

"Is that your schoolteacher voice?"

She'd purposely been firm. But she never stayed up this late. And she suspected that once she hung up, she'd find it hard to get to sleep.

"It's late," she said, refusing to answer his question.

"I agree. May I call you again?"

Her heart skipped. *A long-distance relationship?* her brain asked. *But he's so easy to talk to, he listens and asks insightful questions,* her heart countered. *He's a lawyer, it's his training,* her brain replied.

The two-way argument pounded in her head. "Yes." Her brain won enough rounds. This time, her heart had the last word.

October 1984

Nancy plucked her copies from the machine and stepped aside so Kate could slide in her originals. "Next time you talk to Ed, tell him we're going to Erica's for Thanksgiving."

She knew from her conversations with Ed that the third sibling lived in Lawrence, Kansas, with her husband and two daughters. Their parents were in Kansas City and Ed said they all visited as much as possible. His one regret about working in New York was that he couldn't be a regular part of the family gatherings. At least there were direct flights from New York to Kansas City.

"Don't you talk to him?" The copy machine hummed next to her, spitting out copy after copy.

"Not much. He's either busy with work or talking to you." Nancy pushed her pages under the electric stapler. "Not that I mind. He's always worked too hard. I'm glad he's finally taking some personal time."

"We're just friends," Kate heard herself say.

Nancy laughed and backed out of the room. "Of course you are. By the way, you're invited to Thanksgiving, too! We can drive together."

"I can't go to Thanksgiving with his family!" Kate moaned to Marcia. Her cousin was home on one of her rare visits and had elected to spend the night with Kate rather than at her mother's. Alice had a new boyfriend and he tended to show up at odd hours. Marcia didn't relish the possibility of bumping into him in the middle of the night.

"Why not? You've been phone-dating for two months. That's longer than most couples in this family. You should be buying a wedding dress and booking a chapel."

"Ha, ha. My mom and dad dated for a year."

"They were engaged within a few months."

"It's not like that with us," Kate said. "Besides, how would this work? He lives in New York, I live in Iowa. We're half a country away from each other."

"So you move. Teachers are needed everywhere. That's what you told me about nursing."

She made a face at Marcia. "People hate to have their words thrown back at them."

Marcia waggled her eyebrows. "Just doing my cousinly duty."

"Your mother will be disappointed you won't be here for Thanksgiving," Marian said. They were baking pumpkin pies for dinner. "She's been fortunate to have you around for this long. By the time I was your age, I'd had all my babies." Her eyes clouded, and Kate knew she was remembering the baby boy who'd died. *My uncle.* She'd never thought of him in that way before. Just another of Grandma's stories.

Her grandmother's mood vanished as quickly as it had come. "Maybe you could bring this young man by the house at Christmas? Let your family meet him."

"I'll see, Grandma." Kate poured pumpkin filling into the pie crust. "But it's nothing serious. I've been invited because I'm Nancy's friend, too."

Marian gave her a long, searching look. "Kate Sanders, your father and mother did not raise a fool." She kissed Kate's cheek. "Have a good time. And remember, you're not getting any younger!"

The banter in the Midgorden household reminded Kate of her house when her father was alive. Football was a main staple of Thanksgiving Day and the entire family rooted for their team. Platters of fresh vegetables and fruit were served during the game, and the family didn't sit down to dinner until the final touchdown was scored.

"You're lucky our team won," Nancy whispered. "You wouldn't want to be around here if we lost."

"I heard that," her father said. "You're going to give our guest the wrong impression." He passed Kate the bowl of mashed potatoes. "We're good losers," he said, with a defiant glare at his daughter. "Just much better winners."

Kate laughed. Mr. Midgorden's style of speaking—and questioning—was similar to his son's. Their mother held her own, reminding her family of their manners with gentle chiding. Because the group was small, Erica's children sat at the table, between their parents, their childish voices blending with the general chatter.

Nancy and Erica shooed Ed and Kate out of the house after dinner. "Walk off some of that food," Erica said. "Nancy and I will take care of the dishes."

"Not too subtle, was she?" Ed said.

"I like your family." She wasn't willing to hear any complaints. They had welcomed her with open arms and, except for a few covert glances, had said nothing about her relationships with their son and daughter.

She knew where she stood with Nancy. Ed was more confusing. He had treated her with kindness, included her in his conversation, and smiled at her when their eyes met. But this was the first time she'd been in the same room with him since the restaurant dinner.

He tucked her hand into the crook of his elbow. "It's slippery on this sidewalk," he explained. "Don't want you to fall."

They walked the few blocks to the university campus. Ed showed her where he'd attended classes, the buildings ghostly gray in the evening light. Clouds floated above the trees, adding to the sense of eeriness.

She shivered in her jacket. He drew her closer, his arm stealing around her shoulders. She snuggled into his warmth.

"Kate?"

"Hmm?" The campus was closed for the holidays and quiet. Sheltered against his side, she felt content to wander for hours.

He stopped under the shadow of a huge oak tree. "We have to talk."

Her heart slowed. Max had said those same words when he broke their engagement. But Ed had invited her for Thanksgiving. And he was holding her close.

"We can't go on like this."

She shrank inside her coat. "Okay," she said in a small voice.

His hands cupped her face, tilting her chin until she could see his eyes. The moonlight glistened on his lashes, turning them a smoky gray.

"What's the matter with you?" he asked.

"You're breaking up, right?" The words stuck in her throat but she was determined to be brave. She could cry later, when she was back in her lonely house.

"Breaking up with you?" His thumbs toyed with her mouth. 'I'm trying to say I want more. Dating by phone is not the ideal situation."

She blinked. His thumbs were stroking her lips and she opened them.

"But what can we do?" Her teaching contract wasn't up until June.

"I've asked to be assigned to the office in Des Moines. It's not the best solution but we can see each other on weekends."

Des Moines. "You have an office in Des Moines?"

"The original branch." He feathered kisses over her cheeks and onto her lips. "I want to make this relationship more permanent, Kate. And if that means I have to move, I'll move."

Her hands slid around his neck. He hadn't mentioned marriage but what could be more permanent?

"My contract is up in June," she said. "That should give us some more options."

His tongue licked around the corners of her mouth. "Right now, let's make up for lost time."

"You look beautiful." Nancy adjusted the veil, then stepped back, smoothing the white train.

Kate clutched her bouquet and stared at the vision in the mirror. "I can't believe this is happening."

"Me, neither." Marcia grinned. She held up a soft blue handkerchief. The material was almost paper-thin, the lace at the edges delicate and fragile. "From Grandma, for your 'something blue.' She said Grandpa Frank's sisters gave it to her at her wedding. I told her you already had a penny in your shoe."

"I do, thank you." She tucked the handkerchief into her sleeve. "Aunt Margaret gave me one she brought back from England."

"What about 'something old, something new'? And 'something borrowed'?" Nancy asked. She and Marcia were the bridesmaids, their gowns a deep gold that suited their coloring. "Or is the handkerchief going to double as the old?"

Kate nodded, then lifted her right hand. A bracelet set with sapphires glittered in the sunlight shining through the church windows. "This is for the borrowed. Dad gave it to Mom when I was born." He had given Anne a bracelet for each of their three children, set with their birthstones.

"Oh, Kate!" Tears sparkled in Marcia's eyes.

She blinked rapidly, peering in the mirror at her makeup. "Don't cry, please. I won't make it if you do."

Her emotions had been close to the surface all morning. She'd always dreamed her father would walk her down the aisle. Uncle Alex was doing the honors, and she appreciated having him at her side. Wearing the bracelet her father had presented Anne at her birth brought her dad into the church with her.

"So, what's new, then?"

"What are you, the tradition police?" Kate asked her cousin.

"Just making sure you have everything in place for good luck."

"She's marrying my brother," Nancy reminded them. "That should count."

"I do have something new." Kate gently lifted her hair off her shoulders, showing them the diamond earrings she wore.

"Whoa!" Marcia reverently touched one of the drops. "Where did these come from?"

"I know, I know." Nancy jumped around as much as she could in a long gown and high heels. "Ed gave them to you, didn't he?"

"Look at that blush!"

Kate's color intensified at Marcia's teasing. "A gift in celebration of our wedding—and him being made partner."

Marcia's blond head leaned toward Nancy's. "Should we ask for details about this celebrating?"

Kate was saved by the door opening. "The music's starting," her mother said. "Oh, Kate, darling, you look lovely!"

The girls stepped aside, allowing mother and daughter privacy. "I'm so happy for you," Anne said, adjusting the veil, pinching off a leaf from the bouquet, straightening the collar. "He's a good man."

"He reminds me of Daddy," Kate whispered.

"Oh, honey." Tears shimmered on Anne's lashes. "I wasn't going to cry, at least not until the reception."

Kate kissed her mother's cheek. "Cry all you want. Just as long as they're tears of joy. Because I'm sure I couldn't possibly be happier."

Her mother led her to the door. "Just wait until you have children," she promised. "Then the world won't be big enough for all your joy."

Summer 2004

G.G. was alone in the sunroom, a magazine upside-down on her lap. Hannah approached slowly and dropped to one knee in front of the wheelchair. "G.G.," she said in a quiet voice.

"Oh, Hannah." G.G. tugged at the lap rug covering her legs. "How nice to see you." She sounded more agitated than pleased.

"I don't want to upset you again," Hannah said quickly. "But could I talk to you about your marriage? Not the party. About you and Grandpa Frank."

"Hannah—" G.G.'s fingers plucked at the pattern on the blanket.

"Shh." Hannah covered the worn fingers with one hand. "Give me a minute. Please?"

She waited and when G.G. didn't pull away or show any other signs of wanting her gone, she started talking. "You and Grandpa Frank had problems off and on. You even separated once or twice."

She patted her great-grandmother's hand, calming the fluttering fingers. "It's okay. Everybody has problems. Mom and Dad argue, and I've seen Aunt Margaret get mad at Uncle Alex. Preston and I are always fighting."

But this vacation had brought her closer to her brother. She'd been willing to overlook some of his idiosyncrasies and she had a feeling he'd done the same thing with her.

"That's what happens when two people care about each other. Mom always says you can't have the highs without the lows." She settled back on her heels, keeping her gaze on G.G.'s face. "The thing is, you and Grandpa Frank didn't call it quits. You didn't let the lows overshadow the highs. You kept working out your differences, you came back together instead of staying apart. You lived your wedding vows. And because of that, I'm sitting here today."

She rubbed the back of G.G.'s hand, feeling the veins, the

wrinkles, the evidence of a life lived long. History was in those hands. A history she shared.

"If it upsets you that much, we won't have a party. But you're a hero to us, G.G. Look what you gave to your daughters. Grandma Anne's love of family. Aunt Margaret's way with words. Aunt Alice's determination. That's all from you, G.G."

G.G. was watching her, and Hannah knew she had her attention. She took a deep breath. This would be her last chance to make her point.

"You and Grandpa Frank stayed together for seventy-five years. You created a family and that deserves a celebration. I know you had a big party for your sixtieth anniversary. But now there's a whole new generation to celebrate. Nothing fancy this time. Just dinner, maybe, with the people who owe their existence to you."

G.G. let out a long sigh and then reached over, tapping Hannah on the chin. "You're as stubborn as your mother."

"That came from you, too, G.G. And Grandpa Frank. You stayed together, for richer or poorer, for better or worse." She paused.

"I notice you didn't add 'until death do us part.'" G.G.'s voice was dry, the words said in her matter-of-fact tone.

Hannah relaxed a fraction. "This is a time to celebrate the living." She didn't want to think about the future. It would come soon enough.

G.G. wrapped her fingers around Hannah's hand. "When you get to my age, Hannah, you stop counting birthdays and anniversaries. It's enough to get up every day and see the sun shining."

Her hand curled more tightly around Hannah's and she relished the feel of G.G.'s warm fingers. "We'll have a small party," G.G. said, her voice resigned. "Just the family." She tilted her neck and fixed Hannah with the firm gaze that had stopped little girls in their naughty tracks.

Hannah didn't flinch. She had tough blood in her veins. "Dinner for the family," she agreed. A burst of happiness flared to life. She had succeeded.

★ ★ ★

"How in the world did you get G.G. to agree to this?" Grandma Anne carried her plate of food over to the couch and sat down next to Hannah.

"I convinced her that she and Grandpa Frank had lived their wedding vows. That they were an inspiration to the rest of us."

"Well, I'm very impressed. I thought she'd given up celebrating any day that reminded her of her age."

Hannah stared at her grandmother. "You knew that was why she didn't want a party?"

Grandma Anne raised one shoulder in a ladylike shrug. "I wondered. It's not easy to think about them being gone."

Hannah nodded. She missed Grandpa Richard and she only had stories to bring him alive for her. Grandpa Frank and G.G. had been part of her whole life.

And they were here now, quietly celebrating a marriage that had impacted all of them.

She grabbed an hors d'oeuvre from the plate her brother carried. He frowned and she popped the stuffed mushroom into her mouth with a big grin.

She waved a hand around the crowded room. The guest list had been restricted to the three sisters and their families, but that still constituted a large group.

"We're all here because Grandpa Frank decided to stop at a small-town minister's house one day and try for a sale. Just think what would've happened if he hadn't gone to Winston." She bit her lip. "Or what *wouldn't* have?"

Anne kissed the top of Hannah's head. "You're a very smart young lady."

Hannah glanced at her great-grandparents. Grandpa Frank had wheeled G.G. away from the group, into a quiet corner. Sunlight gilded her white hair, the curls that had been styled especially for the evening. He bent down, his lips lightly touching her cheek. G.G. lifted her hand and cupped his jaw, her wedding band sparkling in the light.

In that moment, Hannah grasped completely why they were still together. When Frank looked at Marian, all the years fell away, taking with them the troubles, the fights, the disappointments. To him, she was forever eighteen, standing in the sunlight, her hair golden, her blue eyes alight with laughter and mischief.

Hannah leaned against the back of the couch. Someday, she thought, if I'm very lucky, someone will look at me that way. And I'll tell him the story of Frank and Marian and the love they shared for seventy-five years.

The Present

Hannah loaded the dishwasher, turning it on before going into the living room of her apartment. She picked up a framed photograph from the end table and sat down on the couch.

"So, G.G., Grandpa Frank, what do you think?" she asked out loud. "He's a great guy, isn't he? He hasn't asked me yet but I'm pretty sure we're getting married."

She smiled at the young couple in the picture. Their clothing placed them in the early 1930s, decades before the frame had been created. She couldn't recall when she'd started talking to them about her dates. Somehow, it was important to have their opinion and this was the best she could do now that they were both gone.

"You'd like him, Grandpa. He's smart. Works with computers. He helps businesses like yours, keeping them up-to-date with their technology."

She nestled into the cushions, a grin on her face. "He's very handsome, G.G. His kisses…" She sighed. "We're going to be very happy."

She placed the photo back on the table and tapped the glass. "Seventy-five years, G.G. That's my goal. Nothing less. It'll be hard work but we can do it. You showed me how."

* * * * *

Mediterranean Nights

Join the guests and crew of Alexandra's Dream, *the newest luxury ship to set sail on the romantic Mediterranean, as they experience the glamorous world of cruising.*

A new Harlequin continuity series
begins in June 2007 with
FROM RUSSIA, WITH LOVE
by Ingrid Weaver.

Marina Artamova books a cabin on the luxurious cruise ship Alexandra's Dream *when she finds out that her orphaned nephew and his adoptive father are aboard. She's determined to be reunited with the boy…but the romantic ambience of the ship and her undeniable attraction to a man she considers her enemy are about to interfere with her quest!*

Turn the page for a sneak preview!

Piraeus, Greece

"THERE SHE IS, Stefan. *Alexandra's Dream.*" David Anderson squatted beside his new son and pointed at the dark blue hull that towered above the pier. The cruise ship was a majestic sight, twelve decks high and as long as a city block. A circle of silver and gold stars, the logo of the Liberty Cruise Line, gleamed from the swept-back smokestack. Like some legendary sea creature born for the water, the ship emanated power from every sleek curve—even at rest it held the promise of motion. "That's going to be our home for the next ten days."

The child beside him remained silent, his cheeks working in and out as he sucked furiously on his thumb. Hair so blond it appeared white ruffled against his forehead in the harbor breeze. The baby-sweet scent unique to the very young mingled with the tang of the sea.

"Ship," David said. "Uh, *parakhod*."

From beneath his bangs, Stefan looked at the *Alexandra's Dream*. Although he didn't release his thumb, the corners of his mouth tightened with the beginning of a smile.

David grinned. That was Stefan's first smile this afternoon, one of only two since they had left the orphanage yesterday. It was probably because of the boat—according to the orphanage staff, the boy loved boats, which was the main reason David had decided to book this cruise. Then again, there was a strong possibility the smile could have been a reaction to David's attempt at pocket-dictionary Russian. Whatever the cause, it was a good start.

The liaison from the adoption agency had claimed that Stefan had been taught some English, but David had yet to see evidence of it. David continued to speak, positive his son would understand his tone even if he couldn't grasp the words. "This is her maiden voyage. Her first trip, just like this is our first trip, and that makes it special." He motioned toward the stage that had been set up on the pier beneath the ship's bow. "That's why everyone's celebrating."

The ship's official christening ceremony had been held the day before and had been a closed affair, with only the cruise-line executives and VIP guests invited, but the stage hadn't yet been disassembled. Banners bearing the blue and white of the Greek flag of the ship's owner, as well as the Liberty circle of stars logo, draped the edges of the platform. In the center, a group of musicians and a dance troupe dressed in traditional white folk costumes performed for the benefit of the *Alexandra's Dream's* first passengers. Their audience was in a festive mood, snapping their fingers in time to the music while the dancers twirled and wove through their steps.

David bobbed his head to the rhythm of the mandolins. They were playing a folk tune that seemed vaguely familiar, possibly from a movie he'd seen. He hummed a few notes. "Catchy melody, isn't it?"

Stefan turned his gaze on David. His eyes were a striking shade of blue, as cool and pale as a winter horizon and far too solemn for a child not yet five. Still, the smile that hovered at the corners of his mouth persisted. He moved his head with the music, mirroring David's motion.

David gave a silent cheer at the interaction. Hopefully, this cruise would provide countless opportunities for more. "Hey, good for you," he said. "Do you like the music?"

The child's eyes sparked. He withdrew his thumb with a pop. *"Moozika!"*

"Music. Right!" David held out his hand. "Come on, let's go closer so we can watch the dancers."

Stefan grasped David's hand quickly, as if he feared it would be withdrawn. In an instant his budding smile was replaced by a look close to panic.

Did he remember the car accident that had killed his parents? It would be a mercy if he didn't. As far as David knew, Stefan had never spoken of it to anyone. Whatever he had seen had made him run so far from the crash that the police hadn't found him until the next day. The event had traumatized him to the extent that he hadn't uttered a word until his fifth week at the orphanage. Even now he seldom talked.

David sat back on his heels and brushed the hair from Stefan's forehead. That solemn, too-old gaze locked with his, and for an instant, David felt as if he looked back in time at an image of himself thirty years ago.

He didn't need to speak the same language to understand exactly how this boy felt. He knew what it meant to be alone and powerless among strangers, trying to be brave and tough but wishing with every fiber of his being for a place to belong, to be safe, and most of all for someone to love him....

He knew in his heart he would be a good parent to Stefan. It was why he had never considered halting the adoption process after Ellie had left him. He hadn't balked when he'd learned of the recent claim by Stefan's spinster aunt, either; the absentee relative had shown up too late for her case to be considered. The adoption was meant to be. He and this child already shared a bond that went deeper than paperwork or legalities.

A seagull screeched overhead, making Stefan start and press closer to David.

"That's my boy," David murmured. He swallowed hard, struck by the simple truth of what he had just said.

That's my *boy*.

"I CAN'T BE PATIENT, RUDOLPH. I'm not going to stand by and watch my nephew get ripped from his country and his roots to live on the other side of the world."

Rudolph hissed out a slow breath. "Marina, I don't like the sound of that. What are you planning?"

"I'm going to talk some sense into this American kidnapper."

"No. Absolutely not. No offence, but diplomacy is not your strong suit."

"Diplomacy be damned. Their ship's due to sail at five o'clock."

"Then you wouldn't have an opportunity to speak with him even if his lawyer agreed to a meeting."

"I'll have ten days of opportunities, Rudolph, since I plan to be on board that ship."

* * * * *

Follow Marina and David as they join forces to uncover the reason behind little Stefan's unusual silence, and the secret behind the death of his parents....

Look for From Russia, With Love *by Ingrid Weaver in stores June 2007.*

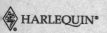

HARLEQUIN®

EVERLASTING LOVE™

Every great love has a story to tell™

Sometimes the love of your life isn't the person you think it is.

After more than twenty years of marriage—twenty
good years—Chloe finds herself torn between two
men. Daniel, with whom she's raised a daughter
and shared the everyday problems and triumphs
of life. And Evan, the man who—she believes—
has always had her heart.

Only now, after two decades of marriage
and a crisis, does Chloe learn what true
love is…and what it isn't.

Pick up a copy of

When Love is True

by

Joan Kilby

Available in June.

nocturne™

IT'S TIME TO DISCOVER
THE RAINTREE TRILOGY...

There have always been those among us
who are more than human...

Don't miss the dramatic first book by
New York Times bestselling author

LINDA
HOWARD

RAINTREE:
Inferno

On sale May.

Raintree: Haunted by Linda Winstead Jones
Available June.

Raintree: Sanctuary by Beverly Barton
Available July.

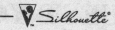

SPECIAL EDITION™

COMING IN JUNE

HER LAST FIRST DATE

by *USA TODAY* bestselling author

SUSAN MALLERY

After one too many bad dates, Crissy Phillips
finally swore off men. Recently widowed,
pediatrician Josh Daniels can't risk losing his
heart. With an intense attraction pulling them
together, will their fear keep them apart?
Or will one wild night change everything...?

Sometimes the unexpected
is the best news of all....

REQUEST YOUR FREE BOOKS!

2 FREE NOVELS PLUS 2 FREE GIFTS!

 HARLEQUIN®

E V E R L A S T I N G   L O V E ™

Every great love has a story to tell™

YES! Please send me 2 FREE Harlequin® Everlasting Love™ novels and my 2 FREE gifts. After receiving them, if I don't wish to receive any more books, I can return the shipping statement marked "cancel." If I don't cancel, I will receive 4 brand-new novels every other month and be billed just $4.47 per book in the U.S. or $4.99 per book in Canada, plus 25¢ shipping and handling per book and applicable taxes, if any*. That's a savings of about 15% off the cover price! I understand that accepting the 2 free books and gifts places me under no obligation to buy anything. I can always return a shipment and cancel at any time. Even if I never buy another book from Harlequin, the two free books and gifts are mine to keep forever.

153 HDN ELX4   353 HDN ELYG

Name	(PLEASE PRINT)
Address	Apt.
City	State/Prov.	Zip/Postal Code

Signature (if under 18, a parent or guardian must sign)

Mail to the Harlequin Reader Service®:
IN U.S.A.: P.O. Box 1867, Buffalo, NY 14240-1867
IN CANADA: P.O. Box 609, Fort Erie, Ontario L2A 5X3

Not valid to current Harlequin Everlasting Love subscribers.

Want to try two free books from another line?
Call 1-800-873-8635 or visit www.morefreebooks.com.

* Terms and prices subject to change without notice. NY residents add applicable sales tax. Canadian residents will be charged applicable provincial taxes and GST. This offer is limited to one order per household. All orders subject to approval. Credit or debit balances in a customer's account(s) may be offset by any other outstanding balance owed by or to the customer. Please allow 4 to 6 weeks for delivery.

Your Privacy: Harlequin is committed to protecting your privacy. Our Privacy Policy is available online at www.eHarlequin.com or upon request from the Reader Service. From time to time we make our lists of customers available to reputable firms who may have a product or service of interest to you. If you would prefer we not share your name and address, please check here. ☐

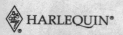

HARLEQUIN®

American ROMANCE®

is proud to present a special treat this
Fourth of July with three stories
to kick off your summer!

SUMMER LOVIN'
by
Marin Thomas,
Laura Marie Altom
Ann Roth

This year, celebrating the Fourth of July in Silver Cliff,
Colorado, is going to be special. There's an all-year
high school reunion taking place before the old
school building gets torn down. As old flames find
each other and new romances begin, this small
town is looking like the perfect place
for some summer lovin'!

*Available June 2007
wherever Harlequin books are sold.*

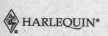

Every great love has a story to tell™

"Joelle and Bobby...I'm aware my visit might have been difficult for you."

Difficult? In fact, nothing will ever be the same again for Joelle Webber and Bobby DiFranco. They've built careers and a home, raised a family. They've shaped a life of trust, understanding and support. It all would have remained rock-solid if not for the unexpected intrusion of Joelle's ex and the long-buried secret he unearths. Joelle and Bobby have leaned on each other through countless crises, but this time the very foundation of their marriage is shaken.

Can they put it back together one more time?

Look for

The Marriage Bed

by

Judith Arnold

available this May.

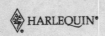

COMING NEXT MONTH

#9. *The Scrapbook* by Lynnette Kent

Anyone looking at Celia's scrapbook would see a portrait of a wonderful marriage, from Celia and Mack Butler's beautiful white wedding—the beginning of her life as a navy wife—to her growing, smiling family. But Celia's life is not so easily summed up in photographs. The true value of these moments frozen in time is found in the stories behind them....

#10. *When Love is True* by Joan Kilby

What do you do when you realize that your one true love has been with you all along? For twenty years Daniel Bennett has been Chloe's rock. But something has always held her back from fully giving him her heart. Suddenly she sees Daniel with new eyes, but does her realization come too late?

www.eHarlequin.com